THE OLD SCHOOL

THE OLD SCHOOL

NEIL RATHMELL

FABER & FABER
3 Queen Square London

First published in 1976
by Faber and Faber Limited
3 Queen Square London WC1
Printed in Great Britain at
The University Printing House, Cambridge

ISBN 0 571 10812 1

FOR LYNNE

Daniel Jones might have had it in mind, when he became Headmaster of The Meadows Preparatory School for Boys in 1932, to use the position as a stepping stone to higher things. Or so his wife had thought. She would even go so far as to say that he had at one time had his eye on the Headship of a certain public school in the South of England with which The Meadows had certain connections. So she could never understand how they still came to be there twenty-three years later. But she didn't ask questions. Her husband's thoughts were no concern of hers. She held her peace, held it grimly, kept a tight hold of it and nearly strangled it, and spent her days dusting. Small and stout, day after day, year after year, she kept the house clean and held her mouth always tightly closed, to keep the dust out and her convictions in, and in the evening read books, about which she never voiced an opinion. The pupils, showing a singular lack of imagination, called her simply Ma Jones, but then they saw little of her. She kept her matronly duties to a minimum, and in latter years refused to leave her private quarters and enter school precincts at all except in cases of extreme illness. When thus obliged to emerge from her own lonely domain, she would enter the sick-room, look at the patient with that mixture of suspicion and cold indifference with which she seemed to view everything, and ask, briefly, "What's the matter with you then?" She did much to encourage a desire for good health among the boys at The Meadows.

The Headmaster was Davy. He had other names, too, which would be in vogue for a while and then fall into disuse, but Davy was perennial. Desperate Dan came in for a year or so, but since there was little that was desperate about Mr Jones he soon became Davy again. He was at other times The Beak, Boyo, Jones the Bones, The Invisible Man and Lloyd George. But in the end everyone always came back to Davy. It is the same with God. He has other names which are used according to the feelings of the speaker or the beliefs of the age, such as the Lord, the Almighty, Our Maker, the Creator, Jehovah, Love and Justice but in the end it comes down to just God, which no one understands. No one understood Davy. Perhaps that is why the name stuck, because it was so vague.

He was a tall man, thin, and in 1955 as nearly bald as makes no difference. There was just a wisp of very thin, white hair left, which lay across his head or fluttered gently in the breeze. Even he seemed not to be aware that he had it. He made no attempt, as some men do, to make a lot of a little and invent a hairstyle which can use a dozen or so strands to some effect. He just let it fall wherever the wind blew it.

He was over sixty and close to retirement. "What is he going to do when he retires?" said Mrs Jones to herself. She asked other questions too, but never voiced them. "What does he think about all the time?" Without looking up from her book, she can see him sitting opposite her, with his arms resting loosely on the chair arms and his eyes abstracted in his bony face, a faint smile on his lips. No answer. "Is he smiling, or is it just stupidity?" No answer. She goes on reading, never looks up. "What does he do all day? What is he going to do when he retires? Does he know he's going to retire soon? Does he know what he's doing?" She never puts a question to him directly, scarcely ever says anything to him at all. She goes on reading. Mr Jones gets up, walks across the room, draws the curtains, walks back to his chair and sits down. She goes on reading, steadily, unmovingly, comes to the last sentence and closes the book. She puts it down, but gives no indication whether she has enjoyed it or not.

"Was it good?"

"It depends what you like."

Mr Jones nods and looks at the fire. He makes no further comment. Opposite him his wife sits and fixes her eye on a dark spot in the corner of the ceiling which she suspects might be the beginning of damp. She stares at it for five minutes, her lips pinched together, waiting to see if it spreads. She goes out after a while and comes back with two cups of hot milk. The dark spot on the ceiling holds her attention again. All the time she is sipping her milk, she stares at that spot on the ceiling. She has the infinite patience of the convinced pessimist, who needs to ask no questions, particular doubts being swallowed up in the general certainty of disaster. The thin wisp of a man sitting opposite her, smiling faintly at the fire, is an irritation which it needs all her patience to endure. But she does so. At last, she takes her eye off the ceiling, stands up and goes to bed.

Mr Jones, still with a faint smile on his lips, still, as it seems by the abstracted look in his deep-set eyes, thinking about something, sits on alone.

Mr Lynch sat in the staffroom in his shirt sleeves, with his head back and his eyes closed. It was late in the afternoon of the day on which the boys returned for the Autumn term. Mr Birkett stood by the window, looking out, with his hands behind his back. His lips formed a thin, straight line and he looked knowingly through the window at the meadows. Behind him, Mr Lynch sank a little lower into his armchair. He was a well-built man in his early forties, a games man, whose muscle was just beginning to go to fat. As he lay back in his chair, his square chin was thrust out in advance of his broad, flat nose and extensive forehead; his big chest sloped away from his chin, but was overtaken by paunch halfway down; beyond that his legs extended, knees spread aggressively wide, culminating in a pair of grubby, bursting plimsolls set squarely on the faded carpet.

"I feel more aware at this time of the year than at any other," said Mr Birkett, "when the new boys arrive, of the lack of initiative and direction at the top. It's when the boys come here for the first time, when they form their first impressions of the school, that a strong discipline needs enforcing. The Headmaster should impress upon them from the very first assembly that we require discipline, that there are certain things we expect from them. But of course nothing of the kind will happen tomorrow morning. So there's no use hoping for it." He sniffed, and continued to stare out over the meadows.

"I don't worry about that," said Mr Lynch, opening his eyes and closing then again. "I make my own discipline."

"It doesn't make for a strong school. It's not personal discipline I'm talking about. It's the total discipline which prevails—or does not prevail, as the case may be—in the school as a whole. That can only come from the top."

Mr Lynch reached out and scratched his knee, blindly, but did not reply. So the Deputy Headmaster, who had turned to his colleague in a kind of appeal, turned again and looked out of the window as before.

Outside, on the other side of the house, Mr Hopper strolled past the bicycle shed, where two boys were examining the chain of an inverted bicycle. "Hello, sir," they said, as he went by. Mr Hopper smiled and walked on. The boys watched him go, unwilling to continue their investigations until he was out of sight. Mr Hopper, with his air of supreme self-confidence, inspired in all the boys a certain bashfulness. They shuffled their feet and smiled shyly whenever he condescended to speak to them.

Mr Hopper continued his progress round the house, glancing casually from side to side as he walked, acknowledging the greetings of the boys with a smile and occasionally favouring them with a word or two, until he came to the archway which led into the quadrangle.

His manner changed when he passed the Headmaster walking through the quad. He became deferential.

"Good afternoon, sir," he said. "A lovely day for the start of the new term."

Mr Jones stopped and looked rather vaguely at Mr Hopper for a second or two before replying. "Ah, Mr Hopper. Nice to see you again." He walked on, smiling faintly and seeming rather to drift on the breeze than to move of his own volition.

"Good afternoon everyone," said Mr Hopper, vigorously, as

he entered the staffroom.

"Good afternoon," said Mr Birkett, turning from the window.

"Afternoon, Geoff," said Mr Lynch, opening his eyes.

A few minutes later, they were all sitting down drinking tea. It was Mr Hopper's function to rouse the other staff from their lethargy, to bring them out of themselves. He considered himself less morbidly involved in school affairs than the others. He did not live there, for one thing, having a wife and daughter and a home of his own to live in. He made no bones about this. He told the others straight out that, in spending so much time at the school, they tended to lose their sense of perspective, to get things out of proportion. The school-master's biggest pitfall, he called it. The only way, he said, was to have a full and independent life out of school. Mr Birkett and Mr Lynch were not in the least bit offended by all this. Indeed, they always agreed most readily with what he said. Perhaps they felt that in so doing they automatically absolved themselves from the charges. Then again, the fact that Mr Hopper took just as great an interest in school affairs as they did seemed to some extent to nullify what he said.

"Family well?" said Mr Lynch.

"Fine, fine," said Mr Hopper.

"Good," said Mr Lynch.

"Good," said Mr Birkett.

"The Headmaster's looking well," said Mr Hopper.

"Do you think so?" said Mr Lynch.

"I do," said Mr Hopper. "I saw him just now as I came in. Looked remarkably well. Hope I wear as well as he has done. He's one of those thin men who look fragile but are as strong as cart-horses really. He's a deceptive man, Mr Jones. There's a lot more to him than meets the eye."

"You're probably right," said Mr Lynch, who then thought for a moment and added, "He's lost a lot of weight over the years."

"Really?" said Mr Hopper.

"Oh yes. Used to be quite a big chap."

"Really?"

Mr Birkett put down his cup of tea, stood up and walked over to the window. If there was one thing which annoyed him about Hopper, it was this ridiculous admiration of his for the Headmaster. Mr Birkett did not like to contradict him openly, but he had his own opinions on the matter and they were certainly not the same as Hopper's. It was difficult indeed to contradict Hopper about anything. He expressed himself so forcibly. Actually, he didn't much care for Hopper, but, of course, he didn't show it. Fred Lynch always seemed to get on with him very well. When Fred and Hopper were talking together so matily, as they were now, he could not help feeling that they were both of them rather like schoolboys, both so absurdly unaware of the dangers that beset the school because of the Headmaster's loosening grip on the reins. Lynch seemed to have a sort of admiration for Hopper which was quite childish. There was an almost ridiculous gullibility revealed in Fred Lynch at such times, which he had always thought silly, but which now began to irritate him. He alone could see how things were going. It was beginning to make him feel bitter. But he was not a man to show his feelings, and at other times, when Hopper was not there, he and Fred got on quite well together. They had been colleagues for over fifteen years, whereas Hopper was a newcomer of only eight years' standing.

"What did you say the new chap's name was, Ron?" asked Mr Hopper.

"Drew," said Mr Birkett, returning to his chair. "Malcolm Drew."

"Is he here yet?"

"Yes," said Fred. "He must be up in his room."

"I'll go and introduce myself," said Mr Hopper. "What's he like?"

"Seems all right. Quiet sort, you know."

"I'll go up and see him."

Mr Birkett, who was feeling peculiarly restless that afternoon, watched Fred Lynch sink down in his chair again and close his eyes, after Mr Hopper had gone, then stood up and walked aimlessly round the room, glanced at one or two anonymous, forgotten piles of books and papers on the table, and ended up once again in front of the window, looking out at the meadows, where two boys were walking.

"They shouldn't be there," he said, half to himself. "The meadows should be out of bounds. But it's up to him. I'm not doing anything. It's up to him."

Fred Lynch either did not hear or took no notice, but sank a little lower in his chair, resting his hands comfortably on his paunch.

There was a brisk knock on Malcolm's door, which then opened to reveal Mr Hopper.

"My name's Hopper," he said, coming in.

"Oh. Hello," said Malcolm Drew.

"Geoffrey," said Mr Hopper, holding out his hand.

"Ah. My name's Malcolm."

They shook hands, Mr Hopper's grip at once establishing his superiority.

"Come down for a cup of tea?"

"Thanks very much," said Malcolm.

They went down to the staffroom, but the pot was empty. "That's all right," said Malcolm. "I'm not really thirsty."

"Sure?" said Mr Hopper.

"You can make some more if you like," said Mr Lynch.

"No. Really. It's all right," said Malcolm.

Mr Hopper smiled. "Feel like going for a walk, then," he said, "before tea? There's half-an-hour yet before we ring the bell. Come on. We'll have a walk round and see what damage is being done."

"All right," said Malcolm. "Thank you very much."

Mr Hopper took him all round the school, explaining it all to him. The new young teacher was a willing listener, anxious to learn about his new surroundings, and Mr Hopper needed little encouragement to expand. He took the youngster under his wing and was full of advice.

"Don't be afraid to ask," he said. "Anything at all you're not sure about, just ask."

"Right," said Malcolm. "Thank you."

But he was too overawed, both by his new surroundings and by his guide, to be able to think of much to say just then.

Outside, near the end of their tour, they walked round to the old stables. Three or four boys, who seemed to be about twelve years old, were standing outside on a cobbled area, talking.

"Hello, sir," they said, when they saw Mr Hopper, and looked curiously at the newcomer.

"Hello, boys," said Mr Hopper. He turned to Malcolm. "This is the committee of the Stamp Club," he said. "Wilkins here is the Secretary. A position of some influence in the school, I can assure you." The boy pointed out as Wilkins grinned and looked at Malcolm. "This is Mr Drew, boys," Mr Hopper went on. "The new member of the staff."

"Hello, sir," said the boys, pleasantly, though still looking curiously at the new teacher.

"Hello, boys," said Malcolm, feeling more important than he had felt for a long time.

"Get round to the quad now, boys," said Mr Hopper. "It's nearly time for tea."

"You've met the Headmaster, of course?" Mr Hopper went on, as they followed the boys towards the quadrangle. They walked slowly. Mr Hopper put his hands behind his back and inclined his head towards Malcolm, who was shorter than he.

"Yes," said Malcolm. "I talked to him for a while in his study when I arrived this morning."

Mr Hopper leant his head closer to Malcolm's. "A very good man, the Headmaster," he said. "An excellent man."

The new teacher was suitably impressed. His new post was fulfilling his dreams with a completeness that seemed almost impossible. He was afraid to breathe, lest the bubble should burst.

They emerged from the shadow of the archway into the quadrangle, where a large crowd of boys was gathered, with more coming in all the time from the buildings and fields. Soon the quadrangle was full with the sixty-odd boys who made up the school's population. Malcolm thought it was marvellous to see them all gathered together there in that one space, with the old horse chestnut in their midst and the old stone of the buildings around them. A bell started to clang and the boys filed in through a door which let into the old house. Mr Hopper put an arm round his protégé and took him in through the door after them.

Later in the evening, after Mr Hopper had gone home, having filled his young colleague almost to satiety with advice and explanations of the school routine throughout tea and afterwards, Malcolm walked out into the quadrangle for a breath of fresh air and a stroll before going to his room for the night. How marvellous, he thought, standing beneath the old horse chestnut, looking up at the stars, breathing in the September scents of evening, to be living here, to belong to all this.

He saw Mr Jones come out through the archway and walk across the quad. "Good evening, sir," he said. Mr Jones smiled vaguely in his direction, nodding his head gently, and walked on by. Malcolm wondered if the Headmaster had realised who he was. He looked up at the stars again, and could not believe his good fortune.

Wilkins stood in the middle of the quadrangle, polishing his spectacles and frowning. He had the air of a man who has several things on his mind and is working through them methodically, from beginning to end. A serious, plodding sort of man, who never panics, never makes a rash decision. Every so often he held his glasses up to the fading light (it was after seven o'clock) and peered through them, but each time he decided they were not to his satisfaction and continued polishing them and frowning.

A few other boys were lounging around in the quad, in twos and threes, but they were mainly new boys—that is to say, nine or ten years old—who had not yet found their way around and felt safest here, in case any unexpected bells should ring. So Wilkins was to all intents and purposes alone, as befits a man who has the weight of responsibility on his shoulders and a difficult committee meeting to deal with in rather less than a quarter of an hour's time. Possibly the presence of the new boys added to his sense of the dignity of his isolation, possibly he felt that they were looking at him with a certain amount of awe and admiration—they must have heard that he was the Secretary of the Stamp Club—but then Wilkins too was human.

The bell struck the quarter-hour, two first formers stood up nervously, looking round, and Wilkins held up his spectacles, put them on and walked away. He went under the archway and off towards the old stables, where a crucial confrontation was to take place between the committees of the Stamp Club and the Amateur Dramatic Society. It was the culmination of two terms of more or less unfriendly rivalry between the two groups, which had caused Wilkins a great deal of distress and appreciably lowered his confidence in the good sense and sanity of his fellow men. He had never been able to understand why the two societies could not coexist amicably, why they could not agree to meet on different evenings, so that those who wished could be members of both, and he considered it a triumph of no small magnitude that this joint meeting had at last been called, since it was what he had been recommending all along. The only trouble was that everybody thought it was Lundy's idea. The first thing Lundy had done yesterday, when they got back to school, was to say that he thought his committee ought to meet the committee of the Stamp Club for talks, and everyone had agreed at once. But that was the difference between Wilkins and Lundy. Even Wilkins admitted that. Lundy was a leader, Wilkins was not. So he contented himself with the thought that the meeting he had wanted all along was at last to be held, and that was the main thing. Reason had prevailed and he had been shown to be in the right, even if he was the only one who realised it.

He climbed up the wooden steps on the outside of the old stables and entered through a small door in the wall. Everyone was there except Lundy, and Wilkins wondered, not for the first time, whether this Amateur Dramatic Society was really a sound proposition, whether it would really last. A lot of the boys who had joined had been attracted mainly by the fact that meetings were held in the stables, whereas the Stamp Club met in a classroom. Nor had they yet performed a play. What had they to show for two terms' work? But that was something he intended to say later.

"Hi, Wilky! Hi, Arnie!" said two people from the Stamp Club.

"Good evening, Mr Wilkins," said one of the Dramatic crew, sarcastically.

Arnold sat down on the Stamp Club side of the table round which everyone was seated. From his jacket pocket he took a note book and fountain pen.

"Take a letter, Miss Wilkins," someone said.

Everybody laughed, including one or two of the Stamp Club people, until they remembered that on this occasion they ought to stand by their Secretary.

"Shut up, Carter," one of them said. "At least we're all here on time."

"Dave'll be here," said Carter.

"Chairman's privilege to be late," said Tomlinson, who was Arnold's opposite number on the committee of the Dramatic Society.

Tomlinson and Carter represented the two extremes of the membership of the Dramatic Society. One was bright and witty and intelligent—that was Tomlinson, who was always somewhere near the top of the form—and the other was tough, dull and uncouth—Carter was not very clever, but he was good at games and would probably be Captain of the rugby team this year. Arnold could not make out how these two both came to be friends of Lundy's, except that Tomlinson could be as rough in his way as Carter could, only Tomlinson hurt with words and looks instead of with fists. If you got on the wrong side of Tomlinson, he could be quite unpleasant.

The room fell more or less silent. What little talking there was occurred only between members of the same side. No one spoke across the table. Carter was reminded vaguely of the way it was in the few minutes of warming up on the pitch before a match started. Tomlinson leaned back with his arms folded, looking as usual as though he knew all he needed to know and could afford to remain silent.

Arnold, who liked reading and knew more big words than anyone else, always thought of Tomlinson when he came across the word, 'sardonic', anywhere. But he could never deal with more than one thing at a time, and just now was writing, "September 9th—Minutes of joint meeting between Stamp Club and Amateur Dramatic Society," in his notebook.

They heard someone running up the stairs outside. "Here's Dave," said Carter. The door opened and Lundy came in.

"Sorry I'm late," he said. "I had to see Mr Lynch about rugby."

A worried look appeared on Carter's heavy face. "What did he say?" he said.

"Tell you after," said Lundy.

Everyone knew that it was either Lundy or Carter for Captain of the rugby team, and if it was Carter Lundy wouldn't mind, but if it was Lundy Carter would be jealous and they would probably fall out. From that point on, Carter's mind was only half on the business in hand.

"Right," said Lundy, "is everyone here? Good. Who's going to start?"

There was a general cry of "You start, Dave" from the Dramatic side, and silence from the Stamp Club. Lundy looked at the Chairman of the Stamp Club, a mild, good-natured boy called Wainwright, and Wainwright was just about to say, "Yes, you start if you like. It was your idea," when Arnold looked up from his notebook and said, "We ought to have a chairman."

"Does it matter?"

"We've got a chairman."

"We've got two."

"One each."

"We've got to have a chairman for the whole meeting." Arnold insisted. "An impartial chairman."

"Listen to the dictionary."

"I suppose you're right," said Lundy.

"Dave for chairman!"

"Dave for president!"

"No," said Lundy. "It can't be either of us. It's got to be someone impartial, like Wilkins says."

"Let him do it, then. Is he imp-thingy?"

"I'm secretary," said Arnold.

"You can be chairman, as well, can't you?" said Lundy.

"Well, I suppose so."

"Get on with it."

"Go on," said Wainwright.

"Oh, all right," said Arnold, moving his chair to the top of the table. "But it's highly irregular."

"Oh, shut up and get on with it."

"Doesn't that give them an unfair advantage?" asked Carter.

"No," said Lundy. "The chairman's impartial."

"Oh," said Carter.

"You'd better take minutes for both societies," said Arnold to Tomlinson.

"O. K.," said Tomlinson. "Can you lend me a bit of paper?"

With a sigh, Arnold handed over his notebook. Imagine a secretary coming to a meeting without any paper!

So Arnold began the meeting. "This meeting has been called by Mr Lundy, Chairman of the Amateur Dramatic Society"—he paused, wondering whether to say anything about his own efforts to bring about such a meeting in the past, but, in view of his position as chairman, decided not to—"in order that the committees of both the Amateur Dramatic Society and the Stamp Club might meet to discuss the problems which the activities of both societies, which have to some extent been in conflict, have brought about in this school. As you know..."

"Get on with it."

Arnold looked aggrieved.

"Let him speak," said Lundy, who liked to see things done properly and was admiring Arnold's gift for public speaking.

"Yes, shut up!" said Carter.

"Thank you," said Arnold. "I will, however, be brief, since this meeting is likely to be a long one. The best thing will be for me to ask the Chairmen of both Societies to give their views and then throw the meeting open to the floor."

"Catch!" someone shouted, but Lundy frowned at him and Carter thumped him and he was silenced for a while.

"Perhaps, since it was Mr Lundy who called this meeting, I should call upon him to speak first."

Wainwright nodded, and Lundy stood up.

"I've been thinking about this over the holidays. Working out what we ought to do. Because when Tommo—Mr Tomlinson, I mean, and Mr Carter and I first started this society, we didn't mean to set ourselves up against the Stamp Club at all. We just wanted to put on plays and things and that was it. But somehow it got so that we were against the Stamp Club—and I don't think it was all our fault—and then that got to be the most important thing about it. So much so, that we haven't actually done a play yet."

Arnold frowned. He could not now make that point himself. That was the trouble with arguing with Lundy. He seemed to be able to give in and win both at the same time.

"Then there was the thing about holding our meetings at the same time as theirs—yours, I mean. Well, at first we did that just because none of us were in the Stamp Club and that seemed fair enough. And I was talking to my Dad about this and he said that there was a lot to be said for a bit of healthy competition. But the way I look at it now, we're cutting our own throats as well, because there are people in the Stamp Club who might be in our Society as well if they were on different nights. And it's the same for you. So that's one thing. But then I got another idea, and that's what I really called the meeting about, because if it was just a matter of changing the nights we could easily have done that and said pax and that would have been it. So what I thought was, why don't we amalgamate?"

David had kept this a secret. Everyone looked surprised, including his own committee. The only one who didn't was Tomlinson, and that might have been because David had taken him into his confidence beforehand or it might have been just his manner—never giving anything away. Certainly Carter knew nothing about it.

"Eh?" he said.

"Amalgamate," repeated David. "Make it the Amateur Dramatic Society and Stamp Club Incorporated. Then there'd be no arguments. We'd just have one committee—all of us here—and we'd be able to arrange everything so that there would be no clashes, and if we wanted any extras we could get them from the Stamp Club, because they'd be members of our Society as well. It would increase your membership and ours. That's what I think, anyway." And he sat down.

At once, everyone started chattering. Arnold, who was not at all happy about this new suggestion, but had not yet found any definite arguments to advance against it, had to shout several times for order, and even then it was only when David also called for quiet and Carter did a little thumping that the room fell silent.

"I now call upon Mr Wainwright to say what he thinks," said Arnold at last.

The Chairman of the Stamp Club stood up and said, "Well, all I was going to say was that I thought we ought to call a truce and have our meetings on different days and everything that you said."

He had begun by addressing everyone, but very soon turned to David and spoke to him as if it were not a proper meeting at all.

"But your idea about amalgamating seems better still. I think we ought to do that. I wouldn't mind doing a bit of acting. And I could swap some of your stamps, Tommo."

Tomlinson smiled and nodded.

"Right, Andy," said David. "You're on."

The two Chairmen grinned at each other, and everyone started talking again.

Arnold was very displeased by the way things were going. Everybody seemed to have agreed to Lundy's suggestion without talking about it at all. It had ceased to be a meeting in any proper sense and the two sides of the table were chatting amicably together.

"Order!" he shouted, and now that everyone was friendly again they all turned and listened to him. "We've heard what the two Chairmen have to say. I now throw the meeting open to the floor."

"Sssh!" said someone. "Listen to the floor. I can't hear what it's saying."

"Tell it to speak up."

"Tell it to stand up before it speaks."

Everyone was laughing. Someone knelt down and put his ear to the floor. "It says, please may it leave the room." The laughter increased, and even Wilkins began to grin after a while, as the humour of the last joke penetrated his sense of dignity.

Seeing him grin, David decided to help him and called for quiet again and Carter went on a tour of the table thumping everyone he could lay hands on, including Wilkins.

When there was silence and Carter was in his place again, looking threateningly round the room, Arnold, rubbing his shoulder where Carter had thumped him, continued. "I think we ought to discuss what Lundy has said before we come to any decisions."

"I think so too," said David.

"And we've got to do it properly, one person at a time."

David nodded, and everyone was quiet and attentive now. Everyone knew that David's suggestion would be accepted—indeed, it already had been—but they were quite interested in playing the game of talking about it. They all looked round, waiting for someone to speak.

Two or three people made short speeches agreeing with David, but not saying much more than that they thought it was a good idea. Arnold was pleased that the meeting was back on an even keel again but was not a little disappointed by the lack of strong reasoning.

"Can anybody see any disadvantages in the scheme?" he asked.

They shook their heads and looked at him suspiciously and Carter glared defiantly round the table.

"If there are any disadvantages, I think we ought to try to find them," said David.

Nobody spoke. They were all very impressed by David's reasonableness.

"Can you see any?" David asked Arnold.

Here Arnold had a problem, because although he did not like the idea of amalgamation at all, he could not find any specific faults in the scheme.

"No," he said, at last, vaguely aware that Carter was staring at him with a rather ugly expression on his face.

"That's it then," said someone.

"What about the Committee?" said Tomlinson.

It was the first time he had spoken and the first time that anything really practical had been said. Arnold began to think that all the best brains were on their side. He was sadly disappointed in his own Chairman, who had given in, he thought, far too readily. He, like everyone else, had been won ever purely by the force of Lundy's personality. But Arnold was not susceptible to charm.

The meeting now became more business-like, and most of the talking was done by Lundy, Tomlinson and Wainwright, who seemed, in the space of a few minutes, to have become great friends. Arnold found, to his increasing dismay, that his former chairman seemed to be showing more interest in the Amateur Dramatic Society than in the Stamp Club, whose interests he was supposed to be there to protect. This was true also of most of the Committee of the Stamp Club. Lundy outlined his plans for the term's activities, which were comprehensive, even grandiose. A great deal of enthusiasm was generated for these activities and more and more the Stamp Club faded into the background. Arnold thought of all those little first formers with their stamp albums being deserted by their leaders. A new post, that of Audition Secretary, whose actual duties remained somewhat vague but who, it was promised, would be closely involved in the running of the Society, was created and to this post Wainwright was unanimously elected. Mournfully, appalled at the turn events had taken, Arnold counted the votes.

Eventually, everything was settled: Lundy was overall Chairman, Carter remained Vice Chairman, Wainwright was Audition Secretary, and the Amalgamated Committee remained unchanged. The Committee members were asked to state for which section of the Society they wanted to have Special Responsibility, and all but one opted for the Dramatic Section, with two, one from each of the former Societies, responsible for Liaison between the two Sections.

There remained the delicate issue of the General Secretary. It had to be either Tomlinson or Wilkins.

"Tommo!" said someone.

"Tommo for General Sec.!"

"I think they ought to decide," said David.

"I don't mind," said Tomlinson.

"Toss up for it."

David looked at Arnold, waiting to hear his views.

"I think I'd rather stay with the Stamp Club."

"Good," said David. "That's easy then. We'll have two Vice Chairmans—Chairmen, I mean. Carthorse for the Dramatic Section and you for the Stamps Section. And Sanders"—he was the Committee member who had opted for Stamps—"can be . . . yes! We'll call him Membership Secretary Stamps Section In Brackets. And Tommo can be General Secretary. That keeps you two about the same level. It even puts you a bit above him, on a level with Carthorse."

Arnold looked at Carter, and Carter, who had been wondering who would be Captain of the rugby team, hearing his nickname, looked up.

"What?"

They were not on the same level at all.

"Go back to sleep."

"Shut up, you!"

"Is that all right, Arnie?" said David.

"Yes. We'd better take a vote though."

"All right. All those in favour of Wilkins being Vice Chairman and Sanders being Membership Secretary both Stamps Section In Brackets put your hands up."

They were unanimously elected, and Arnold, who was still Chairman of the meeting, declared the meeting closed. Lundy, Carter, Tomlinson and Wainwright went off together. The others followed, until only the Stamps Section, in the persons of Wilkins and Sanders, remained in the room.

Arnold was very gloomy. "Well, that's about the end of the Stamp Club," he said.

Sanders was more sanguine. "We needn't bother about them," he said. "I don't see why it should make any difference. We can just carry on as before really."

But he had not suffered a personal defeat, as Arnold had. He felt as though he had failed to make the others see reason, failed in his duty to the faithful members of the Stamp Club, and he considered Wainwright a traitor. To him it was a question of principle, and he was not particularly cheered by the thought that in fact there had been no serious change.

"You're in charge, as well," said Sanders, seeing yet another thing to be thankful for. "You've been promoted."

"That's true," said Arnold, but rather despondently than otherwise. He was not a leader and had never wanted to be, preferring to act in an advisory capacity. He was scorer for the school cricket team and kept a meticulous score book, but he could not have played cricket to save his life.

They turned the light out and climbed down the wooden stairs. The bell was ringing for prayers already.

"Who would have thought that Wainwright would have done that, though?" said Arnold, after they had walked in silence for some time. He was more puzzled than angry.

"Oh, I don't know," said Sanders. "He was never that good as a Chairman."

"Wasn't he?" said Arnold, who had always liked Wainwright and considered that he was the kind of man you wanted in charge—a pleasant sort of person with a nice personality and an even temperament.

"Not really."

Arnold had wondered before the meeting about Wainwright's ability to stand up to Lundy and the Dramatic crew, but he had never really thought of him as being fundamentally unsound. But now, in view of what had just happened, he thought that there might be something in what Sanders said. He took off his spectacles and began to polish them as they walked.

"Well, it's you and me now, Sanders," he said, as they came into the quad.

"That's it," said Sanders. "Couldn't be better as far as I'm concerned."

Arnold was not yet convinced, but he was thinking about it, and as he saw the first formers sitting timidly at the front of the assembly hall, he began to feel that it was his duty to keep things going somehow for their sakes.

The deserter, Wainwright, was sitting with Lundy and the others. Arnold was saddened, but could see a purpose now in going on. He continued polishing his spectacles, thinking it over, and then put them on to pray.

Malcolm's room was small but cosy, brightly painted and with a coal fire. It was on the top floor of the old house, and he presumed it to have been originally one of the servants' rooms. It overlooked the quadrangle and the main classroom block, that rather drab late-nineteenth-century addition to the original building. But it did not seem drab to him. The contrast with smoky Liverpool was too great for it to seem anything less than beautiful, as beautiful as anything he had seen. He felt at once that he was part of something. He was no longer left out on his own, as he had been the past year, living in one place and working in another and liking neither, hating and dreading the journey between them every day. Instead, he would go downstairs in the morning, stroll across the quad and into one of the classrooms; stroll back over to the staffroom at break, sit in one of those old leather armchairs, look out of the window across the meadows; maybe pop up to his room again to fetch a book he had forgotten before going to his next lesson; and in the evening he would still be there, and in the morning he would only have to walk downstairs again and he would be there, in school still. The boys would be well behaved. He would soon know them all. Everyone would know everyone else. How much better this was than the way most people lived, working in cities, commuting, travelling to and fro every day, knowing no one. Why couldn't all schools be like this? This is what life should be like.

It reminded him most of his time on teaching practice with Alice. That had been a good school, though comparatively new, because it was in the country and it was small. The children were all friendly there. There was none of the harshness, the knife-edge existence, the untidy, dirty life of the school in Liverpool. Everything was easy-going and the atmosphere was warm and pleasant. But how long ago that seemed now! It was a little more than two years. Not so long really, but it seemed like twice that time. And that was when he had first met Alice, and now he was back in the same part of the country, near her again, and things seemed to be looking up. She had still not said she would marry him, but they were getting on better. He wondered if he might buy a car, or a motor-bike perhaps—a combination, so that he could take Alice out at weekends. She was teaching at a primary school in the town now. Their term had started last week.

It seemed ages since he had gone out at weekends. The last time was—when? And he was taken right back to the time when his mother was still alive, and almost, so sudden was his recollection, started to cry. He still missed her a lot—his father had been killed early in the war, and he hardly remembered him—but in the four years since her death so much seemed to have changed in some ways, though he could not pinpoint them, that his mother and his old life had faded, at times, almost to nothing. But now, he thought, he was returning to how things used to be. It seemed to him that he had gone on a wide and tedious detour and was only now beginning to see things that he recognised from earlier times.

And the things he recognised were this room, where he was now, being in a place where he felt at home, where he belonged, contentment, a coal fire—he had lived for the last year entirely by shillings-in-the-slot—a quiet life, and Alice.

And all his sense of vocation, that had been so severely tried in Liverpool, was returning now that everything was within his grasp—or only just outside it. He was determined to involve himself as much as he could in the life of the school, and from what he had seen of it so far he did not think that would be so difficult.

The staff, as he discovered, when Mr Hopper took him down to the staffroom later in the afternoon, were friendly and relaxed —especially Mr Lynch—and Mr Hopper himself was very helpful. The boys too, if the group outside the old stables were typical, were very pleasant and respectful. It was quite unlike his first encounter with the boys in Liverpool, when two burly fifth formers had brushed past him in the corridor, almost pushing him out of the way.

And the Headmaster. Returning from his stroll in the quad, he thought how different Mr Jones was from his former Headmaster, who had ruled by fear alone. No one could be afraid of Mr Jones, but everyone would respect him.

The school, and Malcolm's new life there, seemed perfect, and he felt asleep on that first night almost as soon as his head touched the pillow.

He awoke with a start to the tolling of a bell, stared at the ceiling for a second or two, trying to work out what was happening, and then, with a rush of excitement, remembered all about it and got up at once. His first full day in the school! Trembling, he got dressed. The bell stopped tolling. He looked out of the window and saw that the quad was deserted. There was a faint mist, little more than a chill in the air and a dampness which glistened in the early sunlight. He looked at his watch and saw that it was a few minutes after half-past-seven. He realised that he did not know what to do now. He was still largely ignorant of the daily routine of the school. So he lingered for a while in his room, trying to remember if anyone had told him what time breakfast was, and glancing every so often out of his window. But the quad remained empty. At last, he put on his jacket, opened the door and went downstairs. No one was about.

He pushed the staffroom door open and went in, but there was no one there. Still, he decided he had better wait here now until someone came. So he walked over to the window and looked out.

He was spell-bound—an experience normally limited to one's childhood years, when natural phenomena can really seem to be magical. The mist which had been only hinted at in the air of the deserted quad, he now saw lying over the river and the lower meadows, only a few feet high, so that above and beyond it he could see the woods, hazy on the other side of the river.

He stood for ten minutes, just looking, and then the door opened and Mr Birkett came in.

"Good morning, Malcolm. You're up in good time."

"I was woken by the bell," said Malcolm, turning round and feeling very new and innocent. "Am I too early?"

Mr Birkett shrugged his shoulders and seemed to think the question rather pointless. "The boys get up when the bell rings at half-past-seven," he said, "but breakfast isn't till quarter-past-eight."

"We have breakfast with the boys, do we?" asked Malcolm.

"That's right."

Mr Birkett was looking very busy, standing by the table and sorting through some papers in a green folder.

"It's generally rather chaotic on the first day," he said, without turning round. "Make yourself a cup of tea if you like. I won't have one. Too much to do. But you have one, if you like."

"Oh, no. I'll wait till breakfast."

"Fred Lynch will be down soon. He'll be having one."

Malcolm hesitated a moment, then walked over to the corner where the kettle was. "I'll put the kettle on, shall I?"

"If you like. Excuse me a moment." He went out in a hurry, with the green folder tucked under his arm.

Malcolm filled the kettle, put it on the gas ring, found a box of matches on the shelf behind the tea caddy and lit the gas, and each trivial action was like a new discovery. He put enough tea in the pot for two, and then sat down in one of the armchairs waiting for the kettle to boil.

This was marvellous. Here he was, sitting in the staffroom on his own, on a glorious morning, making a pot of tea for Fred Lynch and himself. He still felt new, but here he was and he had a right to be here. It was all, in a sense, his. He lit a cigarette. It was a habit which had been growing with him during his year in Liverpool, and he sometimes thought he ought to try to give it up, because it was a drain on his pocket. But he enjoyed it, and it agreeably increased his sense of independence to light one here, now. He drew the smoke in and felt dizzy, but pleasantly so.

He glanced round the room, and appreciated its well-worn, rather battered, but friendly appearance. The big, old table, the leather armchairs, the faded carpet, the piles of old books and papers. He was to make it all his own.

The door opened and Fred Lynch came in. He looked tired and his hair appeared not to have been combed. He did not notice Malcolm at once and walked with a heavy tread straight over to the tea-making corner. There he stopped, looking uncomprehendingly at the kettle, rubbing one eye with the ball of his thumb.

Malcolm stood up and took a step towards him. "I've put the kettle on," he said.

"Eh? Oh, I'd forgotten about you. Oh. Right." He yawned and tramped over to the settee, on to which he collapsed and lay sprawled out, staring with unseeing eyes towards the window. He scratched his head and grunted, after lying inert for perhaps half a minute, during which time Malcolm had been standing and looking at him with a certain amount of embarrassment and had then walked over to the kettle, which was about to boil.

"Ohhh!" said Mr Lynch, now scratching his stomach. "Strong, not too much milk," he said.

Mr Birkett hurried in, still holding the green folder, but carrying also a pile of text books and holding between his teeth a sheet of paper. He placed the books carefully on the big table, straightened the pile, put down the green folder and took the sheet of paper out of his mouth.

"Morning, Fred," he said, as he leant over him to pin the sheet of paper to the notice board.

"Morning, Ron," said Mr Lynch, shifting his leg out of Mr Birkett's way.

"This is the new timetable," said Mr Birkett, turning to Malcolm, who was approaching with two cups of tea. "You'll have your own personal timetable already, but this has everyone's timetable on. Right," he went on, turning away again and talking now, it seemed, to himself. "What next? Ah, yes. I wonder where he is." He picked up the green folder and hurried out again.

Mr Lynch hoisted himself into a sitting position and took the cup of tea which Malcolm was holding out to him. "Is it sugared?" he said.

"Oh, no," said Malcolm and brought the sugar over. He held it out while Mr Lynch put three heaped teaspoons of sugar into his tea.

Malcolm sat down in an armchair again and watched Mr Lynch stirring his tea so vigorously that it slopped over the side. He tapped the dripping spoon on the edge of the cup, dropped it onto the saucer, and drank.

"Ahhh!" he said, and then yawned.

But the tea seemed to revive him. "Who d'you have first?" he said.

"The fourth form, for English."

"Good bunch there. Some bright lads. They tell me Tomlinson's about the best at English. Lundy's probably good as well. Have you met any of the lads yet?"

"Not really," said Malcolm.

"Well, those two are probably about the best. There's Moorcroft, bit of a swot but not a bad lad. Then there's Wilkins. Professor type, you know. All brain. Hopeless at games. You a games man?"

"I did some games in my last school."

"What's your speciality?"

"Cricket, I suppose."

"Rugby?"

"I've only done soccer, I'm afraid."

"Ah, we don't play soccer, here. I wouldn't mind it myself, but rugger's the tradition, you know. What have we got you down for?" He craned his neck round to look at the timetable behind him.

"I've got the second form on Tuesday afternoon."

"That's right. I remember. Well, I'll run through the rules with you and you can just start a game going. That's all you need to do really. Can't do a great deal with'em at that age. English and what is it you're teaching?"

"Geography, mainly. That's what I did at College. But I've got some maths as well, with my own form."

"What form's that?"

"The first form."

"That's right. Now look. There's bound to be some tears for the first few days. But don't be too soft with 'em. They've got to learn, so it's best to let 'em get on with it."

A bell started tolling and they went in to breakfast. Mr Lynch had suddenly grown very talkative, for one who had seemed when he first appeared to be still half-asleep. Throughout breakfast, he carried on talking to Malcolm and asking him questions, chopping and changing from one subject to another, giving him odd bits of information about the boys and the school and throwing in odd bits of advice here and there. He also consumed prodigious quantities of cornflakes, bacon, tomato, toast and marmalade, and drank several more cups of tea.

Malcolm felt very conspicuous, sitting up on the dais at one end of the dining hall, overlooking the sixty boys all eating their breakfasts and chattering to each other. It was easy to distinguish the new boys—his own form—by their quietness and timidity, as well as by their clean, new blazers. He kept glancing down at all the boys as he listened to Mr Lynch.

Everyone else had finished a good five minutes before Mr Lynch, but no one went out. Mr Birkett had eaten a hurried breakfast and then departed in search of the Headmaster, whom he had so far been unable to locate, as he said, pointedly, to Mr Lynch. But at last, when he had lifted the lid of the teapot and discovered that there was no tea left, he reached out and grasped hold of a large hand-bell which stood on the white tablecloth. He shook it and it rang loudly and at once the boys began to file out.

Mr Birkett called two boys to him in the quad and sent them in search of the Headmaster.

"The Headmaster is nowhere to be seen," he said, as Malcolm and Mr Lynch re-entered the staffroom.

"He'll turn up," said Mr Lynch, and then he roared with laughter. "Morning, Geoff," he said, when his laughter had subsided.

"Good morning, Fred. Good morning, Malcolm. Just suffered your first breakfast?"

"It was very nice," said Malcolm, enthusiastically.

Both Mr Lynch and Mr Hopper laughed loudly.

"I used to do without breakfast more often than not last year," said Malcolm.

"Oh, we can't have that."

"No wonder you're thin," said Mr Lynch.

"Cook's breakfast is probably better than nothing, but that's about all that can be said for it."

"I thought it was very good," said Malcolm.

"For heaven's sake, don't let cook hear you say that," said Mr Hopper. "She'll be giving you extra portions, and you'll never recover."

"My Lynch seemed to like it. He had plenty."

Mr Hopper burst out laughing and Mr Lynch patted his stomach and pulled a wry face.

"By the way," said Mr Hopper, "we're all on first name terms here. Except the Head of course. I'm Geoff. That's Fred. That's Ron."

"Mmm? Oh yes, by all means," said Mr Birkett, and then hurried out again.

"Right," said Malcolm.

A bell started tolling.

"We are summoned to our classrooms," said Mr Hopper. "Do you know where yours is? Good. Have you got your register? Where are they, Fred?"

Mr Lynch shrugged his shoulders.

"Registers," said Mr Birkett, hurrying in with four registers in his hand. "I still can't find the Headmaster. I want to make sure he has all the announcements for assembly. I suppose I shall just have to do them myself."

The three teachers strolled out to their classrooms, leaving Mr Birkett scurrying round the staffroom in ever diminishing circles.

"Sit down, sit down," said Mr Hopper, to his form, blandly.

"Right!" said Mr Lynch to his.

"Hello, boys," said Malcolm. "My name's Mr Drew. I'm new here and so are you, so we must all help each other to find our way about."

The little boys in their rows smiled nervously.

"Did you all sleep well last night?"

"Yes, sir!"

"Yes, thank you, sir!"

"Yes, sir!"

"Please, sir. He was crying."

"Well, never mind. We'll soon get used to it," said Malcolm, remembering what Fred Lynch had said, trying to steel his heart to the miserable-looking little boy pointed out.

"Please, sir. I've been away from home lots of times."

"Have you? And what's your name?"

"Please, sir, Martin Thompson, sir."

"Well, I might be asking you later to tell us all about where you've been, in the Geography lesson."

"Please, sir," said another. "I've been to Africa, sir."

"Have you? Well, that sounds fascinating. It sounds as though we're going to have some good Geography lessons. Now, will you answer to your names when I read them out?"

He went through the register and when he had finished a bell started tolling.

"I expect that means it's time for assembly," said Malcolm. "So will you stand behind your chairs?"

They went into the assembly hall. The Headmaster was sitting alone on the dais at the front and the Hall was empty. Malcolm's form sat down at the front in complete silence. Malcolm walked up to the Headmaster. "Are we too early?" he said, quietly.

Mr Jones smiled and looked up. "No, no," he said. "How are you?"

"Finding my way about," said Malcolm, trying to be affable.

Mr Jones smiled and Malcolm sat down on the bench by the door, where the staff sat.

Mr Birkett popped his head round the door, saw the Headmaster and, with a sigh expressive of both relief and irritation, went up to him and gave him a sheet of paper on which he had written the things he thought Mr Jones ought to say and might forget. Then he sat down next to Malcolm.

The other teachers came in with their classes, Mr Birkett's form, which contained Lundy, Wilkins and the others, coming in last, on their own.

"I want to talk to the new boys," said Mr Jones, after the religious part of the assembly was over. "I want to say only one thing. That I hope you will enjoy your time here, that you will soon find your way around and begin to settle down. It will not always be easy. I hope you don't expect it to be. That would be very silly of you. At times, I have no doubt, you will be unhappy and will probably wish you had never been born. Most of us, at one time or another, have wished that we had never been born. But that's life, and that is what we are here to learn."

He descended from his dais and walked slowly out of the Hall, still holding in his hand the sheet of paper which Mr Birkett had given him, but apparently having forgotten all about it. Mr Birkett set his lips in a thin, straight line, walked to the front of the Hall and dismissed the school.

Two boys lay flat on their stomachs in the grass by the river, their eyes fixed intently on something about twenty yards away. There was a dead silence. The grass stalks touched their cheeks and felt hard to their hands.

One was small and dark-haired, with a round, perpetually grubby-looking face, spattered with freckles. His eyes were ice blue and he had a keen, even fierce, gaze. The other was fair and somewhat taller, or, in their present positions, longer. His skin was pale, his lips were thin and all his features seemed to be elongated, drawn downwards, giving him a blank and despondent look. His eyes were large and watery.

"What is it?" whispered the dark-haired boy, so quietly that only his companion, who was no more than a few inches away from him, could have heard his voice.

"A reed warbler," replied the other, in an equally soft voice. Neither of them removed his eyes from the bird they were watching. "Acrocephalus streperus."

The dark-haired boy repeated the strange sounds, moving his lips but making no sound. He watched the little bird, perched on a low branch overhanging the river, and then glanced out of the corner of his eye at his friend. Two or three yellowing stalks of grass were between their faces, and they blurred as he focused his eyes on his friend's face. He moved his hand gently and pushed the stalks to the ground. He looked back to the river and saw the bird fly away, and he rolled over onto his back. "Acrocephalus streperus," he said aloud.

"That's right." His friend sat up and scratched his knee and then looked at his hands, the palms of which had gone yellow and were creased with tiny criss-cross lines where they had been pressed on the grass.

"What does it mean?"

"I don't know."

The one continued to look at his hands and the other to stare up at the sky.

"Look at my hands. They've gone yellow." He held one of them over the other boy's face.

"Oh yes." He held up his own hands. "Mine are the same."

He rolled over in the grass two or three times and stopped with his face two inches above the earth. "How long do you think it will take you to save up for your binoculars?" he said, to a little insect that was crawling up a blade of grass.

"I don't know. I've got three pounds now and I could buy a pair with that, but they wouldn't be much good. The kind I want cost twelve pounds."

"It'll take you years."

"I know. At the end of every week I give whatever I've got

left over to Mr Birkett to keep for me."

"You'll have to cut out sweets," the dark-haired boy said, vaguely remembering something he had heard his aunt say to his uncle. Then he suddenly jumped up and stood with his feet planted wide apart staring at the river. "It would be good with binoculars, wouldn't it? Are you in the Stamp Club or the Amateur Dramatic Society?" he said, with barely a pause between the two quite unrelated questions. It was a way he had, but his friend had not had time to discover that yet, because they had only known each other for two days, the dark-haired boy being new to the school.

"Neither," he said.

"I thought everybody was in one or the other." He looked sternly down at the upturned face.

"Not really. Lots of little kids are in the Stamp Club, and Wilkins and Wainwright and Sanders and one or two others in our class. And the Amateur Dramatic Society is really just Lundy and Tomlinson and Carter and that lot. They don't really do anything."

"Why don't you form a bird-watching club?"

"Nobody else is interested. If anybody was, they could come with me. There's no need to form a club. Anyway, nobody else is interested."

"How do you know? What's Lundy like?" he said, not waiting for an answer to his first question.

There was a pause, while the fair-haired boy, whose mind would not move as rapidly as the other's, plucked a piece of grass and gave himself time to catch up. He could not be hurried.

"Everyone likes him," he said, at last.

"Don't you?"

"Yes. Everyone does."

"Why?" He stood with his legs apart, looking down at his friend, shooting these questions at him almost fiercely.

"I suppose because he's friendly and not mean. He's good at most things, but he doesn't crow about it. He's good at games. The teachers like him as well."

"Who's the one who's good at things and crows about it?"

he asked, picking his friend up on this point like an inquisitor.

"No one, really. Perhaps Moorcroft a bit."

"Not Tomlinson?"

"No. Tommo's all right."

"Does everyone call him Tommo?"

The fair-haired boy nodded and stood up.

His companion looked at him and grinned at his pale face. "They call you Blue Tit, don't they?" he said.

"Sometimes."

"Because of your name. It's funny you being called Finch and being an ornithologist, isn't it? Do you mind being called Blue Tit?"

The other boy shrugged.

"They used to call me Fishen in my last school. Fishenchips. From Minchip."

"Did you mind that?"

"Yes." The fierce look came into his face again.

"I won't tell anyone."

"I know you won't. That's why I told you."

"Thanks."

They both smiled, a little solemnly, and began to walk away towards the school. John Finch and Philip Minchip, the new boy, were now firm friends.

It was Sunday afternoon. The boys were scattered round the school, some inside in the House common rooms, others on the fields, others in the yard playing cricket and touch-and-pass or just standing and talking. Some had been given permission to go out riding on their bikes and some had gone up into the woods or down the road to the village, having first reported to Mr Lynch, who was the Master on Duty, and given him their names and destinations. John and Philip walked into the quad and saw David Lundy sitting by himself on the wooden seat which encircled the trunk of the horse-chestnut tree.

"Let's go see Lundy," said Philip.

David looked up when the two boys walked up to him. "Hello," he said.

"Hello, Dave," said John.

Philip reserved the right, as a new boy, to say nothing until he was spoken to and stood looking at David's pleasantly smiling face.

"Been for a walk?" said David to John, avoiding Philip's stare. John nodded. "Bird watching?" John nodded again. "See anything good?"

"A reed warbler."

"Is that good?"

John shrugged. There was silence for a moment, and Philip continued to make David feel uncomfortable by watching him. Then, "Hey!" said David. "I was meaning to ask you. Do you want to join the Dramatic Society? That is to say, the new Incorporated Society." He was speaking to Philip and looking him for the first time full in the face. One dark and grubby-looking, the other fair and handsome, with bright eyes and long lashes, they looked at each other.

"No," said Philip.

"Why?" asked David, disconcerted. But he continued to look him in the face, because he felt as if he were being challenged and was determined to give as good as he received.

"We're thinking of forming a Society of our own," said Philip.

David looked at John in disbelief, but John was looking at Philip, and so David turned back to him. "A bird-watching society?" he asked.

"That's right," said Philip.

"Do you want to amalgamate?" David asked him jokingly.

"No thanks," said Philip. "Come on, John. We'd better start making plans."

David watched them go, wondering what made the new boy act so fierce and unfriendly. He decided he didn't like the look of him, but couldn't help thinking there was something about him that—he didn't quite know what—something impressive.

"I doubt if anybody'll join," said John.

But that didn't matter to Philip. "We'll have a Society on our own then," he said. "You're Chairman and I'm Secretary. I'll get a book and we'll keep a record of the birds we see. We'll have regular expeditions and you can tell me what to write down. I might be getting a camera for Christmas. Then we can take photographs as well."

"I've got some books," said John, beginning to get caught up in his quiet way with Philip's enthusiasm. "You can borrow them if you like."

"Thanks," said Philip. He seemed overwhelmed. It could hardly have been by John's generosity, but he certainly felt something very deeply. They did not speak for a while. John went for his books and Philip looked through them with great interest. They sat in their formroom looking through them and talking until the bell rang for tea.

Evening prayers on a Sunday were held immediately after tea and they were a much longer affair than they were on weekdays, with bible readings and a sermon. Sometimes a minister came to take the service. Otherwise it was taken by Mr Birkett, occasionally, but rarely, by the Headmaster, and never by Mr Lynch or Mr Hopper. In the morning, the whole school was marched down the lane, after breakfast, to the village church, a distance of about a mile.

The assembly hall was very old. At one end, on a dais, was a big, highly polished and uncomfortable chair, with a carved lectern in front of it. The body of the hall was filled with rows of wooden benches with desks attached, the original seating with which the school had been furnished when this was the schoolroom where all the teaching was done by one man and an assistant. They were not individual desks, but long ones, accommodating ten boys each, and the desk tops did not lift up, they merely provided a surface to work on, pitted now with age and engravings. The long seat was attached to the heavy, cast iron frame by hinges, so that it tipped up. With the seat down, it was not possible to stand up unless you bent your legs at the knees where the seat pressed against them. If a boy misbehaved in assembly he was sometimes told to stand on the seat—a humiliating experience. There were four high windows down one side only, and two windows at the back. The four windows faced due east, since the assembly hall occupied one wing of the old house and the front of the house had a southerly aspect.

On sunny mornings, the hall had a look of bright and cheerful antiquity, like a jovial old man with a face of creased leather; in the afternoon it looked mellow, warm and soft; but in the evening, it was dark and forbidding, the rows of hard, black desks and the dark wooden panels of the walls creating an atmosphere of monotonous severity, like the unrelenting frown of an old-fashioned puritan preacher dressed all in black. On cloudy days, the hall was merely dull and colourless, whatever the time of day.

Mr Birkett took evening prayers on this Sunday. There had been a time when his sermons were long and impassioned, delivered in a loud, rhetorical voice, which worried some of the smaller boys and put into them, if not the fear of God, then at least the fear of Mr Birkett. But over the years his sermons had been diminishing and his voice had lost some of its former resonance. His sermons were no longer long and impassioned, but merely short and tetchy. The effect they had on the smaller boys had changed accordingly. No longer awed by the majesty of his full-throated anger, they felt it would be advisable to keep out of his way because he was clearly very irritable. The older boys never listened to a word he was saying.

Philip, showing none of the timidity which might have been expected of him as a new boy, read one of the books which John had lent him throughout the service. John, sitting by his side, glanced at the book from time to time and glanced at Philip's face, but he sang the hymns and murmured the Lord's Prayer, none of which Philip did. In four years he had not learnt the carelessness which Philip seemed to have acquired in two days.

David Lundy, sitting in the row in front, glanced round at Philip once or twice, but Philip never once looked up from his book.

John took it all as a mark of the deepest friendship.

If the service was short, the boys had five or ten minutes to themselves afterwards. Otherwise, they had to go straight to their formrooms for Letter Writing. This lasted until eight o'clock.

"Please, sir," said Wilkins, when Mr Birkett came in and saw everyone settled with pens and writing-pads, "may I have permission to go round to the other forms and make an announcement later on?"

"Write your letter first," said Mr Birkett, looking vaguely at Philip Minchip.

"Yes, sir. I'll go at about five-to-eight, shall I, sir? Can Sanders come with me, sir? Sir?"

"What? Yes, yes. Sit down and write your letter."

"Thank you, sir," said Wilkins and nodded at Sanders as he returned to his desk.

Mr Birkett's gaze had fixed more determinedly on Philip, and one by one the boys noticed it and turned to look at him as he sat back in his desk reading the book.

"What do you think you're doing?" said Mr Birkett, when it had become obvious that Philip was not going to look up.

"I'm reading a book," said Philip, turning it over and looking at the cover, as if in confirmation of the fact. But there was no insolence in his voice; rather, anger at being asked the question. A fierce look of resentment appeared in his eyes and his face contracted and grew darker, more grubby.

"Oh, yes," said Mr Birkett, who had remembered something. "Well, there's no need to write a letter this week, of course. But you will next week. What have you all turned round for?" he went on, turning impatiently to the rest of the form. "Get on with your letters. I'm not staying with you the whole time, but I shall look in now and again to make sure there is no noise. If there is, I shall punish you. Now get on."

He went out. After he had gone, there was some whispering and most of the boys turned round to look at Philip, who, however, did not look up from his book. The whispering continued, though in fits and starts, because if anyone had not written the required amount by eight o'clock they would have to stay in until they had done. They seemed to know by instinct when Mr Birkett was approaching, because whenever he came in there was always dead silence.

To begin with, the apparent coolness and insolence of Philip's reply had made all the boys thrill with excitement in admiration of the rebel. But when Mr Birkett gave way, they guessed that it was not a matter of simple rebellion but that there was some reason why Philip did not have to write a letter. They puzzled about it and some of the whispering was on this subject. John Finch was no wiser than the others, and he puzzled about it even more than they did—with the possible exception of David Lundy—but he whispered to nobody about this or anything else. Instead, he wrote in his letter home about his new friend, who was short and had dark hair and freckles and whom he was teaching about ornithology and with whom he had been bird-watching that afternoon and with whom he was going to form a bird-watching club.

Arnold Wilkins' letters were a source of delight to his grandmother and father, and of a mixture of amusement and concern to his mother. On this Sunday, he wrote as follows:

Dear Mother, Father and Grandmother,

I fear my letter this week may prove to be somewhat single-minded. All that has happened during the four days we have been back is as nothing compared to what happened on Friday evening.

The first thing that greeted my ears on Thursday afternoon when I walked into the dormitory with my suitcase was the sound of Carter's voice proclaiming that Lundy had magnanimously agreed to a joint meeting between the Stamp Club and the Amateur Dramatic Society, though he did not say it in exactly those words. I will not bruise the paper with an exact quotation.

Imagine both my pleasure and my dismay! You know how ardently I had worked during the last two terms of last year to bring about just such a meeting and with what little success my efforts had been rewarded, and now at last my dreams had been realised, but at the hands of another. I have learnt by this that the real reward of righteous effort is not to be found in public acclaim but in the private knowledge that one has done right. But I must confess that at the time it was small comfort. I contented myself with planning for the success of this so-long-hoped-for meeting. But even in that I was to be foiled again.

Friday passed in a haze of intense thinking. I was so preoccupied that I misconstrued a line of Caesar which it would not have been remarkable for a second former to understand!

That meeting! I sometimes wonder if any of them have ever heard of the Rules of Debating! They would have gone on without a Chairman, if I had not pointed out the lack of one. For my pains, I was elected Chairman myself, which ought to teach me to keep my mouth closed in future. Still, better me than no one!

To begin with, Lundy made all the proposals which I could have wished him to make, and, if it had ended there, I would have had nothing to complain about. Then he dropped a bombshell which really caught me napping and took the meeting by storm. He suggested that the Stamp Club and the Amateur Dramatic Society should amalgamate. For some reason, everybody agreed at once. I think the reason can be no more than that everybody likes Lundy. Nobody stopped to think, but just jumped at his suggestion, and that was that. I was too surprised to be able to do anything about it. But I doubt if I could have swung the meeting in any case, everyone was so strongly behind Lundy.

There is something about people like Lundy that seems to make everyone do as they want. I suppose Lundy is what they call a 'born leader.' But I wonder what it is that makes him one. I have been thinking about this, but can find no answer.

But I must try to find an answer soon, because the upshot of it all is that I am now Chairman of the Stamp Club. "Some have greatness thrust upon them. . . ! ! !" Wainwright—whom I have always liked—was bribed over on to the other side by the offer of a place on their Committee. I suppose you could say that this has been a salutary experience for me in revealing the basic unreliability of human nature. I would never have thought it of Wainwright. My new Secretary, Sanders, says he suspected this all along and seems not to have been surprised by anything that has happened. He seems to take it all in his stride. I suppose you could say that he is the realist and I am the eternal dreamer!!

So now I have to try to be a leader, like Lundy. I shall do my best, and with the help of Sanders perhaps we shall make a go of it. But I am breaking new ground here and I feel very unsure of myself. But someone has to keep the flag flying.

Anyway, I have been carried away as usual and spent the whole time talking about my own problems and have not given you any of those interesting little bits of news and information that you—especially Grandmother—are always asking for! And now I have no time, because I have to go and call a meeting of the Stamp Club (or Stamps Section, as we must call it now) for eight o'clock. I will not pretend that I am not apprehensive.

So now I must finish. I will try and write a more varied letter next week.

Love,
Arnold.

The rest of the form were poor letter-writers by comparison.

"Why weren't you writing a letter?" asked Carter, after the Letter-Writing period had ended.

A number of possibilities ran through Philip's mind. "My parents can't read," he said, without looking up from his book.

Carter, who was very touchy about some things, stood looking down at him, trying to make up his mind if this were a sarcastic reference to his own lack of ability in that direction. He was still undecided when Lundy called to him to hurry up, and he decided to give Minchip the benefit of the doubt this time, and went away.

"I'm going to read this in bed tonight as well," said Philip to John as soon as they had the formroom to themselves. "It's great!"

John smiled. "I'm glad you like it," he said.

Philip put the book down and sat on a desk by the window, with his arm on the window-ledge and his feet on the desk seat.

"I like this school," he said.

"It's all right, isn't it?" said John, following him and sitting down near him.

"It's better than my last one," Philip went on. "There was this little village school in Wales, only one teacher and everybody in the same class, no matter how old you were or how clever. It was a little pokey room with cobwebs up in the corners of the ceiling, and mice. You could hear the mice sometimes, during the day, if there was a silence, when we were all working. This little scratching sound. Sometimes you saw one running along by the wall. Then it went into its hole again. There was this big Welsh boy who always used to have a few stones in his pocket to throw at the mice. He got one once. It was only stunned, so he got it by the tail and banged it on the floor till it was dead, like you do with a fish. It might not have been dead, only unconscious, but he put it in his pocket and when he went out he gave it to a cat to eat.

"Some of the boys only spoke Welsh and the teacher had to do lessons in both Welsh and English. He was as tall as a tree, and thin. Just skin and bone. His face was all bone. And he had long white hair. He used to prod you with these long, bony fingers, and scratch his cheek with his first finger when he was thinking about something. It was like somebody poking at a dead fish with a piece of stick. You didn't learn anything. They didn't like me because I was English. Some of them hardly knew where England was. The ones that only spoke Welsh.

"It was miles from anywhere, this village, and they were all farmers, apart from the shopkeeper. They were all ignorant and didn't know about anything outside their valley. There wasn't any wireless or television and most of them couldn't read, so there were no newspapers either. As soon as they learnt how to read in that school, they forgot again. There was devil-worship too. We lived in this house on the side of the valley. It was built just on this little ledge, with a path going down the hill to the road. It was only small, but it had big rooms. A great big kitchen with a massive fireplace made out of stone. There was a little face like a demon carved in it at the top. It had beams. All the rooms had beams and sometimes you saw a spider hanging down from one of the beams so it looked as if it was floating in mid-air. There were moths everywhere in the summer. But in the winter you couldn't get out. We were stuck inside the house for three days once. You couldn't get down the path, and for a bit we couldn't get the door open. We had to climb out of the window and dig our way through to the coal house to light the fire. We might have frozen to death. A few times people were found frozen to death on the hills after a heavy snow.

"We've left there now. But before we left, the day before, it was a hard, windy day, like it is sometimes in the valleys. I went out on my own to this hill. Have you ever read about King Arthur? Well, I've read a lot about him and Merlin's supposed to have been trapped by this witch under a mountain in Wales. And some people say it was this hill near where we lived. There was this farmer I got to know a bit. He was quite old, but he had eyes like a hawk. His wife had fish-eyes. She used to lie in bed all day. His farm was all falling to bits and he only had a few pigs left and he used to spend most of his time round by the pigsty. Well, I went to see him, and he told me all about the superstitions and ghosts and gods and devils. Because not everyone believes there's only one god. Some people think there are lots. I think there are lots as well, unless there aren't any. But I told him about Merlin and this witch, and he said he'd heard something about it once. He said there was a witch in the village and maybe a witch was making his farm fall to bits. Anyway, one day a little piglet died for no reason at all, and the pigs started fighting, and there was blood everywhere. A pig can bite your hand off. They've got very powerful jaws. So I went to this hill. It was quite big and there were trees some of the way up, but after a while it was just scrub and stones, but there were one or two trees higher up, all dying. They grew so high, then fell down. There were lots of dead branches lying around everywhere. There was a wind, very dry and hard and all the time there was a noise among the dead branches. It was quite frightening. You weren't sure whether there was a noise or not. You could hear it, but you weren't really sure whether it was outside your head or inside. Just these old, dead branches I was sitting on, and the stones, and this hard, dry wind, and it was quite high up the hill, with the other trees down below. Then I thought I heard a shout. I wasn't sure. I sat as still as I could on the branches, listening. But you couldn't be sure. I thought I heard it again, but I wasn't sure. So I walked away a bit to a tree that hadn't fallen over yet. It was dead, though, and quite small, and twisted a bit into the shape of a man. I thought suddenly it might be a sign of where Merlin was trapped, and I began to be afraid that the witch might be there. I could feel the wind pressing on my back like a big hand pushing me. I didn't want to turn round, in case there was someone behind me. But at last I did. I turned round quickly, and as soon as I did a big gust of wind suddenly blew and nearly knocked me over, like someone smacking me in the mouth, and there was a noise from somewhere. And when I turned round again, I saw what had made the noise. The tree was lying on the ground."

John just listened and watched, while Philip went on telling his tales, until the bell started tolling for supper.

There had been a time when Mr and Mrs Jones had been visited fairly frequently by friends and relations, especially during the school holidays. The Meadows was a delightful place to spend a few days during the summer and accommodation, obviously, was no problem. But that time was past. Their lives, especially since the death of their son, had become increasingly lonely, and it was some years now since anyone had been to stay. At holiday time, The Meadows was very quiet, very empty. It made not a jot of difference to Mrs Jones whether the pupils were there or not, but her husband, of course, had time on his hands. He did not in any obvious way use this time, but was to be seen—had anybody been there to see him—walking slowly along the corridors from one room to another, pausing for a moment here and there, to look inside a classroom or glance out of a window or let his eyes rest for a moment on a painting hung on a wall. Or he sat on the wooden seat under the horse-chestnut tree in the quad, looking slowly round about him. Or he walked on the path across the meadows down to the river, stopping every so often to let his eyes wander over the scene, to stand eventually by the bridge and watch the water flowing or look at the dark stone patched with green and smile faintly, benevolently, at the darkness.

If the weather was bad, he would sit or stand in his study, reading, writing, doing whatever work had to be done, or just thinking, and his face never showed anything other than that faint trace of humour or benevolence, wherever he was and whatever he was doing. If there was rain streaking the window pane and clashing on the gravel path outside; if there was mist or fog curling round the stone pillars on the front steps and leaning wearily on the stone frames of the windows; if there was snow blurring the sky and piling up on the window-sill; if there was wind, hurrying the river along, flattening the grass, rattling the dead leaves against the window; he would look up and smile and carry on with what he had to do.

He was either in his study, or somewhere in a corridor, or on the river bank, and his wife was in another room with a duster or a mop in her hand, frowning at a chair or a table on which the dust was trying to settle, and at her husband, who was like a human dust bent on settling on her life.

Thus passed fourteen weeks of each year; thus, indeed, for Mrs Jones all fifty-two. Mr Jones had a little more to do in term-time. He had to teach a little, and there was more to do in other ways as well. But his manner did not change, and the way he went about his work in term-time was very little different from the way he went about doing nothing in the holidays. Quite often you would come across him in a corridor somewhere, slowly walking or just standing.

Mr Birkett knocked briskly on the door of the Headmaster's study, opened it and looked in. "No one there," he noted, with exasperation, though it was what he had expected. He turned round and went out.

"Oh, Mr Birkett. Could I have a word with you?" said Mr Jones.

Mr Birkett opened the door and went in again. "I didn't see you there," he said.

Mr Jones, seated in a deep armchair, smiled and nodded his head.

It was Monday morning. Lessons were in progress. The clock would strike ten at any moment.

"We've hardly had a talk yet this term, Ron, have we?" said the Headmaster.

Mr Birkett's face took on a look which is hard to describe. "No," he said.

"Did you have a good summer? You stayed with your sister, as usual, did you? In the hotel? Was business good?"

"Fair, fair," said Mr Birkett.

"You must be invaluable to your sister in the summer. Any problems that come up, you'll be able to deal with them for her. Not much of a holiday for you though, perhaps?"

"She's a very capable woman."

"Ah. Capable. The quality must be a family trait. All the same, she must be glad of your presence in the summer, if only for the company."

"Mmm. You said you wanted a word with me."

"Oh, yes." Mr Jones hesitated, looking at a letter that was lying open on his desk. "But that can wait. What was it you wanted, first?"

Mr Birkett had become over the years something of a defeatist. He had become so accustomed to asking for things to be done, regulations tightened up, restrictions imposed, new school rules instituted, old ones reaffirmed, firm stands and stern measures taken, and having his requests always, always, ignored, that he tended now to give up even before he had started. So often, after a long and exhausting chase, when he had finally cornered the Headmaster, he decided that it was not worth saying what he had meant to say, because nothing ever came of it, or else he said it so lamely that the Headmaster could have been forgiven for thinking it was not important. What often happened though, when Mr Birkett did get round to saying something and making out a strong case for it, was that the Headmaster agreed and said, "Well, I think you ought to deal with that, Ron." But on those terms Mr Birkett would rather see nothing done "If he's not prepared to do it himself," he would say to Fred Lynch, "then as far as I'm concerned it can stay undone and things can stay as they are. Why should I worry? Things will just have to get worse, mark my words. But it's his responsibility, not mine." But, for all that, nothing ever seemed to change, for better or worse, and Mr Birkett did worry.

"Only a few things, Headmaster. Nothing very much."

Mr Jones listened and nodded his head and smiled, as Mr Birkett went through the list of things that had to be dealt with, in all of which Mr Jones shared the opinion of his Deputy so completely that he was able, without hesitation, to tell him just to go ahead and do whatever he thought was necessary. "Is that all?" he said, when Mr Birkett appeared to have done.

"Apart from what you wanted to say."

"Ah yes." He looked at the letter again, and picked it up. "Well, I think that can wait a little. It's not urgent. I'll speak to you later about that."

"Right," said Mr Birkett, standing up, perfectly satisfied that the school was going to rack and ruin.

"I think we must have a staff meeting sometime," said Mr Jones. "In a week or so. There's no hurry. You might let me know when you think it would be convenient. No hurry though. I'll mention it to you again later on."

When the Deputy Headmaster had gone, Mr Jones sat for a little while looking at the letter. Then he walked over to the filing cabinet, hooked his finger through the handle of the top drawer and pulled gently so that the drawer slid smoothly open. He dropped the letter in, smiled even more benignly than usual, and gently pushed the drawer back until it clicked and was closed. He rested his hand on the top of the cabinet for a few moments, like an old man absent-mindedly patting a little boy on the head. At last, he returned to his desk where his morning's work awaited him.

He sat down and opened a big ledger and began making entries. The school was not large enough to warrant employing a Bursar, and it was part of Mr Jones's job to look after the school's finances. But twenty-three years' experience had taught him all there was to know about book-keeping, and the science held no mysteries for him. He was, in any case, a mathematician. The morning passed in a friendly way, with Mr Jones bestowing his smile on a number of bills and invoices and statements, from local tradespeople, local council, suppliers of coke and coal, suppliers of books, Gas Board, Electricity Board, and turning over with careful fingers the pages of two or three different ledgers, and writing during the course of the morning a large number of cheques. But he worked at the dull figures so mildly, so unhurriedly, that he might have been an old age pensioner contentedly planting rows of vegetables in his garden.

At lunchtime he left his study and walked down the corridor to his own dining room, where meals were brought from the kitchen to him and his wife. The table was already laid, but his wife was not there. So he sat down at the table and waited. After a few minutes a maid came in with the meal on a tray. A plate of roast meat, a dish of potatoes and a dish of carrots were placed on the table, and the maid withdrew. Mr Jones looked round to see if his wife had come in, and since she had not he helped himself to the food and began to eat.

Without a word, Mrs Jones came in, sat down, put a very little food on her plate and began to eat.

"Ah!" said Mr Jones. "Hello."

His wife looked up briefly and then carried on eating.

"Won't you take a little more?"

She glanced at him for a moment as though he were an idiot. "What time have I got for eating?"

"You must eat."

"With all these big old rooms to keep clean."

"Another five minutes..."

Mrs Jones shook her head like a horse that is irritated by a fly, and said no more. As she put her knife and fork down, her husband said, "I had a letter this morning which you ought to look at sometime."

"I haven't time now," said Mrs Jones, standing up impatiently.

"No, no, of course not. Perhaps if I remember to bring it in this evening you could look at it then. But there's no hurry."

Mrs Jones turned round and went out, shutting the door firmly behind her. The maid came in with the sweet. "Is Mrs Jones not having any sweet, sir?"

"No. So would you like to put just a small portion of the steamed pudding on my plate and put on it just a drop of custard? Thank you. Now you could take the rest away. Thank you."

"Thank you, sir."

"Thank you."

The maid returned a little later with a cup of coffee and a biscuit, which Mr Jones carried to an armchair in the corner by the window. The maid quickly cleared the table, folded the table cloth and took it all away on a tray, closing the door quietly behind her. For an hour, Mr Jones sat in the armchair, first drinking the coffee and eating the biscuit, and then just sitting with his head back and his eyes closed. But he did not snore, his mouth did not fall open as the mouths of middle-aged and elderly gentlemen generally do during their midday rest, and his face retained all of its waking appearance of mild benevolence and absent-minded good-humour. He scarcely moved during the whole hour, but he did not appear to be asleep.

More time was spent during the afternoon with the ledgers in his study. He read a letter which had arrived by the second post while he had been in the dining room. The letter was long and came from someone in Cardiff. It appeared to give him considerable food for thought, and he sat for all of half-an-hour thinking about it, before taking from a drawer in his desk a writing pad, several sheets of which he used in writing a reply. He folded the letter, put it in an envelope and addressed it to Mr and Mrs Minchip in Cardiff.

The bell rang for the beginning of the last period and, leaving the letter with some others in a pile on his desk, he went out. Mr Hopper gave him a deferential "Good afternoon, sir," when they passed in the quad; he heard from the fields the sound of boys' voices and the sound of Mr Lynch's voice raised above the rest; he entered the classroom where he was to teach Maths to

Mr Birkett's form and all the boys stood up.

"Please sit down," he said.

The lesson began. The boys listened to his quiet voice, explaining and unravelling for them, slowly, carefully, the difficulties of algebra. He gave them a rule to write down in their exercise books and walked round the classroom to make sure that each of them had it written down correctly. He demonstrated to them on the blackboard the application of the rule. He called out several different boys, one by one, to work out on the board an algebraic problem which could be solved by the application of the rule. The lesson was slow and repetitive and demanded patience. The teacher had patience, but some of the boys did not, and so he was teaching them to be patient. The influence of the teacher and the influence of the rule of algebra, being revealed slowly in its simple beauty, had their effect. A mood was being formed throughout the class which touched on everyone: a mood of patience, which is the response to simplicity. Even Wilkins felt it, though he thought he was just enjoying the maths.

Philip thought about John Finch and looked at David Lundy. The Headmaster set him a problem to do on the board, and he went out and, with a little rapid thought, worked out how to do it, solved the problem and sat down. He continued to look at David and think about John Finch and feel a curious resentment against both. Mr Jones watched him scowling and noted that he was not like the others. Minchip was in a different kind of mood. The mood of the lesson had not touched him.

Mr Jones wrote on the blackboard a final problem and told them to copy it into their books and solve it now. They worked for a little while, and when the time was up he solved the problem himself on the board and asked them to mark themselves right or wrong. He counted the result.

"We have had a sixty per cent success rate," he said, "which is not too bad for a start."

He closed the door and went out, as the bell rang for the end of lessons.

The road to the village wound round the school buildings,

crossed the river by the bridge, skirted the low hill and the wood and then continued through undulating farm land, past the church, to the village. Sometimes Mr Jones would ask Mr Lynch to drive to the village with the day's letters, sometimes he would send two boys, but more often than not he went himself, as he did today.

There was a slight chill in the air, a hint of colder regions. Birds, in twos and threes, wheeled through the air, going somewhere or waiting to go. The river, as he crossed the bridge, was putty coloured, reflecting the sky. Leaves fell continuously from the trees. The earth was dark brown in the ploughed fields, and the birds circled in the air overhead. As he walked on, he smiled and his smile deepened. It lodged in his eyes and seemed to settle there. He popped the letters in the letter box and, for a moment, his smile broadened and almost became a laugh. He turned to walk back, always smiling.

After dinner, he sat with his wife in their living room, she reading and he just sitting and thinking. She came very close to asking him on that evening what he was smiling about. She very nearly looked up from her book and confronted him with it: are you stupid, or is there really something to be pleased about? She came very close to it, but she did not. She went on reading.

"I thought you had a letter for me to read," she said, without looking up, when they had been in the room for almost an hour without having said a word to each other.

"Yes," he said, very slowly and thoughtfully. "Yes. I'll go and bring it to you, shall I?"

"If you want me to read it, you'd better."

"I'll go and bring it then."

He stood up and went out. He walked along the shadowy corridor to his study and opened the door. He stood for a moment, looking in at the friendly darkness. He did not turn the light on, but walked over to the filing cabinet, opened it, crooking his finger through the handle and pulling gently, took out the letter and gently pushed the drawer back into place. He went out and closed the door.

His wife waited for him to return, but never once looked up from her book.

Mr Jones put the letter in his pocket and walked down the corridor away from his study and out into the quadrangle. Lights were on in the dormitories. The smile was so deep in his eyes, so fixed in the slight curve at the corner of his mouth that it seemed eternal and unassailable. He walked across the dark quadrangle, watching the shadows under the horse chestnut. He glanced up at the pale streaks in the darkening sky. He walked on, past the bicycle shed, and stood at the top of the path which led across the meadows. The path faded into darkness as it approached the river, and the woods beyond were merging with the sky. He walked slowly down the path, but the falling dark kept pace with him, and the woods remained indistinguishable from the sky. He stayed for a long time on the river bank, walking up and down, thinking.

With an impatient gesture, reaffirming her belief that her husband was stupid, Mrs Jones snapped her book shut and went to bed.

Philip Minchip bumped into something and recoiled from it with a startled cry. He peered through the darkness in the unlit corridor at whatever it was, and made out the shape of a man, tall and thin.

"Can't you sleep?" said Mr Jones, resting his hand on Philip's shoulder.

"I was going for my maths book," said Philip. "I want to study it in the morning. I always wake up before the bell goes."

"And how is Cardiff?"

"All right, sir."

"Don't you like it?"

"Not much. It's all right."

The Headmaster nodded and walked on, and Philip went to his formroom to fetch the book on bird-watching, which he wanted John to see him reading when he woke up.

Mr Jones closed the filing cabinet again, with the letter back inside, then walked out again into the dark corridor, like a benign ghost patrolling the school in the hours of darkness.

It was the practice at The Meadows, as in most boarding schools, to have lessons on a Saturday morning. There was a certain atmosphere in those Saturday morning lessons which made them quite different from any others. However tedious they might be, you knew that you had only to wait until twelve o'clock and lessons would be over and you were free then for the rest of the day. It was even better than if the last lesson had been on Friday afternoon, because there was a tension generated during the morning lessons which made the thrill of freedom that much greater at midday. The staff felt it too and approached their work somehow differently on a Saturday morning. Sensing the elated atmosphere in the classroom, and perhaps thinking of what they themselves were going to do in the afternoon, they rarely attempted any serious teaching. Instead, they would set work to be done in the class or tell their pupils to read or give them learning work, while they finished off the week's marking or strolled around the classroom or looked out of the window wondering if the weather would hold. So Saturday morning lessons tended to be rather more tedious than most, and that in itself created a further tension. It was merely a matter of waiting. The work was just a way of killing time. Everyone was thinking about the afternoon.

At break, the four teachers sat in the staffroom drinking tea and discussing their plans for the weekend. The sun was shining fitfully in between the clouds which a strong breeze was blowing constantly towards the south-east. Already there had been a brief shower, during the first lesson. The water was glistening on the grass over the meadows, shaken by the wind.

It was Mr Lynch's misfortune to be on duty that day, and so he sat in one of the armchairs with a rather glum expression on his face, casting doubts upon the likelihood of the sun's continuing to shine. "Raincoats today," he said. "No boy allowed out without a raincoat."

"It looks to me as though the clouds might blow over and the sun come out properly," said Malcolm, hopefully, since he was going out with Alice in the afternoon.

Mr Lynch shook his head. "Raincoats today," he repeated.

"Got something planned, have you?" said Mr Hopper.

"I'm meeting a friend in town," said Malcolm, blushing slightly. "I thought we might go out somewhere."

"Now who might the friend be, I wonder," said Mr Hopper. "Do you have any idea, Fred?"

"I've got my suspicions," said Mr Lynch, winking.

Mr Hopper tut-tutted and raised his fore-finger in a warning gesture. "Don't let her talk you into anything, now. You don't want to give up your freedom just yet. I was trapped myself by a scheming woman. I know."

"You don't want to end up like him, do you?" said Mr Lynch. "A hen-pecked married man, tied to a wife and children and a home to keep. Look how worn he is."

Mr Hopper swelled his chest, put his head back and laughed modestly.

"So be warned," said Mr Lynch, and relapsed into his former gloom.

Malcolm, blushing, did not know what to say, so he laughed. The situation between him and Alice was so unlike what Mr Hopper had implied as for the moment to appear quite desperate by contrast. This was his third weekend in the school. He had seen Alice twice, and neither meeting had given him any real occasion to hope she might accept his proposal of marriage.

"Fancy a drink tonight?" said Mr Lynch to Mr Hopper.

"Yes, all right. Just for half-an-hour or so. What about you, Malcolm? Are you—er—expecting to be back late?"

He winked at Mr Lynch.

"I don't know," said Malcolm, blushing again. In his present mood, he thought it more than likely that he would be back in time for tea. "What time were you thinking of?"

"Blast!" said Mr Lynch, remembering suddenly that he was on duty. "What are you doing tonight, Ron?"

Mr Birkett looked up from his marking, surprised by what he took to be an invitation to go for a drink. "Oh, no," he said. "I've got work to do. I'll stay in tonight, I think. Thank you anyway."

Mr Lynch could not understand why he was being thanked, but he shrugged it off and went on to say that if he would be staying in anyway would he mind just keeping an eye on things if he popped out for an hour or so about half-past-eight.

"Yes, all right," said Mr Birkett, realising his mistake.

"Thanks a lot. I'll return the favour next time you're on."

"No need, no need," said Mr Birkett, whose credit with Mr Lynch, after several years of similar favours, was by now enormous. There was just a hint of irony in his voice, to which Fred Lynch seemed impervious, but which did not escape Mr Hopper. He smiled, as one smiles at another person's failings, indulgently.

"About half-past-eight, then, Malcolm," he said.

"Yes, well, if I'm back by then, I'd like to come. Thank you."

"Good enough," said Mr Hopper. "We can't ask of a young bachelor more than that, can we, Fred? Eh?"

Fred, who seemed preoccupied all of a sudden, shook his head, and Mr Hopper smiled at Mr Birkett, who, however, was not looking, and then at Malcolm. Malcolm smiled back, without understanding what they were supposed to be smiling at, and Mr Hopper's sense of superiority was thus increased all round.

The boys too were making plans. There was general concern about the weather. Some stayed in the classrooms, where it was easier to imagine that all was bright and sunny and the afternoon would be fine; others stood in little groups outside, trying to ignore the wind and pretend that the spots of rain they kept feeling on their cheeks were just their imagination. A seven-a-side match was to be played in the afternoon with Lundy captaining one side and Carter captaining the other. Mr Lynch would then decide which boy was to be team captain. It was an arrangement which neither of the boys liked, and there was a general feeling that Mr Lynch should have made his mind up already and was taking a cruel delight in playing on the boys' nerves. There was this side to his nature which turned most of the boys against him. But Lundy and Carter themselves said nothing. Their friends said it all for them.

"I think Carter ought to be Captain, anyway," said Lundy. "He deserves it."

Carter grunted. He could not quite bring himself to say the same of Lundy, because basically he agreed with what Lundy had said. He knew he would feel cheated if Lundy was made Captain. Lundy had plenty of other things he could do, but for Carter there was only rugby. He tried to say that he thought Lundy should be captain, but he couldn't quite bring himself to.

The others said it was rotten of Lynch. He was only making them wait to be awkward. This match was a silly idea. How was he going to decide anyway? Was it the team that won, or was it the way the two captains played, or what? They made a pact not to cheer either of the two teams, but just to stand and watch, and they would tell all the other kids to do the same. Any kid caught cheering would be beaten up afterwards. Carter stirred at the thought of a beating up.

"Do you want to go out somewhere, or shall we stop and watch the match?" said John to Philip. They were standing by the window of their formroom, a place for talking which had become habitual with them over the three weeks since Philip had begun his stories. Much had been said by Philip there since that time, and John had listened with unabated interest and surprise, though not always without some doubts and reservations. At the moment, they were looking down into the quad, where Lundy and the others were gathered in a small group, talking.

Philip frowned and could not make up his mind. It seemed to make him angry. He wanted to go and he wanted to stay. He resented the conflict and it made his eyes grow small and hard and his face take on an even grubbier hue than usual. "I don't know," he said, feeling that he would like to kick someone. He pulled hard on his ear so that it hurt. "What do you want to do?"

"I don't mind," said John. Philip waited, and John, wisely, said a little more. "In some ways, I'd quite like to watch the match, but I don't mind really."

"We'll watch the match, then," said Philip, scowling even more angrily as he said it.

The clouds continued to hurry over the sky after break, and

there was another shower, but the sun kept breaking through every so often. At lunchtime it was still touch and go. Spots of rain were blowing in the wind and the clouds thickened a little. A few boys reported to Mr Lynch in the quad at half-past-one and those without raincoats were sent off to get them. But most people were staying to watch the match. At two o'clock, the two teams went off to the changing rooms, which were situated in the cellars of the old house, and Mr Lynch changed into his track-suit in his room. A crowd began to form on the touch-line, and the friends of Lundy and Carter who were not in either of the teams went round issuing their instructions about not cheering and the punishment that would be given to anyone who did. There was silence when the fourteen boys walked on to the pitch.

Malcolm sat in a cafe next to the window. The rain streamed down the glass and the street outside was just a blur. Opposite him sat Alice. They had been talking about their respective schools and had ended by arguing. In fact, they had stopped just before it turned into a real argument, and were now sitting in a huffy silence.

Malcolm was bewildered, and his bewilderment showed frankly on his face. Alice, on the other hand, sat quite calmly drinking her coffee, satisfied that she was in the right. Perhaps to her it was nothing more than a simple difference of opinion, but to Malcolm it was much more than that—or seemed to portend much more. Opinion, to him, was a very personal thing, and a difference of opinion was a difference between him and Alice. If anyone argued with him, he could not help feeling that they disliked him. He kept looking at her now, and as he saw her seeming so composed and apparently indifferent, his own distress increased. How could anyone appear so indifferent after a disagreement such as they had just had? It could only mean that she did not care for him.

The afternoon had started well. She was ready and waiting for him when he got to her house and they set off walking straight away. She was very cheerful and talked a lot as they walked, so that Malcolm had only to listen and think that things were going well. His hopes were brightened immeasurably. They walked into the town and went to the park and the river, and for half-an-hour they sat on a park bench watching the ducks and swans. Then, all of a sudden, the sun, which had been shining fitfully until now, went in and the sky clouded over and it started to rain. He put up his umbrella and they ran through what was rapidly becoming a downpour to a cafe by the side of the road just outside the park gate, and there they sat with two cups of coffee. Neither of them was particularly disheartened by the change in the weather, since it was quite cosy and warm inside the cafe and it had been rather chilly outside. So they took their coats off and settled down to wait until the rain stopped. She asked him how things were going in his new school.

It was his favourite theme and he began to describe everything to her in great detail. He got on to comparing it with the school in Liverpool and pointing out how much better it was in every respect. Better conditions, better atmosphere, better children, better everything.

"How, 'better children'?" she asked, with a slightly puzzled expression.

"Oh, polite, good-natured, respectful, willing to learn, honest by and large."

"Of course, it's easy to be polite and good-natured in a place like that, isn't it?"

"What do you mean?"

"They've no cause to be anything but polite and good-natured in a place like that, have they? If we all lived in places like that I've no doubt we'd all be polite and good-natured."

"No, but..."

"Well, there you are then. What right have you to criticise?"

"I don't know what you're getting at."

Alice assumed an expression and a tone of voice which she might use if she were explaining some quite simple thing to a rather slow child in her primary school. "You're saying how much better your school is than the one you were at in Liverpool without giving any thought at all to the reasons why it's better."

"No I'm not," said Malcolm. "I'm not at all. I know the reasons why it's better. It's because everyone lives together and knows everyone else. Nobody ever rushes about. There's no strain. You take your time over things."

But Alice was not satisfied. She thought this was a silly answer, in fact not an answer at all. He had completely missed the point of what she was saying.

"I know all that," she said. "It's quite obvious. But you've got absolutely no reason to start making big claims for your school and saying you're better than everyone else. You've got all the advantages. Other schools, ordinary schools, have to scrape by with dingy old buildings, cramped conditions, oversized classes, not enough money. It's sheer selfishness and arrogance on your part to sit back in your nice little school and say how much better you are than us. As it happens, we were talking about this in the staffroom the other day, and there's a lot of feeling, strong feeling as well, against schools like yours."

"Well, the answer is to make all schools like the one I'm in."

"That's silly."

"How is it silly?"

"Because so long as there are schools like yours taking all the money, the other schools are bound to stay as they are."

"I don't see why."

"Well, you don't see much, then."

Which is where it had ended. Alice had put on her 'there's-no-point-in-arguing-any-more' expression, and Malcolm did not, in any case, know what to say next. They continued to sit in silence for several minutes. Malcolm did not know either how to change the subject or how to continue with the one that had caused the argument, without merely making things worse.

"Hasn't it stopped raining yet?" said Alice at last, looking out of the window.

Again, the indifference. "No," said Malcolm, rather lamely, also looking out of the window.

"We might as well have another cup of coffee, then. I'll get them." She stood up and walked to the counter.

By the time she had returned with the coffee, Malcolm had decided it was time he tried to face the problem head on. He watched the sugar sinking through the froth and said, "Why do we always have to argue?"

"We're not arguing," she said, a little petulantly. "At least I'm not. It's possible to discuss things rationally without it being an argument, if you mean by that a quarrel." She spoke with rather a superior air, as if she were the rational one, he the one incapable of reason.

"Well, let's carry on discussing it, then," said Malcolm, thinking that might be best.

"Oh, must we?" she said, wearily. "Can't we change the subject?"

"You brought it up," said Malcolm, showing some temper. "If you're in one of those moods, we might as well both go home."

"I'm not in a mood."

Alice shrugged her shoulders. "All right then. Let's talk about something else."

But it seemed to Malcolm there was nothing else in the world to talk about. He looked out of the window. The downpour had ceased, but it was still raining and the water was still trickling down the window. It looked as though the sun might break through again soon. All the signs were that it would be a fine, sunny evening. But Malcolm was not cheered in the least by this thought and saw only the drizzle, which was more fitting to his state of mind than any other weather could have been.

"Who's your best pupil?" Alice said, after a while.

His first thought was to say Lundy. Lundy, however, was not his best pupil. Tomlinson, Moorcroft and Wilkins were all better. He still wanted to say it was Lundy though.

"In the top class there's Tomlinson. He's probably the best. Then Wilkins and Moorcroft, probably. A boy called Lundy as well. He's quite good."

It felt wrong, somehow, talking about the boys with her, and he nearly didn't mention Lundy at all. He wondered whether the match had been played.

"What are they like?"

But he didn't want to talk about it. "Boys, that's all."

"Not very communicative, are you?" She looked out of the window. "It's just about stopped now," she said, "Let's go out somewhere. It's too warm in here."

They walked back into the park, but all the benches were wet and they couldn't sit down. They had to keep walking. So they fell into an easy, relaxed pace, and strolled on the footpaths, past beds of late roses whose scent was brought out by the rain, by the river, beneath trees from which the rain-water dripped, between dark, glistening hedgerows and bushes. Malcolm was thinking about school, about Lundy and the others, wondering whether he would spend the evening with Alice or with Mr Hopper and Mr Lynch in a pub in the village, and, to his surprise, wondering which he would prefer. There didn't seem to be much point in staying with Alice now. He began to wonder how much that letter in which he had proposed to her came out of real feeling, and how much it came out of his desperation and loneliness in Liverpool. Things were changing now.

Alice was talking again, not as cheerfully and not as much as she had been at the beginning, before the argument, but she was talking nevertheless, and perhaps trying to get him talking too, because she kept asking him questions. He tried to reply and tried to think of things to say himself, but he didn't seem able to throw off the despondency which their quarrel had brought about in him, and all the time he was thinking about school and wondering what was happening there now.

The sun had come out, the rain had stopped and it looked indeed as though it would be a fine evening. He thought of his room, and the meadows, and thought how pleasant it would be in the quad just now.

"Let's sit down," said Alice. "That seat doesn't look too wet."

So they sat down. Alice sat close to him, with her arm resting half on his. At another time it would have pleased him, but now it only made him confused.

"Anyway, I didn't know you were a socialist," he said.

"What? Oh, you're not still thinking about that, are you? Can't you let it drop? Anyway, what if I am?"

Malcolm didn't know. He didn't know what to make of it at all. He had never thought about the school from that point of view before.

"I don't see what difference it makes having private schools," he said. "It doesn't make any difference to the others."

"I just don't like privilege, that's all. But don't let's talk about that now." She put her hand on his. "We'll only quarrel."

He looked at her hand. She let it lie there for a moment, and then took it away. He could not fathom her changes of mood. For the moment, it seemed too much trouble to have to contend with them and try to work out what they meant. Too confusing.

"What are you going to do now?" she said. "Are you coming back for tea? Mum's half expecting you."

No, he thought. He didn't know why. Obviously, he ought to be going back with her. He had asked her to marry him, after all. But he didn't want to. He wanted to go back to The Meadows.

"Do you mind if I don't?" he said. "There are some things I ought to be doing this evening at school."

She looked surprised and disappointed, but she took his words at their face value. He would have come if he had been able.

"I've got things to do tomorrow," she said. "So..."

"Well, I'm on duty tomorrow, anyway," he said.

He walked to her house with her, and then walked on to the bus stop to catch the bus back. It took him in about half-an an-hour to the village. As he walked up the lane towards the school, he gladly pushed to the back of his mind all thoughts of Alice and his proposal, which he hoped would soon sort themselves out, and looked forward to the coming evening with his new colleagues, in the pub.

Lundy's team had won, but Carter was Captain. This was ironic, as Malcolm discovered when Mr Lynch was talking to him about it after tea, because he had decided weeks ago that

Lundy would be Captain, and the match had been merely his way of keeping the boys on tenterhooks and adding a little tension and excitement to things. As it turned out, the match had made him change his mind, or rather not the match itself, but two incidents that had occurred during the match.

To begin with there had been no cheering, even though there were over thirty boys there watching. He had not realised at first. He had just had a vague feeling that something was wrong. They had been playing for five or ten minutes before he realised what it was. No cheering. Dead silence. So the next time he blew his whistle for a scrum, he called the two captains over to him and asked them what was going on. Why was nobody cheering? It seemed that they thought it would be unfair to cheer for one side rather than another, because really it was all the same team and Lundy and Carter were friends. Nonsense. Bloody nonsense. How could you have a rugby match with no cheering? So he told them that whoever it was who had started this had better go and stop it now or there would be no match, no Captain, no team come to that. It was Lundy who went. So that was the first thing.

Then at half-time, Lundy had come up to him and had had the bloody cheek to say that he didn't want to be Captain and he thought Carter would be better than him. Damned impudence. "I'll be the judge of who's best and who's not," he told him. "It's nothing to do with you. I'll decide and you'll do what you're told to do. "After that he was sure Lundy was playing deliberately badly. In fact, the whole second half was a complete shambles. It started to pour down just after the game started again and the pitch was just a sea of mud within five minutes. But he made them play on. At the end the score was 5-3.

So the upshot of it all was that he had made Carter Captain, because he was pretty sure it was Lundy who was responsible for the business about not cheering and he wasn't going to put up with that lad's cheek at half-time. The only trouble was, Lundy might think he'd listened to what he'd said. So what he was going to do was let Carter be Captain for two or three weeks and then make Lundy Captain. Carter wasn't a bad sort, but he was as thick as two short planks. Lundy was the natural choice for Captain between the two of them. The whole business had been damned annoying and he'd got soaked to the skin. The afternoon had been ruined.

Although Mr Lynch professed to want to forget all about it, he kept returning to that topic over and over again, while he was sitting with Malcolm at tea, while they were driving down to the village and while they were sitting in the pub waiting for Mr Hopper. He seemed to take it all very personally, and he rejected completely Malcolm's tentative suggestion that perhaps David had meant well.

"Nonsense!" he said. "You don't know these kids like I do. Give 'em an inch and they'll take a mile. Anything like that wants stamping on straight away. You keep on top of them. Don't let them think they can start doing what they like with you, or your life'll be a misery before you know where you are."

Malcolm could hardly believe this could be so at The Meadows, although he had verified it by his own experience in Liverpool. But just then Mr Hopper came in.

"What are you drinking?" he said.

Mr Lynch, in his excess of strong emotion, had already consumed two pints of bitter in quick succession. Malcolm had finished one pint, but had only just started his second.

"Come on, Malcolm, you're falling behind," said Geoffrey Hopper, placing another pint glass on the table in front of him. "I might have guessed you'd have sneaked down earlier," he said, turning to Fred Lynch, "to gain an unfair advantage. How many have you had already?"

"I've had two. I don't know how many Malcolm's had. I've lost count."

"Well," said Geoffrey, "who's our school rugby Captain?"

Fred Lych launched once more into an account of the afternoon's proceedings, and Malcolm had a chance to sit back and look round at his surroundings, at the same time trying to get through his second pint as quickly as he could so that he could start on the one Geoffrey had bought him. Not being used to drinking a lot, it soon began to tell on him.

It was the lounge bar of a small village inn they were sitting in, with an open fire, comfortable settles round the walls, little round tables and heavy old wooden chairs with thick cushions on the seats. The walls were covered with horse brasses and photographs of farmers with prize horses and bulls. Fred Lynch was obviously a regular customer. The landlord knew him as 'Fred', and other people nodded and said hello to him as they came in during the evening. Malcolm thought it must be good to be known like that, and wondered if it would happen to him. The bar was warm and cosy, the fire looked bright and welcoming, the conversations going on around him grew noisier and more animated as the evening went on. He made conspicuous efforts to keep up with the others in their drinking. He felt warm inside, and happy so that he wanted to laugh.

"How's Malcolm then?" said Geoffrey. "How do you like our school after three weeks? Wish you were back in Liverpool, do you?"

"Anything but!" said Malcolm. "I think it's a marvellous place."

"It has its points, I suppose."

"I think it's really marvellous. All this talk there is about abolishing private schools, I think it's terrible. Why should they want to abolish places like The Meadows? I don't know. I mean, I was having an argument with someone this afternoon who thought like that. They seemed to think that we were stopping them from doing something. Well, that's just ridiculous, isn't it? It's them who want to stop us."

"In the name of freedom," Geoffrey Hopper put in. "Absurd, isn't it?"

"Ridiculous!"

"Now, I'll go a long way with the socialists. A long way. Freedom, equality—equality of opportunity—brotherhood. These are noble principles, which of course we all share. These are the principles on which democracy is founded, which we fought to defend in the war. It's not only the socialists who believe in these things."

"Of course not!" said Malcolm, agreeing for all he was worth.

"But the socialists, you see, Malcolm, put equality above freedom, and that's where they go wrong. Look at Russia. Everyone equal, and nobody free. No, freedom must come first. Freedom of thought and action. The only limitation is that what you do must not hurt anyone else. Private schools hurt no one. State education is not in the least bit hindered by them. Mark my words, the people who want to abolish private schools are motivated entirely by jealousy. They can't have it, so they don't want anyone to have it."

Malcolm nodded his head vehemently, partly in agreement and partly in admiration of Mr Hopper's logic and lucidity of speech, both of which at the moment were far beyond Malcolm's scope.

"Let 'em get on with it," said Fred Lynch, somewhat inconsequentially.

"I'll tell you, Malcolm," said Mr Hopper, "the only trouble with private schools, by which I mean boarding schools, is that it's very easy for a man who teaches in one, especially if he's single and lives in, to become too involved. You lose your sense of perspective. Fred will agree I'm sure that this is a danger. Everything gets blown up out of proportion. Now if you're married, like me, you can't get too involved. You have too many other things to think about. But for someone in your position, now is the time to be making sure that you keep some other interest going, outside school."

"Good advice, Malcolm," said Fred. "Pints all round?"

"Old Birkett now," Geoffrey went on. "He's not a bad sort, you know, but ... Well, he gets terribly worked up about things that don't matter. A bit of an old woman at times, you know." He leant across the table and whispered. "Fred's not so bad, but even he, sometimes ..." He didn't finish his sentence, but nodded significantly and then leaned back in his chair again.

Fred returned with another round and started talking to Geoffrey about a mutual acquaintance unknown to Malcolm. Left out for a while, Malcolm tried to think about what Geoffrey had been saying, but his head was spinning too rapidly for cogent thought. He seemed to catch glimpses of things, in no particular order, rather than think about them, as if he was going round on the waltzers at the fair, when the things round about are for most of the time just a brightly coloured blur, but just now and again you see things clearly for a second or two before you are pulled away again into the blur. His physical state also was not unlike that induced by the more violent fairground amusements. He held onto his glass, as it were, to keep himself upright, but only just succeeded.

Mr Lynch concentrated hard and spoke not a word as he drove back to the school with Malcolm. Occasionally, he belched and then groaned. Malcolm was rather concerned for their safety.

He put his head down on the pillow and closed his eyes. The ship he was in sank rapidly into the trough of a wave, rose onto the crest of the next, sank rapidly again. The room began to turn round in a slow circle, descending slowly and tilting over to one side at the same time. He wondered whether he was going to be sick, and then fell asleep.

Philip awoke early as usual, and lay in the half-light looking around the dormitory. It was not yet seven o'clock. He could hear the sound of rain pattering gently outside. So soft and low was the sound that at first he took it to be the wind rustling in the trees, but something in the colour of the light told him it was rain.

To awake at this time was, as he told the Headmaster, habitual with him. He could not remember ever having done otherwise, either at home or away from home. In Cardiff, and in the other places before Cardiff, it had always been the same. What was more, as soon as he opened his eyes he was immediately wide awake. There was no intervening period of drowsiness, no half-sleeping and half-waking. He was either asleep or awake. So he did not try, or even want, to go to sleep again, but often got out of bed at once, washed and dressed quickly and left the dormitory for some other part of the school. This morning, however, he did not stir from his bed immediately, but sat up and spent some time just looking round at the beds and their various occupants, and thinking.

He looked at John Finch, who was asleep in the bed next to his. His friend's face, always blank and hopeless, seemed much more so when he was asleep. The corners of his mouth were drawn down and the face was pale. It looked mournful and pathetic, and John might almost have been dead, Philip thought, so waxen and mask-like was his face. He had stared at the face, on these mornings, sometimes for as long as twenty minutes, studying its every feature, pondering it.

On his other side was Tomlinson. It seemed odd to think of Tomlinson asleep. Tomlinson was an intelligence, a brain, a quick wit, a sharp tongue, a quiet, unrelenting, if unspoken, judgement. Sleep seemed not to be a part of his nature, and Philip saw how, even in sleep, he had the appearance of having merely closed his eyes because, for the moment, there was nothing for him to look at.

So he watched John for a while and then turned to look at Tomlinson, weighing up the difference between them. The one, perhaps, dead, and the other merely hiding wakefulness behind closed eyes.

Then, in strange confirmation of his perception, Tomlinson's eyes opened.

The two boys observed each other for a few seconds. There was no embarrassment and no surprise. It was, in a way, what Philip had expected. He was not surprised to find his imagination proving true. Tomlinson was completely self-possessed, as always.

"Do you want to go for a walk?" Tomlinson asked, still looking Philip in the eye.

"Yes," said Philip.

They were a matter of three or four minutes getting washed and dressed, and then they were walking down the stairs together, without another word having been spoken, and the clock was just striking seven.

"It's raining," said Philip, as they walked downstairs.

"We'll go to the pavilion," said Tomlinson.

They emerged into the quad, which was grey with the rain and the dawn light. Piles of dead leaves lay sodden on the ground, dull and colourless out of the sunlight. Water fell through the branches of the tree and dripped steadily to the ground. They walked at a steady pace, neither fast nor slow, looking ahead, not speaking. There were puddles which they did not see, because there was no light to reflect, and so they did not even attempt to find their way round them, but just walked. No talking could be done until they reached the pavilion. They went onto the field and their feet sank into the grass and the wet earth.

They sat on a bench, under cover, at the front of the little wooden pavilion, which was really little more than a white-painted hut with a verandah, and looked out over the cricket field, through the rain, at the dark woods on the other side and the pallid sky above.

"You're generally up before everyone else, aren't you?" said Tomlinson.

"Always."

"This early?"

Philip nodded.

"Why?"

"I just wake up," said Philip, and shrugged his shoulders.

Tomlinson nodded. "I used to wake up very early at one time, when I was in the first form. That was because I was home-sick. Now I only wake up early now and again."

He waited to see whether Philip would admit to this as a reason for his own early waking or offer any other explanation, but Philip said nothing.

"You're not home-sick, then?" he went on.

Philip shook his head. "I've never been home-sick."

"Where do you come from?"

"Cardiff. At the moment. I'm living with my aunt and uncle in Cardiff, but I don't like them, and they don't like me. I wanted to be sent away. So I made trouble at my school there and got expelled. Well, suspended. They can't really expel you from ordinary schools. So they sent me here. I think Davy's a distant relation of my aunt's, or an old friend, or something."

"Your plan worked then."

"Yes."

Philip smiled. Tomlinson was looking at him with some admiration and a lot of curiosity.

"Are you an orphan?" he went on.

"No. My mother lives abroad mostly. I see her sometimes. I don't know where my father is. I used to live with my grandfather mainly, but he died last year. He lived in Hull. He owned a trawling ship. I liked it better there."

Tomlinson nodded his head slowly, piecing together these bits of information, relating them to what he had observed already, making up his mind. But his questions had an impersonal air, and Philip felt that in answering he was describing not himself but somebody else. It was an odd feeling, one which intrigued him.

"People think you're strange, you know," said Tomlinson.

"Why?"

Still he felt as though they were talking about someone else, not him.

"They think you're secretive. You never talk to anyone except Finch."

"Why should I?"

Tomlinson shrugged his shoulders.

"Do you think I'm strange?" Philip asked, suddenly looking at him.

"I don't really care what you are. But you're—different. People tend to get flustered if they come across anybody who's not just like them."

Philip was pleased somehow that Tomlinson was indifferent to him. There were no feelings between them. They met on neutral ground. It was easy.

"Does Lundy think I'm strange?"

"He can't make you out. I think he'd like to be friends."

For a while, nothing was said. Both boys sat watching the

rain, hearing the endless murmur of it on the grass and the heavy pattering and splashing as it fell from the roof of the pavilion onto the concrete in front.

"You're a loner, aren't you?" said Tomlinson, at last.

"Like you."

"In a way. We're different though."

"Yes," said Philip. Still, he had the feeling that he was talking about someone else. It did not really matter what he and Tomlinson knew or thought about one another, because it was not a personal thing. They were miles apart.

"Finch is a loner, as well," he went on. "He keeps himself to himself, doesn't go along with the others. Why don't they think he's strange?"

"They do. But he doesn't bother them like you do."

"Why?" said Philip, turning to Tomlinson and confronting him with this question.

"I don't know," said Tomlinson, looking interested. He seemed to be rather amused by the fact that he did not have an immediate answer to this problem. "Have you any idea?"

"No," said Philip. "I do bother them though, don't I? I'm glad about that."

The conversation lapsed. They both had things to think about and, almost as if it had been agreed between them, they thought about them separately and did not trouble each other. Gradually, there emerged from the mass of ideas rushing around in Philip's mind one question which Tomlinson could answer for him, but which he was not sure whether he could ask. He did not know whether the neutrality which had somehow been established between them was reason for asking or for not asking. But in the end, he did.

"Does Lundy talk about me much?"

"A lot," said Tomlinson, with no hesitation.

But perhaps the boundaries of neutrality had been crossed, for the conversation ceased there. Some time passed in silence and once again the sound of the rain took over. It seemed to grow louder in the silence, and they both watched the rain and listened to the various sounds it made. There was water everywhere. The whole world was dripping wet. It must have been raining since very early in the morning.

But it was light now. No colour had come into the world, but it was light. They heard the bell strike the three-quarters and Tomlinson said, "We'd better be getting back into school," and they both stood up and set off to walk back across the field.

"I wouldn't normally come out like this before everyone was up," said Tomlinson as they came to the edge of the field. "I've never done it before."

They went back up to the dormitory. Tomlinson sat on his bed and dried his hair on a towel. Philip walked over to the window and stood looking out, with his hands on the radiator. They did not speak again that morning, nor, indeed, for several days after. It had been the first time they had ever spoken to each other. For all outward signs, they still might never have spoken. Nor were they, in any sense of the word, friends. But they were equals, and could come and go as they pleased, a fact which they both recognised and appreciated as they ignored each other now at opposite ends of the dormitory, where the other boys were waking up to the tolling of the eight o'clock bell.

As the days passed, Malcolm felt more and more at home within the confines of The Meadows. He might occasionally take a walk outside the school, to the village perhaps for cigarettes, and he still toyed with the idea of buying an old car, but that was as far as it went. Two weeks elapsed before he even visited Alice again. The weather now did not often encourage excursions, being increasingly damp and foggy as the month of November drew nearer, but even on fine days Malcolm was content just to stay in school bounds. Fred Lynch seemed very quickly to become aware of this and began taking advantage of Malcolm's stay-at-home nature by asking him to take over his duties sometimes in the evenings. Malcolm didn't mind. In fact, he thought of it almost as Fred doing him a favour, rather than him helping Fred out.

Perhaps what gave him most pleasure was the feeling of possession, as both possessor and possessed. Quite often he would just sit in the staffroom, or come to a stop somewhere in the school buildings or grounds, wherever he happened to be walking, and bask, as it were, in the satisfaction of being a part of it all, and, spending so much time there, he soon grew to know the place better than the palm of his hand. Every scratch on the wall, every carving on every desk, every shadow in the corner, entered into his memory. He watched its changing expressions, listened to its sounds and its silences, breathed in its smells. The pleasure it gave him was greater than anything he had known. He had, in short, fallen in love, and he pursued and doted on his beloved school with the ardour proper to a lover.

He fell in love with some of the school's sons, too, and doted on them almost as ardently. But his love of the sons, as of the mother, was from beginning to end pure and romantic, unalloyed by fleshly desires. He no more lusted after the boys than, in cold weather, he flung himself headlong into the school's boiler-house. In cold weather, like anyone else, he would warm his hands on the radiators. An arm resting momentarily on a slender shoulder, a hand tousling the fine blond hair. What are these?

His love was for beauty, freshness, honesty, friendly words and smiles, for air and water, not fire and earth. He fell in love with some of the boys precisely because they were beautiful and not sexual. He loved and courted The Meadows because it was so restful and undemanding and let him feel free. He felt important, as if he belonged there, but also as if it all belonged to him.

But rather than coldly analyse, let us share while we can his enjoyment of it all, short-lived as it was to be, lap up as he did the October glory: the river with its rafts of leaves and branches, the quadrangle aswirl with leaves and kicking feet, grey frost in the morning, the earth hard as an anvil, the air like a hammer, blue fingers caught between the two; and admire with him the puerile beauty which surrounded him, in particular the golden good-looks, yellow hair, blue eyes and friendly smile of David Lundy.

Beauty, freshness, honesty, friendly words and smiles—what a paragon was David, possessing all of these in abundance! How fortunate Malcolm to be able to teach the lovely boy for one lesson every day, six days a week. He would see him, of course, frequently around the school and would speak, perhaps, in passing and be spoken to and smiled upon, but the daily English lesson was the real boon. There, for forty-five minutes every day, David sat, at a desk by the window, in the same room with Malcolm, whose heart was gladdened by the boy's mere presence. When Malcolm asked a question and the hands went up, it was David, more often than any other, who was chosen to answer. But Malcolm did not want to make his partiality too obvious, either to the rest of the class or to David himself—perhaps especially to David—and what he liked most and most often tried to engineer, was when, having set the class some written work to do, he was able to wander about the classroom, in between the rows of desks, and steal glances, from near and far, at the object of his admiration. The straw-yellow hair, the fine, almost invisible, eyebrows, the slender nose, the smooth, high-boned cheeks, pale blue eyes and long, thin lips that smiled so pleasantly, imbued Malcolm's spirit with happiness as he strolled about the room.

In this way, October passed. Malcolm's new world gained substance, and the old began to decay. Alice, especially, lost significance. In those two weeks which passed before their next meeting, the school and all its charms were able to have their way with Malcolm unhindered by any outside influence, and at the end of that time Malcolm was entirely under their spell. Unconscious of any change himself, except that he was happy, he presented a very different appearance to an outsider, and Alice was startled and bewildered when she saw him again.

It had registered with her as odd when Malcolm had not tried to fix up another meeting before he went back to the school that afternoon in the park, although she hadn't really thought about it at the time. Then, when the days went by without any communication from him, she began to be upset and to give consideration to what had never struck her before—that

Malcolm might break off their relationship. She had felt very sure of him, though not sure that she wanted him, and had paid no heed to her mother's cautious warnings that one day he would tire of waiting for an answer and withdraw his proposal. Now, suddenly, she felt that he might do that, and even though she was still not sure what her answer should be she began to panic. She wondered what to do. She waited. She tried to make up her mind whether she wanted to marry him or not. She waited for a letter, and every time the letter didn't come her doubt and her panic grew. At last, after waiting ten days, she telephoned the school.

The Meadows, being such an old-fashioned place, had only one telephone, which gathered dust on a high shelf (out of the reach of small boys) in the corridor outside Mr Jones's study. On the rare occasions when it rang, it was a matter of chance whether it was answered or not. At first, Alice was unlucky. The school was in the dining hall eating lunch. Mr Jones himself had taken an early lunch and was now walking towards the village with some letters for the post. The phone rang to an empty corridor and then gave up. Mrs Jones, upstairs, had heard it ringing but ignored it.

Five minutes later, Alice tried again, and this time she had more success.

"Hello! Meadows Preparatory School."

Alice pressed Button A. "Hello," she said. "I'd like to speak to Mr Drew."

"I'm sorry, Mr Drew is having lunch at the moment. Can I take a message?"

"Oh. Yes, all right. Tell him Miss Raynor rang, and that he is invited to tea on Saturday at the house of one of Miss Raynor's friends. Tell him I'll send him a note with the address and time and everything."

"Miss Raynor rang, and he is invited to tea on Saturday at the house of one of Miss Raynor's friends, and you'll send on a note with all the details. Is there anything else?"

"No thank you," said Alice. "That's all. Thank you very much. Goodbye."

Philip reached up and put the phone back on the hook. Grinning, he continued on his way down the corridor to the Headmaster's study. He knocked but, as he had guessed when no one came out to answer the telephone, there was nobody there. He had been first out from lunch, in a hurry to get ready for the bird-watching expedition he was going on with John that afternoon, (it was Wednesday—a half-holiday at The Meadows, to compensate for Saturday morning lessons), but Mr Birkett had waylaid him and put a letter into his hand to give to the Headmaster to take to the post. When the phone started to ring as he came down the corridor, and when no one came out to answer it, Philip naturally answered it himself, rather unnaturally, however, assuming a smart, secretarial voice for the purpose. So it was not surprising that Alice had taken Philip for the Headmaster's secretary.

He knocked on the study door but, as expected, received no reply. So he opened the door, went in and dropped the letter on Mr Jones's desk. He feared that if he returned to Mr Birkett with the letter, he might be made to go down to the village with it himself.

A few minutes later, he met up with John and they reported together to Mr Drew, the Master on Duty, to tell him where they were going that afternoon, but Philip decided to save his message till later. It was too good to waste.

So the two boys set off together, leaving Malcolm sitting on a low wall in the quadrangle with a queue of boys in front of him, writing down in a little book their intended destinations for that afternoon. The sun shone white behind the clouds, and as Philip and John passed through the school gate and turned down the road it finally broke through and the clouds began to give way to the pale blue sky, and warm October sunshine filtered down on them through the tattered branches.

"Have you looked at that History we've got to learn for tomorrow? I don't know how he expects us to get it done by then. It's a whole chapter. Do you know how many pages it is? Ten pages. Ten whole pages! For one homework. We've got those Latin verbs to learn as well. I don't know how he expects . . ."

John chattered on as they walked, and Philip walked by his side listening.

A curious thing had been happening lately, what amounted almost to a transfer of personality. The normally rather quiet, slow and undemonstrative Finch had been quickened, perhaps in a desire to emulate his more excitable friend, into something altogether more outgoing and communicative: almost, in fact, a chatterbox. Philip, by contrast, had withdrawn and taken on the passive, listening role which at first John had played. And now John was really enjoying life. He was proud of their new Ornithological Society—which had remained rather exclusive, with a membership of two, new members by invitation only—and felt that he and Philip were definitely a cut above the rest, with their Stamp Clubs and Amateur Dramatic Societies.

Naturally, the rest of their form resented this. Philip and John held themselves so aloof that the others had begun, in the last few days, to be openly hostile. Their exclusive society had been the object lately of a number of sarcastic remarks.

It was unfortunate, because John had always been well-liked before. Always a loner, with no real friends, but so good-natured that the form had never taken it out on him for preferring his own company to theirs, as children often do. So it was Philip who took the brunt of their animosity, for being a bad influence on John.

Philip considered this, as he walked along beside John, and felt it unfair.

"We go through here," said John.

Holding onto a convenient branch to steady himself, because the thick carpet of damp leaves underfoot made the going treacherous, he stepped across the ditch which ran alongside the road and pushed his way through a narrow gap in the hawthorn hedge, thus gaining entry to the wood which covered an area of a square mile or so behind the school. He waited for Philip, who was soon by his side again.

"This is good," said Philip. "What a smell!"

He breathed in as deeply as he could the rank odour of decaying leaves on damp earth, the close, musty, mysterious smell of a wood in Autumn.

They tramped slowly through the wood, John leading the way, still chattering, calling over his shoulder to Philip, who followed on behind in silence.

In ten minutes they were through the wood and standing at the edge of a large pond or small lake, a stretch of water perhaps a hundred yards wide and two hundred yards long, where the boys hoped to observe wild life. The pond, and indeed the wood, were both out of bounds, and they had not given this as their destination to Mr Drew. Most of the things Malcolm had written down in his book that afternoon were totally untrue.

Philip surveyed the pond. It looked desolate. The countryside just here was flat, rising just slightly on the far side of the pond, and with just the hint of a hill in the distance. The margins of the pond were reedy. The ground on which they stood was soft. The water was a still, silvery sheet. It was very quiet.

Philip's imagination was stirred by the scene, redolent as it was of things strange and sinister. He stood and stared over the water, rapt, absorbing the powerful atmosphere, a small fire kindling in the back of his mind.

John too stood still, scanning the pond and its reedy edges for signs of life. He had stopped chattering as soon as they had emerged from the wood and now, all other interests and feelings routed in the face of his passion for bird-watching, his proper seriousness and taciturn manner returned. He did not forget Philip, but took it for granted that he would know what to do and would prefer, as he did himself, to be left alone. So, without a word, he turned aside and walked quickly and quietly towards a tree which stood right on the very edge of the wood, by the water's edge. He climbed, with practised agility, into the lower branches of the tree and lodged himself there, commanding an excellent view of the pond and surrounding countryside. A strange figure he looked, staring disconsolately over the water with that expressionless, almost death-like, face that was his most striking characteristic.

Below, Philip smouldered, his hands thrust into his pockets. He was suddenly filled with resentment against John and everyone, and a rage quickly grew inside him. He picked up a stone and flung it as far as he could out over the water.

John looked down, startled.

"Hey!" he said.

But Philip was already throwing another stone. His face set in a scowl of pent-up fury, he threw stone after stone, sometimes far out over the water and sometimes almost at his feet, to make a bigger splash. He threw harder and harder, trying to make a bigger splash.

After his first exclamation, John remained silent, staring down at Philip, afraid and bewildered. But at last, as Philip went on in his frenzy of stone-throwing, John found it in himself once again to remonstrate.

"Stop it!" he said.

Philip turned and looked at John, still perched in the tree, still, even in his anger, expressionless of face, and that seemed to anger Philip still more. After a moment's pause, he ran at the tree. John gave a start of surprise and gripped tight hold of the branch, as Philip jumped up from below and caught hold of the end of the branch and began swaying it up and down and from side to side, apparently trying to dislodge the other boy. John rocked and bounced about among the twigs and dying foliage, and hung on for dear life. Then, suddenly, Philip let go. He turned, threw one more stone as far as he could out over the pond, and then ran off into the wood.

John clung onto his branch, staring about him in bewilderment and fear, with that blank and mournful face, not daring to move, for several minutes after Philip had gone.

Philip ran as hard as he could through the wood, until it hurt, and then he stopped. A stitch cramping his side, his body cold with sweat, he leant against a tree until he had recovered sufficiently to be able to go on. He walked, then, dragging his feet through the leaves, to the edge of the wood. He jumped across the ditch and turned in the direction of school. His breathing became more even, his face less agonised, and by the time he turned in at the school gate the fire that had so suddenly flared up in him had been extinguished.

He ambled through into the quad, hands in pockets. The afternoon sun still shone down warmly. The quad was empty. He set off for the playing fields, still at this unhurried pace, hands in pockets. When he reached the fields, he saw there was rugby practice in progress—lines of boys tackling each other—and, near the touch-line, Mr Drew with a group of boys watching. He stopped where he was, bent down to feel the ground, and then sat down.

"Who do you think should be Captain, sir?" one of the spectators asked Malcolm.

"Oh, it's very difficult to say. Both Lundy and Carter have . . ."

But the boys butted in with their own views again and the argument continued around Malcolm. The issue of the Captaincy still loomed large in school affairs, and not only among the pupils. It was still staple conversation with Fred Lynch, and Malcolm was as interested as any of the boys, though for different reasons.

Philip sat and watched the practice, a few yards away from Mr Drew's little group and apart from the others, scattered in twos and threes round the edges of the pitch, silent and seemingly more detached than they.

Once or twice, boys glanced round at him, stared for a moment, murmured something to their neighbours and then turned back to the practice. He had achieved a certain notoriety throughout the school for being different, funny. But the reasons for his difference were as yet intangible, more to do with what he did not do than with what he did. His continuing to do nothing was sufficient therefore, for the time being, to cause his reputation to grow. So he sat quietly and watched the practice.

Mr Lynch at last grew weary and brought the practice to an end. He sent the boys on a circuit of the field, whilst he set off to plod back up to the school. One by one, the boys completed the circuit and soon were sprinting past him, before he was yet halfway to the school.

But the Captain and his friends did not rush off. They preferred to stay on the field for a while longer to talk about the practice, discuss the team and generally relish the feeling of being celebrities, watched and admired by the spectators still dotted along the touchline.

A figure appeared round the corner of the cycle shed, and stood there surveying the whole field and meadows and river beyond. It was John Finch, face as dead as a fish.

Philip, still sitting on the grass, watching the players who had remained behind, did not notice him.

Malcolm listened to the chatter of the boys round him and looked at David.

The star-players stood self-consciously on view near the middle of the field, unwilling to bring their performance to an end. Then, gradually, they drifted across the field in the direction of the main group of supporters.

Malcolm, of course, led the chorus of congratulation and uncritical comments on their various performances during the practice.

"I'm not sure which is the strongest section of the team, the forwards or the three-quarters," said Malcolm. He glanced round the group. "What's your opinion, David?"

"Mmm, I don't know, sir. Our passing was a bit ragged today, I think. The forward line's pretty strong. It's got Carthorse in it, hasn't it?"

Everyone laughed and looked at Carter, who, with his face streaked with mud and his feet set wide apart, looked more than usually brutal. He grunted and took the compliment as his due.

"What do you think, Carter?" asked Malcolm.

Carter looked up. "What about?"

There was a snigger, Carter's dim-wittedness being proverbial and having been the subject of a number of sarcastic comments by Mr Lynch during the last hour.

"Where do you think the team's strengths and weaknesses lie?"

"It hasn't got any weaknesses, sir. It's a good team."

One or two of the boys agreed, chiming in with, "Yeah, yeah, it's a great team. The best."

Carter raised his head at this and looked around, his confidence bolstered by the unexpected support. But it was dashed again a moment later as David interupted the crowing of the sycophants.

"Don't be silly! It can't be great yet. It's going to be, of course. The greatest! But there's bound to be things wrong with us at the moment. Aren't there, sir? We've only been practising for three weeks."

Murmurs of approval from the other team-members accompanied Lundy's words. Carter had subsided almost visibly. He stared at the ground again. The captaincy had been the worst thing that had ever happened to him. The jibes at his dullness had more of malice in them nowadays. There was no open hostility yet, but it was a growing undercurrent.

"You've got to study tactics haven't you, sir?" David went on.

"Certainly," said Malcolm. "Brute strength without brains is of no use at all, even in rugger."

He had not intended any insinuation about Carter, but it was obviously taken as such, and all eyes turned upon him. He swallowed, more hurt by this cruelty than he would have admitted, and conceived an enormous hate for the teacher. All, it seemed, were turning against him. Lynch, the team, his friends, and now this Drew. He wanted to beat them all up. He remained silent.

"You need the strength, of course," said David, to break the silence, but added, in case he should be thought to be soft, "but it's not everything."

Carter looked up slowly and turned his eyes on Lundy. He just looked, thinking, "I want to beat someone up," and David felt suddenly nervous.

He looked away again.

The other boys exchanged glances which said, "Fight!" All began to wonder where and when it would be. Imaginations began whirring and spinning like little electric motors.

Carter, who had issued his silent challenge without fully realising it, now, as he sensed its effect, saw that he could no longer stay. He turned abruptly and strode away.

David gave one, short laugh, which convinced no one, least

of all himself.

"Do I sense a certain atmosphere?" said Malcolm, who had no idea what was going on.

"Carter's in a huff," someone said.

"Why?" asked Malcolm.

But they all remained silent.

"Sir! Excuse me, sir! Mr Drew!"

Philip ran up to the group.

"Yes?" said Malcolm.

"A telephone call came for you, sir. A young lady. I'm to say that Miss Raynor rang—I think that was the name—would that be right, sir?"

"Yes, I think so," said Malcolm, confused and embarrassed. The other boys were grinning.

"Miss Raynor rang, I was to say, and you are invited to tea on Saturday at the house of one of Miss Raynor's friends, and she will send on a note with—er—all the details."

Philip smiled brightly. All the boys were giggling. Malcolm had turned bright scarlet.

"Th-thank you, Minchip," he stuttered. He coughed, looked away, blushed deeper. At last he mumbled, "I'd better be going," turned and walked hurriedly away. He heard the boys laughing as he went. They were rolling about on the field, giggling uncontrollably.

Philip, suddenly a popular hero, stood and smiled in their midst.

"Did you make it up?" asked Lundy.

"No," said Philip, and told them what had happened.

The laughter began again. They began imitating Mr Drew's reaction. Gradually, the laughing, shouting, jostling crowd of boys made their way up to the school, with David and Philip in their midst.

John Finch saw them come into the quad, and stood at the formroom window watching them.

Friendship is almost always exclusive. It was coincidence, of course, that Carter had been expelled, or had expelled himself, from the group at the moment of Philip's arrival, but it seemed, not only to Carter but to everyone, as though Philip had replaced him, or even ousted him. And gradually everyone else in the group began to feel the pull of exclusion working on them too. Things were not the same.

But to begin with nothing seemed changed beyond the expulsion of one member and the election of another to the ranks of the clique, and a sudden increase in the general level of excitement brought about by these events.

And indeed excitement did run high. Philip was the centre of a growing circle of boys in the quadrangle before tea, all waiting to hear about and to see enacted The Comedy of the Telephone Message for Mr Drew and—when David rejoined the group after changing out of his rugby togs—The Drama of Carter's Challenge and Desertion. Both Philip and David played to packed houses until the bell rang for tea.

Carter was seen sitting at another table with two third form boys who were members of the rugby team and who were to be the first members of what came to be known as Carter's Gang. This left a place vacant at David's table, which was filled, naturally, by Philip.

Conversation at the table revolved mainly around Carter's probable course of action now, and the likelihood or otherwise of its coming to a fight. It was Wainwright who pointed out one important aspect of the situation that had so far gone unnoticed, which was that Carter's post of Vice-Chairman of the Amateur Dramatic Society and Stamp Club Incorporated must now fall vacant.

"Oh yes!" said David. "Philip—you can be Vice-Chairman now. We'd better have a meeting. After prep."

Word soon spread, and soon after seven o'clock the room above the old stables was packed with boys, the biggest turnout since the revolutionary first meeting of term. Carter, naturally, was not there. He was lounging, with the beginnings of his gang, against the wall of the cycle shed, frightening enough in the dark to make two first formers, who had come out to fetch the lamps from their bikes, stop, hesitate, then turn and flee to the comparative safety of their classroom. The only other person of note who was missing was Tomlinson.

"Arnie," shouted David over the noise of talking and laughing, "Tommo's not here. Birkett's nabbed him to do a job. Will you take the minutes? This has got to be official."

Arnold sighed. Where would they be without him?

Minutes of the Extraordinary General Meeting held on 12th October, 1955, at 7.12 p.m.

The meeting was called to order, with some difficulty, there being a very large attendance, by the Chairman, who then called upon the Secretary to read the minutes of the previous meeting.

Mr Wilkins, standing in for the General Secretary at the Chairman's request, attempted to do as he was asked, but was forced to stop after only a few sentences in view of the lack of silence and frequent interruptions *from all quarters*. It was decided therefore to postpone the reading of the minutes until the next *ordinary* meeting.

The Chairman then announed his reason for calling this *extra-ordinary* meeting, which was to elect a new Vice-Chairman (Dramatic Section) to replace Mr Carter, who was *presumed* to have resigned.

(The Acting Secretary's request for actual evidence of this was ignored.) The Chairman proceeded to nominate Mr Minchip for the post, Mr Wainwright seconding the nomination.

Mr Minchip then stood on a chair and delivered a speech in which he promised to serve the Society to the best of his ability and proposed that the Society put its efforts into the production of a play or revue to be performed in the School hall at the end of the Autumn term.

This proposal being well received (in such a manner as to cause the whole building to tremble) and in the absence of any other nominations, Mr Minchip was duly elected Vice-Chairman (Dramatic Section).

Loud cheers ensued, and with the sudden departure of the

Committee from the room, the meeting was presumed closed.

A. Wilkins.
Acting Secretary,
Vice-Chairman (Stamps Section).

The Committee's "sudden departure" took them, with their followers, back to the formroom, where Philip's propsal of some kind of Christmas entertainment was eagerly discussed. As enthusiasm for the day's other excitements began to wane, this new topic took over and kept them going until the bell rang for prayers.

Carter went to bed in silence. The others were subdued in his presence. Sooner than usual, all were in bed and quiet, which surprised, and relieved, Malcolm, when he came along to turn out the lights. He was expecting more smirks and giggles.

"Goodnight boys," he said, nervously, just before he switched off the lights.

Murmurs of goodnight, and the sound of boys turning over in their beds, came to his ears.

Click—darkness, which came as a relief to them all.

There followed two weeks of really beautiful October weather, exactly as October should be. A fine, light mist in the morning, quickly dispersed by brilliant, golden sunshine, which picked up and played with all the colours of the dead and dying leaves, and in the afternoon grew warm. In the evening, the long rays of the sun lay slantwise across the meadows, and all seemed peaceful. To Malcolm, it was perfection.

On Friday afternoon, two days after the events just related, when the bell rang at four o'clock, Philip and David sauntered down into the quadrangle and sat together on the low wall. It was warm and quiet.

The excitement had died down. It had been losing momentum steadily all the previous day and now, in the absence of any action on Carter's part, there was a lull. The members of the group lost interest in each other and, at four o'clock on Friday afternoon, the very time when you could count on finding Lundy, Tomlinson, Wainwright and the others together, they all went their separate ways without a word being said. The charm that had bound the circle together seemed to be fading. Tomlinson had gone up to the dormitory to find a book, which he then took down to the fields to read. Wainwright was down at the river with two others throwing stones at the opposite bank. Carter was somewhere else with his twin third-form shadows. Philip and David sat on the wall in the quad.

The shadow of the classroom block edged its way over their bodies; the sun lit their hair.

Malcolm opened the door to his room and went in. He put his books down on the table, and then walked over to the window to look out once more on the idyllic afternoon before settling down to mark the books. He stood there for a long time, transfixed by the vision of David's innocent beauty in the Autumn sunshine.

"What other places have you been to?" asked David.

Philip thought for a moment. "I stayed in France for a few weeks once, with my mother."

David looked at him, expectantly. He had heard many stories of people and places during the last two days.

"A small town called Pitot in the Midi. That's what they call the South of France."

"What was it like?"

"It was hot. Really hot. You stayed indoors in the afternoon. I was there in August. Really hot. Like, as if somebody had a big magnifying glass held up to the sun and it was focussed on that town. Blistering. Paint peeled off houses. You closed the shutters in the afternoon. It was always hot there in the summer, but this was a real freak heat-wave. Sweat. It poured off you. People were ill. People fainting from the heat. Dying even."

"Phew!" David gasped, mopping his brow. He looked at the sun, then back at Philip.

"In the morning, and in the evening, people were out. Most of the men just wore shorts. Sometimes a shirt as well. Mostly the women go barefoot. It's a port, a little fishing port, with a harbour. Very nice. White stone, seagulls, little boats. Just sailing boats, most of them, without engines. I used to spend most of my time round the harbour."

Malcolm could not move until they did. The sight of the blond hair in the sunshine had dazed him.

The boys stood up and began to walk slowly away. They stopped while Philip gestured, demonstrating something, and then moved on again until at last they went round the corner and out of sight.

Malcolm turned away from the window and sat down at the table. Feeling as though he were in a trance, he picked the first book off the pile, opened it and began to read the essay.

Philip and David walked slowly across the Meadows to the river, while Philip continued to paint his picture of the little Midi town of Pitot.

". . . took me out in his boat once. A big man with a big, bushy moustache. Big chest. He tried to talk to me all the time, in French, and laugh. I didn't understand a word he was saying, but he didn't seem to mind."

". . . when I was out walking once and I got lost. I must have taken a wrong turning somewhere. I had to stay the night. I slept on the kitchen floor with the dog. But the soup they gave me at supper-time was delicious."

". . . found me on the floor of the boat. I must have fainted. I remember climbing into the boat after everyone had gone. I must have been there all afternoon."

They stood on the bank of the river for a while, watching Wainwright and his friends throwing stones, and then walked on along the river bank, under the bridge.

"Why did you come to this school?" asked David.

"I was in trouble at my other school in Cardiff. They suspended me. I might have been expelled. My aunt and uncle wanted rid of me, anyway. So they sent me here. Davy's a friend of the family."

"What were you in trouble for?"

"Playing truant. Breaking things."

They scrambled up a bank at the end of the field beyond the bridge, ran across a field, climbed over a fence, and stood in a narrow lane which led only to a farm and was out of bounds.

"What about tea?" said David, looking at his watch.

"Let's skip tea," said Philip. "Nobody will notice. I've got some tuck we can have later."

"What if they check up?"

Philip shrugged his shoulders. David took a deep breath, feeling much as one does when about to take one's first dive from the spring-board.

"O. K.," he said.

Philip went on talking to David, answering his questions, describing people and places he had known, as they walked along. David was fascinated, and envied Philip's exciting life. They walked not towards the farm but back along the lane to the road and then into the wood where John had taken Philip two days ago. They tried to walk round the pond but were halted by marshy ground. They climbed and sat together on the branch of the tree where John had sat. Philip called it "The Finch's Perch" and told David what had happened that day. They sat on the branch of the tree, swinging their legs, discussing friends and acquaintances.

Mr Hopper said grace. There was complete silence. Then the single word, "Servers!" produced a sudden scraping of chairs and a cacophonous babble of conversation as ten small boys were catapulted from their tables to the hatch and then hobbled back bearing trays of food which seemed many sizes too large for them.

Malcolm sat at one end of the staff table next to Mr Hopper, who seemed preoccupied with something. Birkett and Lynch sat at the other end, deep in conversation. So Malcolm was left alone to eat a leisurely tea of bacon and eggs. As he ate, he glanced about the room in search of the lovely boy, and was rather worried when he didn't see him there. Remembering he had seen him leave the quad with Minchip, he looked around for him and his anxiety deepened when he couldn't see him either. He did not know what to do. He didn't want to 'tell' on them, but he knew he ought to. But his dilemma was solved for him.

When the meal was nearly over, and the boys were filling up on bread and marge, Mr Hopper beckoned a boy from the table nearest the platform and handed him four form lists. The boy knew what to do without being told, and proceeded to work his way slowly up and down the aisles, ticking off names as he did so.

At last, the boy returned and handed the lists back to Mr Hopper. Mr Hopper left the lists lying on the table whilst he finished his cup of tea, and then ran his finger slowly down the first form list, stopping at a name near the bottom which was not ticked. Malcolm, who was looking over his shoulder, told Mr Hopper that the boy was unwell and was lying on his bed in dorm, on his instructions.

Mr Hopper took out his pen and wrote, "Sick," against the boy's name.

"Teacher-on-duty should be told, you know," he said, without looking up.

"Oh, I'm sorry. I didn't know."

He put the first form list on one side and checked the second form list, which was complete, and the third form list, which was also complete, and then came to the fourth form list.

Mr Hopper leant over and touched Mr Birkett's arm.

"Lundy and Minchip—any reason why they should be missing?"

Mr Birkett thought a moment. "Not that I know of. Aren't they here?"

Mr Hopper shook his head. "Not here."

"Hmmm." Mr Birkett frowned. "You'd better check."

Mr Hopper stood up, picked up the hand-bell and rang it aloft. The boys looked up and screwed their heads round to face him, and the hubbub fell to a murmur.

"Silence!" he shouted, and the murmur ceased.

"Lundy?" he said, and his eyes roamed over the faces in front of him, some of which also scanned the room.

"Minchip?"

The same survey of faces, and an expectant pause. The boys

glanced at their neighbours, with looks that showed hope of some excitement.

"I don't suppose any of you have any idea of the whereabouts of these two?" drawled Mr Hopper, laconically.

The boys looked at each other again and shook their heads.

Mr Hopper looked down at Mr Birkett, who frowned.

"All finished?" he asked, turning back to the boys. They looked at him. "Dismiss by tables. On you go."

The boys shot away, table by table, down the corridor which led to the quadrangle, like water pouring down a funnel. They were replaced, as the last drops disappeared down the corridor, by two fat ladies in grubby white aprons who set to work at once clearing the tables and re-laying them for supper.

Mr Birkett was still frowning. Mr Hopper had sat down. Malcolm looked anxiously across the table, biting his lip, and Fred Lynch buttered another slice of bread, spread it thickly with raspberry jam, folded the slice in half and ate it.

"Minchip and Lundy," said Mr Hopper, at length. "Are they friends?"

"They've been sitting next to each other since yesterday," said Malcolm.

"Have they?" said Hopper. "I hadn't noticed."

(He managed to imply by this that no one of any standing in the world would notice such things.)

"Another whim of the Headmaster's," said Mr Birkett. "There was bound to be trouble."

"What's that?" said Mr Hopper.

Mr Birkett shook his head. "You'd better inform the Headmaster, Mr Hopper," he said, standing up, "and meanwhile I'll send some boys to search for them round the school grounds."

He walked quickly out of the dining hall, followed by Mr Hopper.

"Minchip's a strange boy, isn't he?" said Malcolm to Fred Lynch.

"They're all strange, if you ask me," Fred replied, pulling his mouth this way and that to try to get at the last fragments of his tea. "What goes on inside boys' minds doesn't bear thinking about. So I try not to. That's where Ron goes wrong, you know."

He stood up.

"Best just leave things be. Like old Danny Boy," he said, nodding at Malcolm and tapping his finger against his nose. "He knows what's what."

Suddenly chatty, and almost fatherly, he put his arm around Malcolm's shoulder and led him, still talking, out of the room.

Mr Jones was as phlegmatic as Fred Lynch, and exasperating to Mr Birkett, but by no means unconcerned.

"If the school rules have been broken," he said, "as seems to be the case, then they must be severely punished."

Mr Birkett, who had arrived at the Headmaster's study very soon after Mr Hopper, interjected, "Very severely. Breaking of bounds is a serious offence. An example must be made. Minchip, especially, must not be allowed to get away with this. He is obviously leading Lundy astray. Lundy has always been a model pupil. That, at any rate, is my view."

"A view I share entirely," said Mr Jones. "But there are offences still more serious. Let us hope that breaking of bounds is as far as it goes."

Mr Birkett looked up quickly.

"Not that one has any reason to fear otherwise," smiled the Headmaster.

"What do you suggest we do, sir," said Mr Hopper, "if Mr Birkett's search-party return empty-handed?"

"The police must be informed," said Mr Birkett.

"As Mr Birkett says," said Mr Jones. "We must consider the boys' own safety. It is a dark night. I think, however, we could legitimately wait for perhaps—" he looked at the large old clock in the corner, which showed ten minutes past six—"fifty minutes, until seven o'clock, before we take that step. In the meantime, if our initial search proves fruitless, I would suggest that we make our own search in the immediate vicinity of the school. Mr Lynch could be asked to drive slowly down the lane to the village and back. Mr Hopper, would you go and ask him to do that, while Mr Birkett checks on the search-party?"

A rabbit, startled by the headlamps, bounded away down the

road in front of Fred Lynch's car, and then suddenly veered off into the hedgerow.

"If I'm the one to catch 'em," muttered Fred to Malcolm, who was looking anxiously to right and left as they drove slowly down the road, "I'll thrash 'em myself first before I take 'em back, then Ron and the Boss can do what they like. And I hope they thrash 'em again. Little buggers, bringing me out like this."

They reached the village, turned at the green and drove more quickly back.

"Lundy's been a bloody nuisance all term," muttered Fred. "He was a good lad last year. It's being in the top class. It goes to their heads. Happens every year."

Mr Birkett's search-party had scoured the grounds to no avail.

"No sign of them," said Fred Lynch to Mr Birkett, who was standing in the quadrangle awaiting their return.

Mr Birkett looked at his watch. "The police it is then," he said, and strode off in the direction of the Headmaster's study.

Fred made straight for the staffroom, but Malcolm stayed in the quad, peering into the darkness and allowing the cool night air to relieve, as far as it could, his state of nervous tension.

Twenty minutes later a police car pulled up at the front of the school and two policemen walked into Mr Jones's study. They sat down, in the unhurried way that policemen always have, and waited.

Mr Jones briefly explained the situation.

"Should we look near or far, do you think, sir?" asked the policeman who did the talking.

"In the case of one of the boys, I must say that I'm surprised you're having to look at all. In the case of the other—well—the boy, to use your own jargon, has a record of truancy."

The policeman who did the talking raised his eyebrows. The other appeared unmoved.

"A difficult home situation. He has played truant—not from us, but from previous schools—on several occasions, and has once or twice run away from home. He has only been with us a few weeks."

The policeman waited, but Mr Jones said nothing more. "I see, sir," the policeman said at last. "It's difficult for us to do much at night, but we'll see what we can do. We'll put out a call and have a scout round. So long as there's no danger of abduction or anything of that sort?"

"Oh, I would hope not," said Mr Jones.

"No reason to suspect anything?"

"I don't think so."

"Good. Well, we'll see what can be done, sir. We'll be back later. We'll find our own way out. Thank you, sir."

His silent companion followed him out, and a few moments later the car was heard drawing away.

The clock in the corner chimed nine. David and Philip sat next to each other on a small sofa, their eyes cast down. Mr Jones surveyed them, like a scarecrow sadly observing two small birds who had not heeded his warning.

"You have put us all to a great deal of trouble," he said, softly, "and disappointed me."

"Yes, sir," said David, who was close to tears.

"It was a silly thing to do. One understands why, I think, but still it was silly."

"Yes, sir," said David, with a sob rising in his throat.

Mr Jones, amused by David's readiness to agree with whatever he said, turned his back on them and thought for a moment.

"Minchip," he said, at last, turning round, "do you still descend to your classroom in the dead of night, when all good things of the world, except me, are at rest, to fetch work to do in your bed?"

David looked at Philip in surprise.

Philip grinned, then frowned. He liked Mr Jones. "Yes, sir," he said. "Sometimes."

"I hope you sleep better tonight, after your exertions in the fresh air."

David half-laughed, and the laugh brought a rush of tears from his eyes, which he hurriedly brushed away.

"You are both gated until half-term and will report to me

every day at four o'clock until then. Now go to your beds."

"Thank you, sir," said David, more relieved than he could express, not at the nature of the punishment, which was not light by any means, but just that it was over.

Philip said nothing, and the two boys went out and made their way quickly to their dormitory.

Intense and excited whispers filled the dermitory until late that night. David and Philip were heroes again, even more infamous now than they had been on Wednesday, and David thoroughly enjoyed it. While they had been out he had enjoyed the thrill of breaking rules, then, when they were found and brought back by the police, and during the whole series of reprimands from all the various authorities involved, and while their fate was still unknown, he had been scared and tearful and wished it had never happened, but now that the worst was over and he was a celebrity he enjoyed himself again and lived the daredevil part to the full with his friend.

This escapade, and especially the gating, bound the friends even more closely together. People, from now on, always thought of Lundy and Minchip together, and both boys gloried in the association, though for different reasons.

So, in the darkness of the dorm, their whispers were heard, recounting over and over their whole adventure, from first setting out, to the dark sojourn in the wood (they sat in the tree for fully two hours) while bats fluttered round them and owls swooped on mice and young rabbits below them, to their walking down the lane back towards school and being caught suddenly in the police car's headlamps and being brought back to school in the car, and so on up to the conclusion: gated till half-term. Philip's whisper goes on longest, while David is beginning to doze, and the boys nearest Philip's bed make a rapt audience till very nearly midnight.

Mr Jones lingered in his study for almost an hour after the boys had gone, thinking about what had happened, and especially about the character and behaviour of his young relative, Philip

Minchip. Eventually, he walked over to the filing cabinet, opened it and took out the letter which he had promised to show to his wife at the beginning of the term. He hesitated a moment, looking at it, and then, seeming to reach a decision, closed the filing cabinet drawer and left his study, with the letter in his hand.

He found his wife sitting in their living room, reading, as usual. She didn't look up when he came in.

"I have that letter here," he said, "if you'd like to read it."

"What letter?" she said.

He held it out to her and she took it.

"The letter I was going to show you before."

Mrs Jones took the letter out of its envelope and read it.

"I might have known," she said, when she had finished. "I might have known. Well, what now?"

Mr Jones smiled wanly. "I don't know, dear," he said. "I'm sure I don't know."

"Dear Malcolm,

I hope you got the message all right. In case you didn't, this is to invite you to tea this coming Saturday—not at our house, but at the flat of a friend of mine. There will be two or three other people there probably. Come to our house at about three o'clock and we'll walk round together.

I hope everything is all right.

Love,
Alice."

The letter did not arrive until Saturday morning, by which time Malcolm was beginning to wonder whether Minchip had fabricated the whole thing, though how he had got hold of Alice's name he couldn't imagine. But the arrival of the letter put his mind at rest and, since none of the boys had made any further reference to the business, he now forgave Minchip.

Alice was waiting for him at the bus-stop. Partly out of anxiety as to whether he would come or not, partly to escape from her mother and partly because it was a gloriously sunny afternoon, she had decided to come out and meet him. She greeted him with a smile and took his hand at once.

Malcolm's feelings were confused. It was the first time she had ever met him at the bus-stop. He was pleased, but puzzled. Her warm smile and her eager taking of his hand both flattered and disturbed him.

"Is that a new dress?"

"Yes," said Alice, delighted that he had noticed. "Do you like it?"

"Mmm. It's very nice. It suits you."

Alice glowed, and began to feel that everything was going to work out. But this did not reduce the nervous tension she felt, rather it increased it. She had gone to great pains to make herself look attractive, had bought the dress on Thursday, with shoes to match, had made an appointment for that morning at the hairdresser's, and had spent ages in front of the mirror before coming out, putting on her make-up. Once the invitation had been made to Malcolm, her one thought, her only ambition, was to be sure of him.

Malcolm missed most of the details, but the overall impression was by no means lost on him. As the bus drew up and he saw her standing on the pavement, he almost did not recognise her. That is to say, he did recognise her, but with surprise, so that in the next moment he wondered if he had made a mistake. He put it down to not having seen her for some time.

As they walked along, Alice told him about her friend, with whom they were to have tea. She was a young woman, two or three years Alice's senior, who taught at the town's principal girls' Grammar School, or High School, as it was known. Alice had met her at a meeting of their Union. Her name was Joan Malling. She was a graduate of London University, and she taught History.

But Malcolm was only half-listening. His confused feelings were trying to sort themselves out. He had given no thought to Alice during the past three weeks. Their last meeting had been a failure. Other things had pushed her from his mind. He had been just beginning to accept that state of affairs and, had a complete break come, would have been ready for it—almost glad of it. Indeed, he had thought it more than likely that the reason for the invitation was for Alice to bring their relationship to an end, which would explain why she had not wanted to speak to him personally on the 'phone, but had left a message instead.

He had spent some time that morning, and on the bus, considering what might lie behind the line in Alice's letter—"I hope everything is all right." It would seem to point in a different direction. But then it could be taken in a number of ways.

Now, however, it seemed he had been wrong. Unless Alice was being especially nice in order to soften the blow.

Such was Malcolm's state of mind, as he walked along the sunny, busy streets in the middle of the town, with Alice. It seemed to grow more complicated every minute, as every minute he found himself becoming more and more attracted to her. He did not remember ever before experiencing such a physical liking for her. Their relationship had never been passionate.

"It's just along here," Alice said, as they turned around a corner which marked the end of the shopping centre and into a street of mainly eighteenth- and early nineteenth-century town houses. Three-storey houses, in the main, terraced, and very handsome. Some had been turned into flats, some had been converted into business premises—dentists, solicitors and the like—but the majority still served their original purpose.

Malcolm's eyes travelled admiringly over the houses on either side as they walked down the road.

"Does she live in one of these?" he asked, surprised.

"Yes," said Alice. "It's a really lovely flat. Wait till you see it."

"How does she afford it?"

"I think she has money."

"She must have."

A little over halfway along the street, Alice stopped and mounted the two broad stone steps which led up to the imposing front door of one of the houses. Standing back and looking up, Malcolm saw that the building had three storeys, like most of the others, surmounted by a small attic window projecting from the roof. Alice was pressing on the first of three bells, by which was a card bearing the name, Miss J. Malling.

"It's really lovely," said Alice, turning and looking down at Malcolm, who was standing with his head back and his mouth open, staring up at the tall building. She smiled. "You'll love it," she said. "Like your school."

The door opened. Alice and Joan exchanged greetings. Joan looked with interest at Malcolm, who was introduced to her. They shook hands, and she bade them follow her upstairs.

Joan had the top floor and the attic rooms above.

"Sorry about the climb," she said, as they ascended.

"That's all right," said Malcolm. "I'm used to it. My room's up two flights as well."

"Oh, well, that's all right then. The High School's all up and down stairs, too. Lucky Alice, teaching in a modern, single-storey primary school!"

They emerged onto a spacious landing, whose white-painted walls were hung with a number of old prints and maps, which served as Joan's hallway.

"Would you like to see the flat first?" asked Joan. "No one else is here yet."

There was a kitchen, with an array of cupboards and shelves all around, all, it seemed, filled with heavy old utensils of iron and earthenware. An enormous dresser held quantities of blue and white crockery. In the middle of the room stood a heavy, old-fashioned, solid, scrubbed kitchen table. Under it and around it were half a dozen three-legged and four-legged stools of various shapes and sizes. This was at the back of the house, and the window commanded a not uninteresting view of the rooftops of an old part of the town, including a couple of church spires and a bell-tower.

The bathroom, also at the back and as large as the kitchen, was carpeted and painted a deep red, but was not otherwise unusual.

Joan's bedroom, at the front of the house, was prettily feminine, with lace curtains covering the windows, pillared on either side by floor-length curtains of deep, midnight blue. There was a brass bedstead and a large bedcover. There was no wardrobe, but a cupboard in one corner presumably served that purpose. A couple of antique-looking chests stood against one wall, and over one hung a mirror in a gilt frame. Two or three antique chairs and a small occasional table by the bed completed the furniture. The wallpaper was a delicate pattern in pale-blue on white. On one wall two oil-paintings hung, one of violets, the other of an elderly lady.

Alice enthused over the room, and Malcolm, too, admired it greatly.

The living room was awash with bits of furniture, paintings, objects and bric-à-brac. But the total effect was far from being cluttered. It was interesting, lively, even refreshing. It was a large room and could well cope with all it contained. A settee and two armchairs, with faded covers, very soft, capacious and inviting, were the basis of the furnishing. To these were added an old-fashioned rocking chair, a very low stool and a small fireside chair. In front of the window stood a long oak dining table, surrounded by six high-backed chairs. On the table stood an oil lamp. The walls were buttressed all the way round the room by other items of furniture, large and small, chests, tables, chairs, bookcases, cupboards, and a grandfather clock. Most of these were surmounted by other objects, such as vases, cups, candlesticks, pictures, books, ornaments, *objets d'art* and plants. On the walls, above these and in between them, were pictures, so many that it would take less time to describe the spaces between than the pictures themselves. There were also on the walls two or three mirrors. The walls themselves were plain. There was no carpet. The floor was polished wood, covered only by one or two small rugs. In front of the hearth was a brass fender. The fire was laid but not lit. The room was warm and full of life. Malcolm looked forward to seeing it by fire-light. He had had the fire in his own room lit two or three times recently and had enjoyed the friendliness of the open fire, the colour and movement it imparted to the room. What would it do to this room!

They went upstairs and saw the attic rooms, which were simply but cosily furnished as bedrooms, one with a double bed and one with a single. Just after they had gone up, they heard the doorbell ring.

"I'll leave you to come down yourselves," said Joan, and went quickly downstairs to answer the door.

"Lovely, isn't it!" said Alice.

"Beautiful," said Malcolm. "She must be very wealthy."

"Both her parents are dead. I think she inherited quite a lot from them. But it's lovely, isn't it."

Malcolm agreed. "Marvellous." He looked round the small bedroom in which they were standing. "This is quite like my room at The Meadows, you know," he said.

"Is it?" said Alice.

He moved over to the little window and looked out, down into the street.

"My room looks out onto the quad," he said.

"I'd like to see it sometime."

Malcolm wondered about this. He was not sure whether he wanted her to see it. He remained where he was, looking out of the window, and said nothing.

"I love you, Malcolm."

Malcolm was rendered by this even more unsure of himself. The confusion which had begun as he was stepping off the bus was becoming unmanageable. He tried to search out his reaction to Alice's words, but could not. It was as though he and his feelings had drifted apart in space and, reach out as he might, he could not touch them. Something, however, was demanded of him.

He turned round and saw that Alice was sitting on the bed, looking down. He felt again the physical attraction to her which had been no part of his feelings towards her until now. He sat down by her and put his arm round her. She turned to him and they kissed. She kissed him harder than he had known her kiss before, and he was surprised. They drew apart slightly.

"I love you, Malcolm," she said. "I wasn't sure before. But I know it now. I'm sorry if I've been cruel to you in the past."

Malcolm still said nothing. They kissed again, for longer this time, and Malcolm's hand went up onto Alice's breast. He had never touched a woman's breast before. They drew apart again.

"We'd better go down," said Alice, quietly.

They stood up, Alice smoothed down the bed-clothes and they went downstairs.

"Malcolm, this is Freda," said Joan, as they entered the living room again. "Malcolm teaches at The Meadows, a little prep school near here."

"Oh, yes, I know."

Malcolm shook hands with a small, rather dumpy young woman with freckles and curly hair. She seemed quite bright and friendly, but her voice was surprisingly strong and deep, and her accent was rather hearty.

"Freda teaches History and Geography at the High School."

"Pleased to meet you, Malcolm. Alice, what a splendid dress. Is it new?"

"Do sit down, Malcolm," said Joan.

"By the way, Joan, Terry and Dot said they might be a little late. Something's cropped up to do with Terry's brother. Don't ask me what. Anyway, they said not to wait but to start without them and they'll get here as soon as they can."

"Oh, well," said Joan. "In that case, we might as well start. Are you all hungry?"

"Say yes, Malcolm," said Freda.

"I thought Arthur was coming," said Alice.

Joan nodded. "He is, but he's going to be late too. He rang me yesterday to say he would have to catch a later train. He won't be here till seven or eight o'clock. Make yourselves at home then, and I'll go and perform a few miracles in the kitchen."

"Forget about the fishes," said Freda, "just bring in the loaves."

The afternoon and evening passed, for Malcolm, in alternating periods of waking and sleeping—or so it seemed. There were times when the conversation around him seemed to drift away onto the edges of his consciousness, while he became absorbed in his own thoughts. At other times, he was drawn into the conversation and everything seemed perfectly normal. He told them about The Meadows, and about the terrible school in Liverpool. He swapped Training College experiences with Freda and Alice and, later, with Dot, who was a student now at Alice's old college. He discussed motor-bikes with Terry, who owned one. Then again there were times when the room, or one of the many objects in it, claimed his whole attention and seemed to grow larger than life and fill his being.

Thus, it seemed to him, as time went by, his soul either went out of him and fixed onto some object in the room, or returned and sank deep out of reach inside him.

After tea, the fire was lit. Alice sat on the little stool, while Malcolm sat in an armchair next to her, and she leaned against his legs.

Terry and Dot sat together on the settee. Joan sat in the other armchair, opposite Malcolm, while Freda sat on the fireside chair, roasting herself.

Until it was quite dark outside, the only light was from the fire. Then Malcolm asked if the oil lamp was ever used. Alice protested that the firelight was enough on its own and much nicer, but Joan got up and lit the oil-lamp. Alice admitted then that she had been wrong and said that the room looked even prettier now. All agreed that electric light, after this, would seem odious.

They talked about teaching, about mutual friends and acquaintances, about houses and furniture, London, the countryside, parents and children, freedom. It was a little after the lighting of the oil-lamp when they got around to freedom. Freda was its most vocal champion and the most extreme. Terry thought there were limits. Joan Malling said less but held views very much the same as Freda's and expressed them more tellingly, Malcolm thought, for making less noise about it.

Malcolm listened whenever Joan was speaking, and watched her a good deal. Since the oil-lamp had been lit, he could see her better. She was tall and slender. Her hair was tied back rather severely, however, and her features were also severe.

Indeed, she had rather a bony face, but it was not unattractive and it was certainly striking. Her eyes especially caught his attention, for they were large and very blue. The firelight that flickered over her exaggerated the bone structure but softened with shadows any angularity it might otherwise have possessed and made the face seem softer.

"The war," she said, "Nazism, Fascism, should have made it clear to everyone that oppression, totalitarianism, almost any form of authoritarian rule, is dangerous and wrong. All sorts of prejudices and unquestioned dogma which held good before the war are disappearing now, and should disappear. People didn't realise what these things could lead to."

Malcolm listened and thought she was right, though he didn't trouble to think of any specific issues to which her words might be applied.

Freda launched out into a defence of the doctrine of free love, and spoke scathingly of marriage as a repressive and conservative institution. "The end of a person's development as an individual," she said. If she were to write a story, she said, she would end it with the words, "And so they got married and lived miserably ever after."

Terry, who worked for an estate agent, argued vehemently against Freda on this point.

Joan agreed that marriage often seemed to close a couple's eyes to what was happening outside the four walls of their own home, but pointed out that it need not be marriage itself which caused this, since there were cases where it didn't happen, and plenty of narrow-minded single people about. On the issue of free love, she agreed that there was much prejudice and stated that she herself could see no objections to pre-marital intercourse—provided one took precautions.

Terry seemed a trifle embarrassed, but appeared to agree with this point of view.

Freda proceeded to talk about ignorance of contraceptive devices and of sex generally, and the conversation turned to the subject of sex education in schools. Each of them described what form this had taken in their own schools, and much hilarity resulted. Terry gradually lost his embarrassment and spoke almost as openly as the enlightened Freda, but always with an air of surprise.

Malcolm remained noncommittal throughout. There was a puritan strong and deeply rooted in him, but there was also a kind of detachment from himself, very much in evidence this evening, which made that puritan remote enough to seem a different person. He said little, and by his silence was probably assumed by the others to be on the side of freedom. Indeed, he felt himself emotionally much more attracted to Joan's point of view—or even Freda's—than to Terry's. There was a reasonableness about Joan, something calm and civilised, which appealed to him.

He was thinking along these lines about Joan, watching her and dwelling on her image, only half-listening to what was being said, when, faint and far away, he heard the doorbell ring. Joan was wrenched out of his vision, and he sat staring at her empty chair. Terry and Freda were growing very vehement about something. Alice turned her head round and looked up at him. She smiled, took his hand and squeezed it gently. His eyes moved away from the empty chair and onto Alice, who looked, in the soft light of the oil-lamp and the open fire, very warm and appealing. He smiled and his heart began to beat quickly.

Joan returned and introduced them all to Arthur. The men stood up and shook hands. Chairs were offered, but he took one of the high-backed chairs by the table instead. As a result, the cosy little semi-circle around the hearth was broken and the atmosphere, conducive to discussion, was destroyed. Now they talked about British Railways, the weather, and other matters which none of them cared about.

Arthur suited the high-backed chair, Malcolm thought. He was a Captain, it seemed, in the army, and suitably military in appearance: tall, thin, erect, with a small moustache, sociable, but unbending, impersonal.

"Are you hungry, Arthur?" asked Joan.

"I am rather."

"I'll go and make you some dinner."

"Come on, chums," said Freda, standing up briskly. "Time we were going."

Joan insisted that it was not necessary for anyone to go, but none of them believed her and, in any case, they were all now more or less anxious to leave. So, within moments of Freda's standing up, the five original guests were emerging onto the lamp-lit street with noisy farewells, thanks and promises to come again soon.

Terry and Dot were soon thundering away on Terry's motor-bike, and then Malcolm and Alice set off walking down the street with Freda.

"What did you think of Joan's little homestead, then, Malcolm?"

"Marvellous! Absolutely!"

"Nice, isn't it? Pity Arthur had to come and kick us all out. I can't stand him. God knows what Joan sees in him. I expect he'll be staying the night too. No accounting for taste, is there?"

They walked on a few paces in silence.

"You going back to The Meadows tonight, Malcolm?"

"Yes," said Malcolm. "The last bus is at ten."

"Aren't the buses terrible? Ten o'clock! That's dismal."

They reached the end of the street, where Freda turned one way and Malcolm and Alice the other.

"See you again, Malcolm. You must do something about a bed for the night next time. Ten o'clock's ridiculous. Cheerioh!"

Malcolm and Alice walked away through the almost empty but brightly lit centre of the town. For a while neither of them spoke.

"You're very quiet, Malcolm," said Alice, at last.

"Am I?"

"Didn't you enjoy it?"

"Oh, yes. Yes I did. Very much."

"Something on your mind?"

"Not really."

"Oh well."

They walked on in silence again. Malcolm was feeling peculiarly depressed all of a sudden, but he couldn't put his finger on the reason.

"It's quite a nice town, isn't it?" Alice said, breaking the silence again. "At one time I really hated it, and I thought about going somewhere else. But I like it now. I suppose I'm making new friends. I don't see my old friends any more. And I'm near you."

He felt scared. A sudden panic came upon him.

Alice stopped and looked up at him. "Malcolm, do you still . . . I mean . . . ?"

"Of course," he said. "Of course."

She kissed him and held him tight. "Oh, Malcolm. I've been so worried. I thought maybe you were changing your mind. I'm sorry I've made you wait so long."

He didn't know what to say.

"So the answer's yes," she said, "if you still want me."

"Of course," he said. "Of course I do."

"I love you, Malcolm," she said. "Oh, I'm so happy. Everything's all right now."

Something was happening at The Meadows, some slight, subtle change in the atmosphere, which everyone felt but no one understood. It manifested itself most strongly in the behaviour of the fourth form, with whom the teachers became increasingly impatient. Either the form was restless and quick to lose concentration, or they were so subdued as to seem in a trance. The whole form sometimes seemed to be daydreaming. Mr Birkett became particularly irritated with them and spent as much time haranguing them, lecturing them on the vital importance of this final year at the prep school, as he did in trying to teach them. One day, he kept them all in for an hour at the end of afternoon lessons. Soon, everyone was longing for half-term, which was now only two weeks away.

In a vague way, the boys knew that it was Philip's fault. They did not know how or why, but they felt it, and the heroes of the week before found themselves becoming increasingly unpopular. Philip didn't mind, indeed he seemed almost to welcome and encourage it, but David was disconcerted and tried, variously, appeasement and self-assertion to cope with the situation, which he had never met before. Philip was merely scornful. Conflict seemed to nourish his ego.

Friday lunchtime saw the most open attack so far on the two friends. It came from an unlikely quarter. A boy called Andrew Wilson, quiet, hard-working, ordinary in appearance and, it had always been assumed, in all other respects, suddenly emerged as an individual.

The day was sunny and warm, one of the last such days of the year, and after lunch most of the school stayed out of doors. Carter and his team cronies had changed into their rugby togs and were on the field practising kicks. Philip and David sat, with some others, among them Wilson, on the slope which led down to the playing field. They talked of this and that and joked about 'the carthorse'.

In fact, David had intended changing and going onto the field himself, but Carter had beaten him to it. He had been on the point of suggesting it to the others, when he had seen Carter heading for the changing rooms. So he was annoyed with Carter, but also, obscurely, with himself, and the latter annoyance perhaps went deeper.

So David joined in with Philip's jibes, but hated himself for doing so, and, trying to expend the hate somehow, joined in the more. It was a vicious circle.

"Look at that! He must have a stone in his hoof!"

"Send him to the blacksmith!"

"Send him to the knacker's yard!"

"What's that?"

"Where they chop up useless old carthorses and sell them for dog food."

The other boys laughed and joined in, taking their cues from Philip and David. But at last Carter and his friends came off the field and went to get changed ready for the afternoon lessons. The entertainment came to an end.

"That was a good show," someone said.

They all nodded and murmured agreement. After the noise

and hilarity, a lull set in.

"What about the other show?"

Everyone turned to look at Wilson, who sat on the slope a bit higher than the others.

"What show?"

"The Amateur Dramatic show we're supposed to be doing for the end of term."

"Oh yeah."

"What's it going to be?"

Philip shrugged his shoulders. "Don't ask me," he said.

"It was your idea," said Wilson.

"So what?"

"So you ought to do something about it."

"He can't do it on his own," said David. "We'll sort it out at the next meeting. We want everyone's ideas."

"And when's the next meeting going to be?" asked Wilson. "When you and Minchip feel like it?"

"'Course not."

"That's what it seems like. And whenever we do have a meeting, it's only to elect your friends onto the committee. We never actually do anything."

"There hasn't been time."

"And as for the—'amalgamation' . . ." He laughed briefly, and did not bother to finish the sentence.

The others looked expectantly at David.

"What about it?"

Wilson laughed again. "The societies aren't 'amalgamated' at all. Wilkins and Sanders have just carried on with the Stamp Club like before. Only better. Better than the Dramatic Society anyway. At least they do something."

It was David's turn to laugh. "Yes! Wilkins and his first formers!"

"Well?" said Wilson. "What's wrong with that?"

David laughed again.

"I agree," said Philip, to everyone's surprise. "We'd be better off without the Stamp Club people. We only want people who are really keen."

There was a pause. Everyone was wondering whose side they were on. David seemed to have lost his footing for the moment.

"Well, you can count me out, whatever you do," said Wilson,

"Good riddance!" said Philip.

The bell was ringing for afternoon lessons. Wilson turned and walked away. A few of the by-standers quickly followed him, others stayed to hear what David would say now. But David was still puzzled.

"Do you think we should split?" he said to Philip.

Philip shrugged his shoulders.

"Perhaps we should have a meeting tonight," said Tomlinson, who had been watching in his usual detached manner.

"Yes," said David. "We'd better."

The bell had stopped ringing.

"We're going to be late," someone said.

"Come on, or he'll keep us in again."

They ran.

Shortly after four o'clock, Mr Birkett came across David and Philip standing outside the door of the Headmaster's study.

"What do you want?" he said.

"We've to report to the Headmaster, sir," said David. "But I don't think he's there."

Mr Birkett knocked on the door and looked in. There was no one there.

"Well, there's a staff meeting starting shortly," he said. "What does the Headmaster normally do with you?"

"Nothing, sir."

Mr Birkett frowned. "I see. Well, you can't wait now. I'll tell him you reported. You'd better run along now."

"Thank you, sir," said David.

Mr Birkett watched the two boys go, hovered for a moment, undecided, outside the door, and then went in, leaving the door open. He sat down in the armchair next to Mr Jones's desk and took out of his pocket a piece of paper on which he had made a note of the issues he wanted to raise at the meeting. He had decided that the time had come for him to air some grievances, and, in going over the various points in his head during the afternoon, he had worked himself into a state of high irritation. Every so often, as he sat there now, his head would tremble slightly, and he drummed his fingers on the arm of the chair.

Fred Lynch stood at one end of the quad, just outside the doorway which led through to the staffroom, surveying the sunny afternoon scene. He was on duty and, for once, glad of it, because it meant he would be able to keep popping out of the staff meeting whenever things got too tedious. Staff meetings bored him to tears.

"Excuse me, sir."

It was David and Philip trying to squeeze out between the doorway and Fred Lynch.

"What?" He turned round and stepped out of the way.

"Sorry, sir."

The boys hurried away.

"Mind you stay in bounds," he called after them. "*I'm* on duty today."

They made no reply, none that he could hear anyway, and were soon round the corner out of sight.

"Should have collared them and given them something to do," Fred Lynch muttered to himself, after they had gone. He looked at his watch, turned and went inside.

Geoffrey Hopper was cramming books into his briefcase. "Damn nuisance, this staff meeting," he said. "We've got people coming to dinner."

"What do you think it will be about?" asked Malcolm, who stood by the open window enjoying the breeze and the view of the meadows.

"Oh, just the usual. Nothing important, you can be sure of that. I expect Ron will spout a bit. The Head will take no notice, thank the Lord. There'd be no peace if Ron had his way, I'm afraid."

Malcolm laughed.

The door opened and Fred Lynch strolled in.

"No one put the kettle on?" he said, astonished. "Come on,

come on! If I've got to sit through a bloody staff meeting, I'm going to have a cup of tea while I'm there. Fall asleep otherwise."

It was just quarter-past-four when the kettle boiled.

"Come on then," said Mr Hopper. "Let's get it over with."

"Hang on, hang on!" said Fred Lynch, pouring the boiling water into the teapot. "Goodness me! Don't you want a cup? Malcolm?"

"Yes, all right," said Malcolm.

"The Head won't be there yet, anyway."

"That's true," said Mr Hopper.

Mr Jones was, in fact, half-a-mile away, walking back from the village, where he had been to post the mail. He didn't hurry, and when he entered his study all four members of his staff were there waiting for him.

"Good afternoon, gentlemen," he said. "Don't stand up. I'm sorry I'm late. I took a walk down to the village to post some letters. It's a lovely afternoon. I'm afraid we won't see many more like it this year. So I took my time and made the most of it. I hope you'll forgive me."

"Of course, Headmaster," said Mr Hopper.

"Thank you. Now, let me see." He sat down at his desk, pulled open one of the drawers, looked inside, closed it again and then looked round the room at them all, smiling.

"I shall probably forget half the things I meant to say to you," he went on. "I always seem to do that. But I find making lists and agendas and so on very banal, somehow. Still, Mr Birkett, perhaps if you were to begin by raising any points that you want to deal with, that will allow me time to collect my thoughts."

"Very well, Headmaster," said Mr Birkett, ominously, but before he could continue the Headmaster began speaking again.

"Oh," he said, "it's just occurred to me—so sorry, Mr Birkett—that I've never formally welcomed Mr Drew to the school, this being the first staff meeting we've had this term."

He smiled. Malcolm looked down, embarrassed. Mr Birkett raised his eyes to the ceiling, and his head trembled.

"We do welcome you, anyway," Mr Jones went on. "How's it going? You're coping very well, I'm sure. How do you like the school?"

"Oh, very much indeed!" said Malcolm, with great enthusiasm. "Really, very much!"

"That's splendid," said Mr Jones, smiling. "I'm very glad. It's a delightful old building, isn't it? I've been here over twenty years ... and ... I wonder ... One has really got to know it very well. Very well. So you like it then?"

"Very much," said Malcolm, a little disconcerted by something in the old man's voice, a certain sadness, despite the smile.

"That's splendid. Welcome anyway. I hope the whole of your time with us passes enjoyably."

"Thank you, sir. I'm sure it will."

Fred Lynch sat with his tea cup held close to his mouth, taking frequent, and not altogether silent, sips and staring absent-mindedly out of the window. Geoffrey Hopper glanced at the clock in the corner.

"Mr Birkett. I'm sorry. Please continue."

Mr Birkett consulted his notes. "First," he said, "I think we should confirm some dates."

"Certainly," said Mr Jones, leaning forward and opening a large diary which lay on his desk. The others took out pocket diaries and pens from their pockets.

"First, the end of term exams..."

Mr Birkett read out the dates he had arranged for these and other events that were to take place that term. The others copied them dutifully into their diaries.

"There are one or two other points that I would like to raise now," he said, when that business was completed. The Headmaster looked at him expectantly. So did Malcolm. But the other two did not appear to be taking much notice. "First of all, there is the matter of dress. I've raised this before many times, I know, but I think it is an important point, one that needs stressing, and needs stressing to the boys. First, general tidiness—shoes, socks, ties, and so on—and here I think we should have a clothes inspection first thing tomorrow, with our own forms. Send any boy with dirty shoes back up to dorm, to clean them. That's the first thing. But one inspection isn't enough. We must continue to take this sort of action, all the time. That's the first thing. The other thing about dress is leisure wear. Some of the boys are beginning to stretch the rules here, and with this kind of thing it's the thin end of the wedge. I think you, Headmaster, should make an announcement about this in assembly. What I'm thinking about is things like bright red sweaters, gaudy shirts, that sort of thing. The boys must be made to live up to the standards we lay down. And this is not just the older boys. If it were just my own form, I would deal with it myself and that would be that. This thing is more widespread."

"If you'll excuse me, Headmaster," said Fred Lynch, standing up. "I'm on duty. I'd better go have a look round."

"Certainly, Mr Lynch," said the Headmaster.

Fred Lynch hurried out of the room and walked away down the corridor, shaking his head. "I don't know why he bothers," he said to himself.

But Mr Birkett did bother, and went on bothering to the end. Having dealt with the matter of dress, he went on to talk about such matters as politeness, punctuality, laziness, slipshod work, noise in the dormitories, frequenting the sweet-shop in the village, handwriting and underlining the title, all of which put together amounted to a disastrous and very nearly fatal decline in standards. And the upshot of it all was that he wanted the Headmaster to speak to the school about it in assembly.

"Very well," said Mr Jones. "I will do that at the very earliest opportunity."

Mr Birkett's head was still trembling with the vehemence of his speech.

"Well now," Mr Jones went on, "I think Mr Birkett has said just about all there is to say. Thank you very much, Mr Birkett. As far as what I have to say goes... Oh, but Mr Lynch is not here now. I think he ought to be here really, for what I have to say. Perhaps one of you could go and fetch him."

But there was no need. At that moment, the door burst open and Fred Lynch rushed into the room. "Somebody's let my tyres down!" he said, as if he could hardly believe what he said. "Somebody's let my tyres down!" he repeated, as they all just sat staring at him.

"Good heavens!" said Mr Jones.

"When did this happen?" said Mr Birkett.

"I don't know. Sometime after lunch, it must have been. It's not even the end of term. I always keep it locked away in the garage at the end of term."

"We must find the culprit," said Mr Birkett.

"Damn right we will!" said Mr Lynch.

"I'd better start asking questions now."

"You had, and I'll come with you."

"What about this other business, Headmaster?" said Mr Birkett.

"I think, under the circumstances," said Mr Jones, "that can wait until another time. It's not so terribly urgent that it can't wait a little longer. You'd better see about Mr Lynch's tyres. We'll call the meeting closed, I think."

Fred Lynch marched off rapidly with Mr Birkett, and Geoffrey Hopper and Malcolm followed them out, leaving the Headmaster sitting in his study alone. For once, the smile had left his face, and he looked very troubled.

"Dear Mother, Father and Grandmother,

Good news! The Stamp Club is again independent! I have just returned from *another* extraordinary General Meeting of the now defunct Amateur Dramatic Society and Stamp Club Incorporated, called by Lundy, who has done a complete about-face, to propose that the two societies go their separate ways again. I was amazed, as you can imagine, but very pleased. At last 'our leaders' have seen reason! Or have they? Anyway, at least we are left on our own again, and the pretence of 'amalgamation' has been dropped.

Wainwright has stayed with the Dramatic Society, so I remain Chairman of the Stamp Club, with Sanders as Secretary. I must say everything has been going very well since we took over (modesty—hum, hum!) and we have a good membership. (I doubt whether the Dramatic Society people could say the same, but more of that another time. All they seem to do is fall out with one another—and they *still* haven't done a play!)

It has been an eventful day. This afternoon, someone let down the tyres of Mr Lynch's car. All four! (I'm not sure about the spare.) So we all had to stay in after tea, while Mr Birkett lectured us. He was very angry. He has been interviewing suspects this evening, and I suppose he is hoping someone will 'inform' on the culprits. But I doubt if anyone will. No one knows for sure who did it, but, of course, we have our suspicions.

Everybody here is a bit quarrelsome at the moment and we'll all be glad when it's half-term. Mr Birkett has been in a terrible mood all week, and today's prank has just made him worse. Still, Sanders and I are getting on pretty well. I think, 'mind your own business', is good advice here at the moment.

But I must stop now as the bell is ringing for supper. I will be writing again on Sunday, of course, with more news. I wonder what else will have happened by then!

Love,
Arnold."

The lights were out, but the boys in the dormitory were talking.

"And that's just the start," said Philip.

"What else are you going to do?"

"Lots of things."

"Like what?"

"Oh, all sorts of things."

"Why don't you—break into Davy's study."

"We might do that," said David. "That would be easy."

"You'd have to bring something back as proof."

"His cane, maybe."

"Or his gown."

"Something off his desk."

"A picture off the wall."

"Mrs Jones."

"Get lost!"

"When I've been in Davy's study before," said Philip, "I've

always felt a kind of atmosphere. A weird atmosphere."

"How do you mean?"

"Well, I was once left alone in his study for a few minutes. But all the time, it felt as if someone else was there. It was all dead silent, and nothing moved, but—I kept wanting to look behind me. I could tell there was someone, or something, there. I could feel it watching me. You know how it is, when you can feel someone looking at you."

"You're round the twist, Minchip."

"Ooooooh! I'm scared!" somebody said, in a mock-terrified voice.

"I reckon there must be a ghost in this place," said Philip. "A place as old as this is bound to have a ghost."

"Get lost! There's no such thing as ghosts."

"Well, I think there is."

"So do I."

"Me too."

"Ooooooh, don't! I'm scared!"

"I believe in ghosts," said Philip. "If there were a ghost here, shall I tell you what I think it would be?"

"Don't bother."

"Yeah, go on."

"I think it would come up from the river on misty, moonlit nights. It would be the ghost of someone who was drowned in the river, and it would climb up onto the river-bank and drift over the meadows, dripping water behind it, and it would come into the quad, and the water would be constantly dripping from it as it stood there looking round with hollow eyes, and then suddenly it would cry out, in a horrible, mournful voice, 'Somebody pushed me! Somebody pushed me!' Then it would pass through the door into the school, and it would begin to drift down all the corridors, searching for the person who pushed it into the river, leaving a trail of water behind it. And in the middle of the night, when we're all asleep, it probably passes down between the beds, looking at us all, searching for the one who pushed."

"I shan't be able to sleep now."

"And then, just before morning, at first light, it returns to the river, drifting down over the meadows in the mist, and sinks under the water again, and lies down until the next night."

"Let's talk about something else, can we?"

"Phil's right, though. I bet there is a ghost."

"All I know is," said Philip, "that there was something very strange in the atmosphere that time in Davy's study. Something very strange."

Suddenly the door opened and twenty hearts gave one massive thump in unison.

"Shut up and get to sleep!" shouted Mr Lynch.

There was absolute silence.

"If I hear another word spoken, I'll give the lot of you a thousand lines."

He walked out and slammed the door. The whole dorm breathed a gentle sigh of relief, but no one spoke again.

Mr Lynch quickly completed his final tour of inspection and then went to his room and to bed. All lights were extinguished. Nothing stirred. Darkness and silence reigned in every room in the school, save one.

Mr Jones, like some ghost of Philip's imagination, still hovered within the precincts of his study, where he had remained since the staff meeting had ended, before its climax. Disconsolately, like one stranded on a rock in the midst of the cold waters, he wandered about his room.

"The best thing," he said to himself, "is to do nothing."

A coal fire had been burning but had now crumbled away almost to nothing, a small grey heap on the grate. The room grew chilly. At one o'clock, he opened the window wide to the cold, dark night and stared out. The chill that enveloped him seemed to strengthen him, like metal cooling.

"It's just a matter of waiting," he said.

It cheered him. He felt a lightening of his spirit, and the smile returned to his lips.

"Patience."

He closed the window. He opened the door, went out and closed the door behind him. Calm now, he set off to walk about the school. Slowly, calmly, he walked along the corridors of the old house, switching the lights on and off as he went. A nocturnal watcher, outside the house, would have seen two or three windows at a time suddenly lit up and then, a few moments later, darkened, to be replaced by the next section, and so on, little by little, around the whole building. And he would have seen also, from time to time, a tall, thin, black figure, stooping slightly, pass slowly behind the lighted windows.

Philip saw the lights, and hid. He watched the Headmaster go by. As soon as it was dark again, he made his way quickly back to the dormitory, postponing his raid on the Headmaster's study to another night.

At two o'clock, Mr Jones stood in the quadrangle and listened to the hooting of an owl. The air grew colder. The last remaining leaves shivered on the branches.

Mr Jones shivered too and, at long last, made his way back inside to the house and to bed.

"Davy's gone mad," said Philip.

The boys were sitting in their formroom at break on Saturday morning. Outside a ferocious wind was blowing. The tree in the quad was being bent this way and that. Leaves were swirling round in frantic eddies and whirlpools.

"Eh?"

"He's gone mad."

"What do you mean?"

"What I say. Listen! I couldn't sleep last night. So, at about two o'clock in the morning, I got up and came down here."

"Blimey! Weren't you scared? It must have been dead spooky."

"You might have met that ghost you were talking about."

"I wasn't scared. I quite often do it. Anyway, I was in here, when suddenly the light went on outside. I hid behind a desk. That one, it must have been."

He re-enacted it.

"I got down like this and watched the corridor. And it was

Davy. He was walking along and smiling to himself. He kept stopping and looking around, and smiling all the time. Weird! And the way he walked—dead slow, just sort of drifting along."

"Sure there wasn't water dripping off him?"

"The Mad Headmaster!"

"Innocent children murdered by mad Headmaster! Read all about it!"

"You never know!"

"Seriously though, Phil. You're not making it up?"

"Of course not. Anyway, it's quite likely, because insanity runs in his family."

"How do you know?"

"Because I'm related to him. He's my great-uncle ten times removed, or something. And I've heard that quite a few people on his side of the family went mad."

"Honestly?"

"Honestly."

"Blimey! This place isn't safe any more."

"Hey, Phil! If insanity runs in his family, and you're related to him, that means insanity runs in your family too, doesn't it?"

"I suppose it does," said Philip. "You'd better all watch out."

Malcolm hurried out after lunch, wrapped up in a long raincoat, college scarf and gloves, to battle his way down to the village. He stood at the bus-stop on the village green, along with two or three other people, pushed this way and that by the wind. Then, sitting on the top deck of the bus, he could both hear and feel the wind buffeting the vehicle, and he felt most precarious and vulnerable.

It all added to his uneasiness. He was as nervous about the afternoon's meeting with Alice as if he were going out with her for the first time. He wondered how she would behave, what she would expect. He tried to decide what he should do. He wondered whether she had told her parents yet. Presumably they would be expected to 'name the day' soon.

He tried to think about something else. But the wind rocked

the bus and seemed intent on destroying his concentration and and making him edgy.

He tried to devote his attention to the problem of Minchip and Lundy, and the letting down of Fred's tyres, of which they were strongly suspected. But he couldn't concentrate on anything for long, and throughout the journey his thoughts were jolted about from one thing to another, and at no time did he feel any kind of certainty about anything.

But as soon as he had stepped off the bus, it needed all his concentration and strength to keep on a straight path in the struggle against the wind. By the time he reached his destination, he felt almost exhilarated and much less troubled in his mind.

"What a day!" he said to Alice, when she opened the door.

"Oh, your hair!" she said.

"Is it a mess?"

He looked in a mirror in the hallway, and saw that it was.

"It's blowing a gale out there. Have you been outside?"

Alice shook her head. She took his coat and scarf and hung them up.

"Mum and Dad in?" said Malcolm.

Alice shook her head again. "No," she said. "They've gone to a funeral."

"Oh, I didn't know."

"A cousin of Dad's. I'd never met him."

She went into the living room, and Malcolm followed her. Although he was relieved that her parents were not there, his unease was returning. Neither of them knew what to say.

"Sit down," said Alice. "I'll make a cup of tea, shall I? Or would you prefer coffee?"

"No, tea would be very nice," said Malcolm.

She stood smiling at him for a moment, and then went out to the kitchen. Left alone, Malcolm sat looking round the room at the wedding photographs and little ornaments which covered most of the available surfaces. How different, he thought, from Joan Malling's living room. But then Joan was rich. A coal fire burnt rather raggedly in the grate, and every so often a cloud of smoke billowed out into the room. It depressed him, and he wished he was outside again. He decided he would suggest going for a walk when they had finished their tea. To escape from the smoke, and to try to ward off the depression, he went out to join Alice in the kitchen.

"Is the fire smoking?" she said.

"Yes," said Malcolm.

"It does that when it's windy. It'll be better when it's got going properly. Perhaps we'd better stay in here."

"I think we'd better. Then let's go for a walk."

She looked surprised. "In this wind?"

"Blow the cobwebs off."

"All right, then," she said, smiling brightly. "Whatever you say."

"It's quite pleasant really. I enjoyed my walk here from the bus-stop. It's exhilarating."

"We'll do whatever you want, darling," she said, leaning across the table and kissing him on the cheek.

Malcolm smiled, a little shakily, and sipped his tea. She was obviously very happy, and he could not help but feel flattered that her happiness was because of him, but what of his own feelings? He didn't know.

"Had a good week at school?" he said, at last.

"Mmm—not bad. How about you?"

"Yes O. K. We had a bit of excitement yesterday. One of the teachers had his tyres let down."

Alice burst out laughing, a reaction Malcolm had not expected.

"He didn't think it was funny," he said, rather put out.

"I bet he didn't," said Alice, still laughing. "I just wasn't expecting it, that's all. It sounded funny."

Malcolm thought about it. He hadn't realised there was a funny side to it. No one had laughed at school. He recalled the expression on Fred Lynch's face when he burst into the Head's study. He began to laugh too.

"You should have seen his face when he told us," he said. He imitated him. "'Somebody's let my tyres down!'"

This made Alice laugh even more, and they infected each other with their laughter. Malcolm repeated his imitation. Their laughter became uncontrollable, and it was a long time until it subsided. Malcolm felt better now.

"Finish your tea and let's go out," said Alice.

Both wrapped up in coats and scarves, they went out a few minutes later to do battle with the wind. It was impossible to do much talking.

"Did they find out who did it?"

"What's that?"

"Did they find out who did it?" shouted Alice.

"No. We've got a pretty good idea though."

"What?"

"I said, we've got a pretty good idea."

"Oh."

It suited them both to be out in the wind, shouting and struggling along. They held hands and the wind whipped up their circulation and gave them rosy cheeks and made them feel alive. Malcolm began to feel as though everything was all right. They walked into town and joined the throng of Saturday afternoon shoppers. All the men seemed to have one hand on their heads, holding their hats on, and all the women seemed to be in need of at least four hands, what with handbags and shopping bags to carry and hats to keep on and skirts to hold down. It was impossible. They passed many flustered and embarrassed faces as they threaded their way along the pavement.

Alice window-shopped, and Malcolm was frequently jerked to a stop and asked for his opinion of some article in a shop window, or, more often, given Alice's opinion and asked whether he agreed. He didn't mind. He was happy to be relieved for a while of more serious thoughts. He allowed his mind to be entirely occupied by the things going on around him. Everything else was in abeyance, shelved for the time being.

So the afternoon passed, and, for once, he forgot all about The Meadows.

Philip and David were trying to sweep up the leaves in the quad, a well-nigh impossible task which had been given them to do by Mr Lynch. It was a particularly malevolent imposition, even by his standards, but then he was feeling particularly malevolent, for a whole host of reasons. First, there was the letting down of his tyres; then there was being on duty for two consecutive days (he was standing in today for Mr Birkett, having been asked for once to pay off a small—very small—portion of his debt); then there was the weather, which for some reason irritated him; and then there was his general annoyance with Lundy; and beyond all that, the feeling that the term so far had been a wash-out and that probably the whole year would be the same. He felt as if he were somehow ill-starred, as if to get through the year unscathed would be a lucky escape. He spent the day wishing he could go for a drink in the evening and decided that as soon as young Drew got back he would ask him to take over after tea.

When the two boys reported to him after lunch, as the rules of their gating demanded, his evil spirit breathed inspiration into him and he sent them to fetch brooms. He almost smiled. It made the afternoon almost tolerable. Every so often, he would come out into the quad, and watch them fighting their losing battle against the swirling leaves. He found it a satisfying sight. In between times, he sat with his feet up in the staffroom and thought about it and thought about going for a drink in the evening, and felt better. He made the boys continue until half-past-four, when it was falling dusk and boys who had been out were returning to report to him.

"Maybe you'll think twice about breaking bounds now," he said, "or doing anything else you shouldn't. Take your brooms back, and report to me in the dining hall before tea."

Everyone would know that he knew they were the culprits, he would make sure of that.

Philip and David, of course, were thoroughly miserable throughout the afternoon. They grumbled and cursed and called Mr Lynch all the foul things they could think of. But as the afternoon wore on and they grew more weary, they stopped talking and their venom wore away. Instead, they brooded, and resentment began to grow between them.

Although David had cursed Mr Lynch with Philip, he did not really feel justified in doing so. He could not really blame Mr Lynch, because he knew they had done wrong and Mr Lynch had every right to punish them. So he began to blame Philip instead, and once the feeling had germinated it was quick to grow. Accusations against Philip came rushing in from all directions. He had got him into trouble; he had turned people against him, like Wilson; he had split the two societies; he had been rotten to Finch. His anger made him feel better: it seemed to purge his feeling of guilt. He was filled with a sense of righteousness. Thoughts of confessing to Mr Lynch entered his mind. But he was not sure about that. It would be like sneaking, in a way. No, he would not confess. He would just bear the suspicion of Mr Lynch and the others. But he would break with Minchip. He had had enough of him.

"It's victimisation," said Philip, throwing his broom back into the cupboard.

"Of course it's not," said David. "He knows it was us, so he's got every right."

"What?" Philip looked at him incredulously. David began to walk away. Philip laughed, scornfully. "Why don't you go say you're sorry?"

David stopped and wheeled round. "That's what we ought to do."

"Go on then. I don't mind."

"I'm not going to sneak, don't worry."

"It doesn't worry me. I don't care what you do."

"Well, I'm not going to. But I'm not going to join in any more of your stupid jokes. Trying to be big, that's all it is. You just spoil things."

"I can manage on my own," said Philip. "I don't need you. See you." He walked past David—who stood back warily as he passed—and went outside. He walked across the quad, keeping his head down against the wind, and down across the meadows to the river. The wind blew cruelly over the fields and hurried the dark waters along. Philip, torn between anger and tears, stood beside a tree which leaned at a dangerous angle out over the river, and stared down at the broken, racing stream. He turned and pushed against the tree, as if he were trying to push it into the river.

But after a while he stopped that, and searched around for a stone. He found a big one, which he could hardly lift, but he struggled to raise it up in the air over his head and then thrust it out into the river. It fell and was swallowed up. The splash was hardly noticeable on the disturbed waters in the dark, and, with the wind and the water making so much noise, it sounded scarcely at all.

So he turned and plodded back up to the school, with the wind trying to wrap itself round him and trip him up. He shrugged it off, ignoring it, as Carter might have shrugged off an ineffective tackle. He just kept on walking.

Malcolm sat on the low stool, leaning against a leg of the dining table. The leg was hard and pressed uncomfortably against his spine, but it was the best he could manage and the discomfort didn't really trouble him. It seemed, somehow, distant from him. He sat with his head tilted back, resting against the edge of the table-top, and held in his hand a glass of wine, which he raised at frequent intervals to his lips—or rather, first to his cheek or his nose, and then to his lips. He didn't really know what was going on. He knew that Alice had gone away somewhere in tears, and he thought that Joan or Freda or someone was with her, but he wasn't sure. He couldn't remember exactly what he had said to make her cry, but he thought it was something to the effect that he wasn't really one hundred per cent sure that he still wanted to marry her, and perhaps they should wait a little while before telling her parents. She hadn't told them yet. That was a relief. So he had tried to explain his feelings to her honestly, but it hadn't worked. Now she was away crying somewhere. Oh well. He took another sip of wine. He felt a sudden urge to giggle. He didn't know why. He tried to keep a straight face and took another sip of wine. He had a feeling that some of it had not quite got into his mouth. He looked down and saw that there was a streak of red wine down his shirt. Not much though. That was all right. A simple mistake. Nothing to worry about. Could happen to anyone. He giggled. Something—he wasn't exactly sure what—was very funny. He giggled again, and this time he couldn't stop. Someone took the glass out of his hand. People were looking at him. They were laughing too. He laughed up at them. Then Freda came and sat down on the floor next to him.

"Having a good time, Malcolm?" she said.

He nodded, vehemently. "It's rea . . . real . . ." He stopped, surprised by the difficulty he was having in pronouncing the word 'really'. He actually sounded drunk. He hadn't thought that one's speech would be slurred, just like a stage drunk. "It's—real—ly—funny," he said at last.

Freda laughed. "What is?" she said.

"I've forgotten," he said, and snorted.

"Alice isn't so bad now. She's stopped crying."

"Who's Alice?" he said, and snorted again.

"You've had far too much to drink, you know."

"No I haven't. Someone has taken my glass away."

He was pronouncing his words very deliberately and with an exaggerated correctness, in an effort to overcome the tendency to slur them.

"I must get myself another drink."

"Don't you think you ought to stop while you're winning? We don't want you being sick all over Joan's carpet, do we?"

But Malcolm was trying to stand up. He was determined now to show that he was not drunk, and it really did seem to him as though he was walking quite normally—well, almost. The wall collided with him in the hall, but he reached the kitchen eventually. He looked at the bread and cheese on the kitchen table, but decided against it. Concentrating hard, he poured out a glass of wine, white this time, to match his shirt. He drank some. It tasted peculiar. He caught a glimpse of what looked like Alice, outside the kitchen door, but he couldn't be certain. She didn't seem to be there any more, anyway. The voices of the other people in the kitchen sounded at one and the same time deafening and a long way off. He took another sip of wine, and it tasted better this time. Suddenly, he felt almost normal. He remembered something he had heard about empty stomachs and decided he would eat some bread and cheese. He cut a small piece of each, and ate them. He began to realise that he ought to be doing something about Alice. He hadn't meant to hurt her. He was only being honest. He had thought that would be best. He went off in search of Freda.

But Freda was with Alice again, in Joan's bedroom. Alice was feeling better and had begun now to worry only about her red eyes and the state of her make-up. Freda kept up the good work of cheering her up.

"I'm afraid poor old Malcolm's in a bit of a pickle," she said, laughing.

"Is he?" said Alice, looking up, half worried but, since Freda obviously found it funny, half amused too.

"Oh, dear me, yes! Absolutely pickled, in fact."

"Oh, dear!"

"Mind you, it's not surprising, the amount he's knocked back tonight."

"I don't think he's used to it."

"I hope he never does get used to it. He's drinking like a maniac!"

Alice laughed. "Oh dear," she said. "I'd better go and find him."

"Oh, he's all right," said Freda. "Leave him alone for a while. I'll keep an eye on him. You carry on sorting your face out in here."

"Oh, thank you, Freda. I don't know what I'd have . . ."

"Never mind about that," Freda interrupted. "Get your face stuck into that mirror, and I'll go check up on your alcoholic friend out there."

"Make sure he's all right, Freda."

"Don't you worry. He'll pay for it in the morning."

Freda went out in search of Malcolm. She found him sitting on the stool again in the living room, but he was not giggling any more. He had turned very pale.

"Alice is all right now," she said, sitting down beside him, as before. "She'll probably come out soon."

Malcolm said nothing.

"Are you all right?"

He nodded, but his face looked like a death-mask.

"For goodness sake, don't be sick on the carpet."

Malcolm stood up.

"Mind your wine!"

Leaving his wine glass in Freda's hand, he went quickly out of the room, keeping his mouth tightly closed.

"Oh Lord!" said Freda, watching him go.

"Had a drop too many, has he?" said a young man who was standing nearby.

"I think he's going to be sick. Go see if he's all right, will you? I hope no one's in the bathroom."

Malcolm leant over the lavatory bowl, vomiting. He seemed surrounded by cold and silence. Every so often, he winced and shuddered with the bitter taste in his mouth and the effort of vomiting. The sick was still in his mouth and nose. He stayed leaning over the lavatory, waiting for more and recovering his strength. The taste was awful and he felt completely drained and he was cold with sweat, but the drunkenness was gone and he felt immeasurably better. He was amazed at the speed with which his drunkenness had disappeared: one moment his head had been reeling and the next he was sober. Weak and shaken, but sober.

Someone tapped on the door and a voice said, "Are you all right?"

"Yes," he called back. His voice sounded very weak. Now the ignominy, the embarrassment. He didn't want to see anyone. He wanted to be left alone now, to go away somewhere. He wished he could stay in here on his own. But he would have to go out.

"He says he's all right," he heard a voice say.

Thank goodness they weren't coming in. Then he noticed the door was locked. He didn't remember locking it. He was safe anyway, until he had prepared a face for going out.

He rinsed his mouth out, and washed his hands and face with cold water. Now that the initial feeling of relief had faded, he realised that he still felt far from well. Sober he might be, but his inside was still in a mess and, looking in the mirror, he saw that his face looked absolutely washed out.

He looked around to make sure that he had left everything clean, and then unlocked the door. Whoever it was that had been asking if he was all right had gone. He went quickly upstairs to fetch his coat and scarf, found them under a pile of other coats on one of the beds and went downstairs again. But in the hallway Freda saw him.

"Malcolm," she said, in a voice which sounded to him strangely accusing, perhaps because he felt guilty.

"My bus goes at ten o'clock," he said.

"Have you seen Alice?"

He shook his head.

"Don't you want to?"

"Not really."

Freda nodded, as though she understood, but sighed too. It helped to disperse some of Malcolm's guilt. "Oh well," she said.

"I don't know," he said. "Perhaps I should."

Freda shrugged her shoulders.

Then Alice came out of the bedroom.

"Are you all right, Malcolm?" she said. "Are you going?" she added, noticing his coat and scarf.

"I'm O. K. now," he said. "My bus goes at ten o'clock."

"I'll go get my coat," she said, and ran upstairs.

Malcolm stood in the hall with Freda, feeling rather awkward, holding his coat and scarf. Freda looked at him.

"Foiled again," she murmured.

Malcolm laughed, and felt ashamed.

"You look a bit better than you did, anyway. I thought you were going to die, or worse, throw up on the carpet."

"I'm afraid I'm not really used to it."

"Practice makes perfect. Are you sure you're all right now, though? I daresay you could stay the night if you wanted. Joan wouldn't mind."

"Oh no," said Malcolm. "I'd better get back. I'm on duty tomorrow anyway."

"Oh yes. I'd forgotten it was a boarding school. How awful, having to work on a Sunday. Don't you mind?"

"No, not at all," said Malcolm. "I like it."

"Really?" Freda shook her head, in wonder. "I suppose I ought to admire your dedication," she said. "Can't say I do though."

Alice reappeared wearing her coat. "We'd better hurry," she said. "We ought to say thank you to Joan, though."

"Don't worry about that," said Freda. "I'll say your goodbyes for you. Take care, Malcolm. Toodle-oo!"

Malcolm and Alice walked down the street in silence. The wind had not abated. In fact, in anything, it had grown strenger. Malcolm longed to be safe back home in his room at The Meadows. That was all he thought about. Sixty boys sleeping in the dormitories, safe and peaceful, the wind outside, locked out, and him too in his own room, safe. He felt as if he would like never to have to go out again, never to go beyond the bounds of the school, ever again.

"I'm sorry I was so silly," said Alice, after they had walked some way in silence.

"It was my fault," said Malcolm.

"Oh no! You were only being honest. It was all my fault. I've spoiled everything."

"No. No you haven't."

But their struggle with the wind made it impossible to say much. They walked on again in silence. Malcolm, for the second time that day, was grateful for the wind. It helped to complete his sobering up, too. They came to the bus stop.

"I'd take you home," said Malcolm, "but I'd miss my bus."

"That's all right."

"You don't need to wait with me."

"No, I'll wait. I don't mind."

"It shouldn't be long."

They fell silent again. Both wanted to find something to say, but couldn't. There was no easy starting-point.

"When will your mum and dad be back?" asked Malcolm, to break the silence.

"Not till tomorrow. Tomorrow afternoon."

"Oh. I didn't know."

"They're staying overnight at Dad's brother's."

"Oh, I see."

Silence again, while they looked down the road for the bus.

"Malcolm—you could stay the night if you wanted."

"Oh, no, I've got to get back. I'm on duty tomorrow. Thanks anyway."

"Oh."

The wind howled around the buildings. A tall tree in a garden nearby was being bent nearly horizontal by the wind. Leaves and litter flew lurching down the road.

The bus was a long time coming. Malcolm looked at his watch and grew uneasy.

"Something might have happened to it, in this wind," said Alice.

"I hope not," said Malcolm.

But still the bus did not come.

"Perhaps we'd better go to the bus station and ask," Alice suggested, and eventually Malcolm agreed.

It turned out that a tree had been blown down, blocking the road, earlier in the evening, bringing some telegraph wires with it and causing chaos in the vicinity. The last bus had been cancelled. So he went home with Alice.

She made cocoa when they got back, and busied herself with the fire and chattered away quite brightly and cheerfully. The strained, uneasy atmosphere began to evaporate, and they forgot about what had happened earlier. At least, no mention was made of it. They sat on the sofa in front of the fire, drinking their cocoa. Alice talked and Malcolm listened. Half of him was still in his room at The Meadows, but half of him was here, enjoying the comfort and the warmth.

"Freda's nice, isn't she?" said Alice.

"Yes, she is," said Malcolm. "She doesn't mind a bit what she says, does she?"

"Oh, not a bit! She always speaks her mind. But she's very kind. She was very nice to me this evening."

"To me, too."

"Was she?"

He nodded. "I'm afraid I made a bit of a fool of myself."

She smiled ruefully. "So did I."

"Good old Freda! Looking after both of us. Quite a handful for her. I was sick, you know."

"Were you?"

"I'm afraid so."

"Poor Malcolm! And it was all my fault. I am sorry."

She took his hand and held it.

"Oh, it wasn't your fault. It was me."

"I do love you, Malcolm."

"I love you, too."

He put his arm around her, and they kissed. For the time being, he was glad to forget his doubts and let himself believe what he said. He held her body and stroked her hair and fondled her. She was very soft and compliant.

"I love you," he said again.

"I'm so glad you've come home with me," she said. "It would have been awful otherwise. I thought I would probably never have seen you again if you'd gone."

The likelihood of this struck Malcolm quite hard, so that he tried not to think of it.

"But you're here," she said, "and everything's all right."

Malcolm made himself stop thinking of what might have happened if the last bus had been running, blocked out all thoughts of his room at The Meadows and the sixty boys sleeping under the same roof. The blood ran faster in his veins. He began fondling her again and started to unbutton her blouse, but he was all fingers and thumbs. She helped him, and after a while they went up to Alice's bedroom and made love, after a fashion.

Half-term was nearly upon them. Always welcome, it was looked forward to this year with more eagerness than usual, but in the event it brought none of the expected relief.

The gales that had forced Malcolm into staying the night at Alice's home marked the end of the spell of good weather. The maturing sun sank rapidly into old age and darkness. The earth swallowed up the old leaves in mud. There was rain, there was fog. The days were cold and the nights colder. The last fourteen days of the first half of the term dragged like the last minutes before half-time in a rugby match in which no one has scored and neither team is making any progress and the players themselves have become indistinguishable one from the other in the mud in which they flounder. Or like the last minutes of a rugby practice, continued into the darkness, despite the boys' protests, by an angry and despotic coach, as happened on the last Tuesday before half-term, when Fred Lynch was determined to make them suffer and when, under cover of the growing darkness, Carter kicked the ball hard into David's stomach, winding him badly. So passed the last few days.

Loyalty was short-lived, friendship unstable. The only semblance of solidarity was that of the boys in opposition to Mr Lynch, who had decided that the whole bunch were a bad lot. When he made Philip and David serve all the other tables at tea on that windy Saturday, all the boys were ready afterwards to rally round the two victims. But Philip and David were enemies now.

Philip might have had his supporters if he had wished, but he didn't seem to want them. So for a time he was more or less ostracised, while David paraded his regained popularity. But things had changed. The magic circle, having once been broken, would not hang together again. David's supporters soon drifted away. For one thing, he did nothing but talk about Philip, calling him names, accusing him of one thing and another. Nothing but Minchip. His friends quickly tired of this, and he too began to find himself often alone. He didn't like it, and he didn't know what to do.

He wrote a rather mournful letter to his parents on the Sunday before half-term, saying he was fed up and was looking forward to going home. No one seemed interested in anything any more. The Amateur Dramatic Society was abandoned. He called a meeting on the last day of the half-term, but no one came. He felt like crying, sitting in the old stables all alone, but managed not to. He blamed it all on Philip, and his anger kept the tears at bay.

Only Mr Jones seemed untouched by the depression which weighed upon everyone else. His smile grew more and more far-away. He drifted through the fog as if it were sunshine.

"I'm surprised, Mr Jones," said the Chairman of the Governors, "that you should have allowed things to reach this stage before you informed us. Had we known earlier, we might have been able to do something."

"Had we known earlier... had we known earlier..." said Mr Jones, smiling.

"But you must have known."

Mr Jones did not deny it. "Yes, oh yes. For some time."

"Then in that case, Mr Jones, I fear that the blame must, in a large part, attach to you."

"Certainly, certainly. But there was nothing to be done. Nothing to be done."

The Chairman of the Governors opened his mouth to say something, but changed his mind and merely shook his head and sighed. It had been like this since he had arrived. The Headmaster was impermeable. There was obviously nothing to be gained from talking to him. Gradually, the truth was dawning on him that Mr Jones was not entirely sane. He seemed to have no conception of the seriousness of the situation. It was very sad. But he was relieved on one point. His initial fear had been that there might be a criminal aspect to the situation, which would have been much worse.

"You have informed the staff, presumably?"

"No, not yet. I was going to..."

The Chairman of the Governors sighed again. "I see," he said. "Well, Mr Jones, we must do what we can. I think I'd better talk to the staff myself."

He was wondering whether Mr Jones should be relieved of his duties as from that day, but that, he realised, was not an easy decision. He would need to consult the Deputy Headmaster, and perhaps a doctor and Mrs Jones too. What was the best way of doing things, he wondered, so as to cause least hurt to those involved? Yet there could be no doubt, in his view, that Mr Jones had, shall we say, lost touch with reality. He was pleased though that no one was to blame. He felt now only sorrow that Mr Jones should have finished like this. Everything possible would have to be done now to make things easy for him. His mind ran on to nursing homes that he knew of and the steps that would have to be taken. The way, though very delicate and needing a lot of tact, seemed clearer now.

"Would you permit me to arrange things then, as I think best, Mr Jones? If you will allow me to take things out of your hands, at any rate for today. And may I also suggest that you put these things out of your mind? They must have been preying on your mind for a long time, and you look tired. How about handing over the running of the school to Mr Birkett for a few days, so you can rest?"

Mr Jones nodded and smiled, and seemed further away than ever.

"Just leave things to me then."

The news came as a shock but no surprise to Mr Birkett. He had been expecting something like this to happen for a long time, he said. He readily confirmed the Chairman's suspicions concerning Mr Jones's sanity and agreed that it would be better if the Headmaster left things to him from now on.

"Bankrupt?" said Fred Lynch.

"I'm afraid so."

"And we'll have to close at Christmas?" said Geoffrey Hopper.

"There's nothing we can do now to prevent it."

"But what will happen to us?" said Malcolm.

The second half of the term was nearly two weeks old. Mist

overhung the river and wreathed the school buildings in pallor. From the river bank, if they could be seen at all, they looked faint and insubstantial. The days were sunless but white. Philip and John found themselves standing next to each other on the river bank.

"Hello," they said.

John had felt no animosity. When things went wrong, he was inclined to blame himself. After Philip had turned on him and made friends with Lundy, he had simply gone back to his old self, withdrawn and alone, and uncomplaining. His face, in the cold and misty air, looked as always expressionless and dead.

"Let's be friends again," said Philip.

There was a slight pause, and then John said, "All right."

Then they fell silent again. Renewal of their friendship brought about no sudden increase in communication or apparent feeling, and in manner or bearing neither boy showed any sign of change.

"Still bird-watching?" said Philip.

John nodded.

"I don't suppose you see much in the winter?"

John shook his head. "Not much."

Some of the boys, David in particular, were surprised when they walked into the classroom together. But their desks were well separated and they made no attempt to move them. At four o'clock, John took out a book from his desk and sat reading. Philip sat and doodled on a piece of scrap paper. After half-an-hour, he stood up and walked over to John.

John looked up and nodded to his old friend. "Hello."

"Hello," Philip nodded too, and sat on the desk in front looking down at John. "I wish I was like you," he said.

"How do you mean?"

"You never seem to get worked up. I wish I was like that. Do you ever lose your temper?"

John thought about it and then shook his head. "Not very often," he said.

"How do you do it?"

"It's just me, I suppose. The way I am."

Philip nodded. "You're lucky," he said.

John looked down at his book again and seemed to go on reading. Philip slid off the desk and walked to the front of the classroom. The word 'morass', relic of an English lesson, was written on the old-fashioned easel blackboard. Philip rubbed it off, reducing it first to 'ass' and then obliterating it altogether. He turned then and walked back to John, who had looked up and was watching him.

"What do you think of me?" said Philip, sitting on the desk again.

"What do I think of you?"

Philip nodded.

"I don't know."

"You must know. I don't mind what you say. You won't offend me or anything."

"Well—I don't know... You—you like people to take notice of you."

Philip nodded. "That's true," he said. "I do. Is that wrong?"

John shook his head. "No. I don't suppose so."

"But you don't. You don't want people to take notice of you, do you?"

"I'm not bothered."

"I'd rather be like you. You don't bother about anything, and everyone leaves you alone."

"Oh well," said John. "Everyone's different, I suppose."

Again, Philip slid off the desk and this time began wandering about the classroom, in amongst the desks, up and down the rows. John rested his head on his hands and went on reading, or seeming to read.

There were two other boys in the classroom, who were playing chess but who naturally listened to whatever Philip or John said. One was called Smailes, and the other was Wilson, the boy who had precipitated the 'de-amalgamation' of the Stamp Club and the Amateur Dramatic Society. Relations between Wilson and Lundy were cool, when they existed at all, but since Philip had been ostracised by his former friends, Wilson had felt inclined to look on him more kindly, although until now he had not shown it.

Wilson moved a pawn and then sat back to watch Philip wander about the classroom.

"Why do you like people to take notice of you?" he said.

Philip stopped and turned round. John looked up from his book.

"Why?" said Philip.

"Yes."

"I don't know. But I do."

"Yes. Finch is right," said Wilson.

Philip sat down on another desk, between Finch and Wilson. "Who would you rather be?" he said. "Finch or me?"

Wilson thought about it. It was an interesting question. Smailes, oblivious to what was going on round him, groaned slightly and shifted his position, trying to fathom out his best move: none of them seemed to hold out much chance of success.

"You, I think."

"Why?" said Philip.

"Well, I should think you'll have a more exciting life, though Finch's will probably be more peaceful."

"If you were him," said Finch, "you'd want to be me."

They all laughed, surprised at Finch's perception.

"Finch might be a famous ornithologist, like Peter Scott," said Philip, "and go on the television."

"He might," said Wilson.

"I doubt it," said Finch.

"What do you think I'll be?" said Philip.

"A writer," John suggested.

"Maybe," said Wilson. "Or an actor."

"I'd quite like to be Prime Minister," said Philip, and then added, "but I'd rather be the king."

"You'd be assassinated," said Wilson. "I think you should be an actor. Or a spy, perhaps."

Philip liked both ideas.

"There!" said Smailes, sitting back.

Wilson turned back to the chess board. "What have you moved? Oh yes, I see." He moved his queen. "Check. Mate, I think."

Smailes's face fell, as he realised his stupid mistake.

"Do you play?" Wilson asked Philip.

Philip shook his head.

"I'll teach you, if you like."

Philip agreed and the pieces were set out again for a new game. John put his book away and came over to watch.

"I'll tell you what we'll do," said Wilson. "Smailesy, you can play against Phil and me, and I'll explain it as we go along. All right?"

So, as the other boys began to drift into the formroom before tea, they joined Finch as spectators to the chess match. It was surprising: Finch, Wilson, Smailes and Minchip, all seemingly good friends. David kept himself ostentatiously apart. But Tomlinson and the others, after a while, went across to watch.

The bell began to ring for tea, and they had to wait until seven o'clock, after prep, before they could continue. The spectators remained to watch. It was a close game, with mistakes made on both sides, Philip's inexperience being balanced by Smailes's over-confidence, and it was made the more entertaining by the running commentary given by Philip's coach, Wilson, and by Philip's own remarks. It was Philip's re-emergence into public life though, and his unexpected association with Wilson, that really drew the crowds. It was as though Philip were a magnet, repelling and attracting by turns.

Smailes only just managed to beat him, with less than a dozen pieces left on the board. It was exciting chess! With relief at having won, Smailes packed the pieces away in their box, but Philip had had a victory too.

"You played well," said Wilson.

"Thanks," said Philip. "I'll have a game with you sometime."

"Sure," said Wilson.

"It's a good game."

But the bell was ringing for supper and the crowd of spectators broke up. Crossing the quad, Philip joined up with John Finch again.

"Can you play chess?" he said.

"Yes," said John. "Not very well, though."

"Well, that's O.K. We'll have a game some time."

"All right," said John, pleased, so that a shade of expression flickered for a moment on his face. He had expected to be dropped in favour of Wilson, as he had been dropped before in favour of Lundy. But Wilson was in front of them with two or three of his own friends, and so Philip stayed with John. They met up again after supper. John was standing in the quad, with his head tilted back, listening to the hooting of an owl. It was a cold, dark night, with no sign of moon or stars. Philip, coming out into the open air from the dining hall, breathed in the familiar smell of mist, which was like a cold, heavy hand in the air, and like iron in the lungs. He made out the shape of John in the middle of the quad, under the tree, and walked across to him.

John looked down, when he heard him approach.

"What are you doing?" Philip asked.

"Listening to the owl."

"Oh."

Philip stood silent, and after a few seconds they heard the long wavering note of the nocturnal creature, unseen, somewhere above their heads.

"I wonder if it's watching us," said Philip.

"Perhaps it goes boy-watching, like I go bird-watching."

Philip laughed. "So long as it doesn't think we're mice or something."

The owl called again, and they listened.

Suddenly, a black shape seemed to float out from behind the tree, and both boys involuntarily gripped each other, but it was only Mr Jones. He drifted noiselessly across the quad, his gown trailing out behind him, and entered the building. The boys had let go of each other and laughed in reaction to their momentary fear.

"He looks like a vampire," said Philip.

"Yes, the way his gown trails, like wings."

"Maybe he is a vampire. Perhaps that's why they're having to close the school. I said he was going mad, didn't I?"

"Come on," said John. "Let's go inside. I bet it snows soon."

"I hope so," said Philip, and followed him inside.

"We've just seen a vampire," he said to the other boys in the dormitory, as he was getting ready for bed.

"What?!"

"It turned out to be Davy," he went on. He propounded his theory of the reason for the closing down of the school, and found it appealed to their imagination if not their good sense. Other theories were put forward. Naturally, the closing of the school was staple conversation at the moment. They had mixed feelings about it, from sorrow and regret to excitement, but the latter predominated. Each day would bring a letter for someone from his parents, telling him what arrangements they had been able to make for next term. Prep schools around the country were profiting by The Meadows' misfortune. But already some of the boys had been told that they were to be entrusted to their local grammar school for the next two terms, if not for ever.

"What will you be doing in January, Chippy?" someone asked.

"I don't know," said Philip.

His aunt and uncle had written, he knew, to his mother, but as far as he knew there had been no reply yet. He had not discussed what might be happening to him after Christmas with his aunt and uncle. Indeed, he had spent as much time as possible during the holiday out of the house, away from them. They didn't ever have much to say to each other.

"Perhaps I'll go abroad with my mother."

"Might you?"

"Maybe."

"Hey, I wish I could go abroad."

"Would you have to go to a foreign school, Phil?"

Philip shrugged his shoulders.

"Why does your old lady live abroad, anyway?"

He shrugged his shoulders again. "She prefers it there, I suppose."

Philip's parentage and family background were a mystery which all of the boys were rather wary of approaching, lest it should prove to be embarrassing.

All the boys were in their beds now. In five minutes, the master on duty would come to switch the lights off. The boys lay in their beds, talking and reading comics. Two, dangerously, played cards, which was forbidden. Philip had picked up a bird-spotting book from the locker beside John's bed and was flicking through it.

"You'll be a chess champion soon."

It was Tomlinson who made the remark. He was sitting up in bed, with his hands clasped behind his head, staring at the ceiling. Philip turned to look at him, and Tomlinson inclined his head towards Philip. Philip tried to assess Tomlinson's attitude and wondered what lay behind the remark. It was weeks since either of them had spoken, and no serious conversation had taken place between them since their early morning walk to the cricket pavilion.

"I doubt it," said Philip.

"Perhaps not chess."

The lights went out.

"What do you mean?" whispered Philip, after a few seconds' silence.

"Nothing."

"Hey, Phil!" someone called, in a low voice.

"What?"

"How can you kill a vampire?"

"Sunlight kills them," Philip whispered. "Or the sight of a cross."

"Do you think we should rig up a cross in here, in case Davy comes in the middle of the night?"

"Shut up, will you?" said another voice.

"Shut up yourself!"

"Come over here and say that!"

"Get lost!"

A book was thrown.

"Hey!"

"Well, shut up! I'm trying to get to sleep."

"Don't blame me then if you wake up in the morning and find someone's been drinking your blood."

"Oh, don't be stupid."

"Just don't blame me, that's all."

"Oh, belt up, you two!"

Eventually, the dormitory was quiet again, until it began to be filled with the sounds of sleeping. But between the hours of one and two in the morning, footsteps sounded in the corridor outside, and stopped at the door, which then slowly opened to admit Mr Jones. He stood in the doorway, listening to the sounds of sleep, but did not advance into the room. After a little while, he stepped back and pulled the door closed again. His footsteps receded. A minute later, the door, which had not been properly closed, sprang open again and swung back, remaining wide open all night. A cold draught blew into the dormitory, and when the boys woke up they shivered. The open door, when it was noticed, gave rise to much speculation about ghosts and vampires.

"Check your necks for teeth marks everybody," someone said, and they pretended to see red spots on each other's necks.

"But seriously, it could be, couldn't it?" said someone else, when they had finished making their beds. "Not a vampire perhaps, but mad, you know, like Chippy said. He saw him walking about in the middle of the night. Didn't you, Chippy?"

Philip confirmed that he had.

"Well, he might be dangerous, mightn't he? We ought to tell someone."

"Don't be daft! Who could we tell? Who'd believe us?"

"But we might wake up one morning and find ourselves murdered!"

They all laughed, and made their way down to breakfast.

But still David kept himself apart. For the rest of the class, they quickly forgot the reasons for their earlier dislike, so that now, when Philip talked and made himself interesting to them and somehow caught their mood, they readily accepted him again. But David held off, and sulked. He felt he had been badly treated. He had begun the term with such high hopes, and for a little while eveything had gone his way, but then, one by one, things had begun to go wrong. His Society, his team, and latterly his friends. His good reputation with the teachers, too, had been destroyed. With that had gone his own confidence in himself. About the school itself coming to an end, he didn't know what to think. Under the circumstances, perhaps it was just as well, but he was sorry too. He had enjoyed his four years at The Meadows, except for this one.

So depressed had he been made by all these changes and misfortunes, that he lost all of his customary buoyancy and seemed like a different person, withdrawn and solemn, and often touchy. His parents had been rather worried about him during the half-term holiday, and wondered if he was sickening for something. He had become an altogether more emotional person. One night, lying in bed at home, he gave in to his misery and cried.

His conscience was often troubled about the business of Mr Lynch's tyres. Once or twice, during the holiday, he came close to confessing to his father, to get it off his chest. But he didn't want to fall in his parents' estimation as well as in everyone else's. So he kept it to himself, and it began to grow out of proportion and weigh heavily on his mind. He had difficulty in getting to sleep at night.

But in David's mind, of course, it was all confusion, one thing mixed up with another. He was too young, too unpractised in the arts of introspection, to be able to sort out causes. In the midst of all the confusion, holding all the threads, it seemed to him, stood Philip. Philip was at the beginning and end of everything. But whether he wanted vengeance or reconciliation was not clear. With every day that passed, and with the accumulation of more and more unspoken thoughts, his attitude to Philip grew more complex, more ambivalent, and more unfathomable.

He had some strange dreams in which Philip figured. A rugby ball kicked into his stomach, picked up to be kicked back and discovered then to be not a rugby ball but Philip's head. Philip, as a ghost dripping water, following him wherever he went. Philip rolling a huge tyre after him across the meadows and then pushing it into the river. They leapt onto it and floated away downstream. All his friends, and his father, stood on the bank waving their arms and shouting, "Out of bounds! Out of bounds!" Then the tyre began to sink. He woke in the middle of the night, sweating and afraid.

But he never spoke to Philip. He ignored him and kept away from him, tried even to avoid being in the same room as him, which meant that his isolation automatically increased as Philip's decreased. Carter saw his chance. The rugby ball in the stomach was only the beginning. Lundy, he said to his friends, was for it.

One afternoon, the fourth form were having a games lesson on the field with Mr Lynch. It was a miserable afternoon, cold and damp, with a sky sheeted over with grey clouds, all twisted and heavy, like damp sheets. There was no rain, but the wind carried moisture with it. Even at two o'clock, it seemed as if it would soon be dark. The field was muddy, and soon the boys were too.

Mr Lynch made them run twice round the pitch as soon as they were all assembled on the field. It was hard work, with boots loaded down with mud. Carter made his intentions known at once. Halfway round the first circuit, he barged into David and knocked him headlong into the mud.

David picked himself up as quickly as he could. "Watch it, Carter!" he shouted.

Carter carried on jogging round the pitch as if he had not heard.

A few minutes later, the class were gathered around Mr Lynch, awaiting his instructions.

"Right!" he said. "You can have a game. Captains—" he looked round the crowd of boys, allowing his eyes to rest for a second or two on three or four faces, one of them David's—"Carter and . . . Tomlinson. Come out and pick sides!"

The two captains stepped out of the crowd and turned to face them. David stood with downcast eyes, waiting to be picked. He felt very hurt at having been passed over. Mr Lynch never stopped punishing him.

"Lundy!"

He was Tomlinson's third choice. Everyone seemed to be against him. He walked out and stood with the rest of Tomlinson's team, never raising his eyes from the ground.

Eventually, when the teams were picked, they moved out to take up their positions on the field. David was walking on, still with his head down, when a lump of mud hit him on the leg. He stopped quickly and looked round, very angry. Carter was walking away down the field in the opposite direction. David stooped to pick up a handful of mud, but changed his mind, and went on walking to his position.

The match began, and David tried to lose himself by putting all his energy into playing. He ran hard and shouted for the ball and did all he could to exhaust himself—and to prove Mr Lynch wrong. But Carter would give him no peace. It soon became apparent to all the boys that Carter was out to 'get' Lundy. No one took sides, no one helped. They just watched what was happening and wondered how it would turn out.

After only two or three minutes' play, Carter's rough treatment of his former friend began. One moment David was running with the ball, and the next he was being swung round and dragged down onto the ground by a big hand holding onto his shirt. But he held onto the ball and curled himself round it. Carter's hand came down on his head and pressed, and a knee was thrust hard against his side. Other players arrived and the ball was kicked loose. David's hand was kicked too, though it may not have been Carter who did that. He picked himself up and ran back to where the play was, rubbing his hurt hand. He could still feel Carter's hand on his head and his knee in his side.

Time and again, David was dragged down, not always when he was holding the ball. Carter was intent only on 'getting' David, and David could not escape. He was no match for Carter. All he could try to do was run and avoid him, but the mud slowed him down and made it impossible to dodge or sidestep. The first time he tried to swerve to avoid Carter's reaching hand, he skidded and fell, and Carter came crashing down on top of him, knocking all the breath out of his body.

"Scum!" snarled Carter, whenever he passed near enough to David for him to hear. "Scum!" He spat the word at him and sneered, and his eyes gleamed nastily.

Perhaps Mr Lynch didn't realise what was going on. It is possible he didn't, because he wasn't following the match very closely, and for part of the time refereed from the touch-line.

At half-time, David stood alone, while the others stood in twos and threes, getting their breath back and talking. He felt like an outcast. He was bruised all over, tired, rather scared, and close to tears. Yet, oddly enough, he felt no anger against Carter. It was just the same as when Mr Lynch had made them sweep up the leaves in the quad. He felt somehow as though the punishment was deserved. Carter was in the right. It was Philip who was to blame.

He didn't think it out. He couldn't have explained it. But inside him, emotion was welling up and when suddenly it broke, it broke over Philip.

The whistle blew and the match re-started. David played sluggishly and ineffectively. His will to resist had gone, and Carter saw that he had won. From then on, he didn't bother to inflict any more physical injury—or not much, anyway—but continued to sneer and to gloat over his victory, laughing at David and calling him "Scum!"

The second half was ten minutes old when they noticed Mr Lynch walking away, up the slope towards school. They went on playing, however, knowing that he would soon be back and would expect them to continue.

Philip did not enjoy rugby or any other sport, and he never exerted himself unduly in games lessons. But he was not inept. At times, in fact, he played very well. It did not interest him though. Tomlinson had picked him for his team and made him hooker, a position which suited Philip as well as any other. Like the other boys, Philip had become aware very quickly of what Carter was doing, and, also like them, he did not appear to take sides but merely to observe. However, in his case, appearances were deceptive. It amused him. He had derived considerable pleasure from watching David's fall from grace. David, he felt, was a self-righteous prig who deserved all that was happening to him.

"Foul! Forward pass!"

The shout came from one of Carter's team and was directed at David.

"It wasn't!" shouted David. "Play on!"

But play had stopped.

Others on Carter's team supported the accusation. No one on David's side seemed very sure. They shrugged their shoulders. Tomlinson hadn't been looking. The boys on the edges of the field began to drift in to see what was going on. Carter stepped up to David.

"Scum!" he said.

"Don't call me that!"

"Who's going to stop me?"

He stared belligerently into David's face.

"You can call me what you like, anyway," said David. "I don't care."

Carter laughed and walked away to pick up the ball. "Free kick!" he said.

"It wasn't a forward pass," said David, turning in appeal to Tomlinson and the rest of the team, but no one was prepared to offer him their support.

"Prove it," said Carter, returning with the ball.

"What do you mean, prove it?" said David.

"What I say," said Carter. "But you can't, scum! So get out of the way scum! It's a free kick to us, scum!"

David's heart-beat suddenly accelerated, making him feel giddy.

"Might as well let them have it," said Tomlinson. "Come on." The rest of his team turned and walked away.

Philip heard or felt or sensed something coming towards him from behind, and found himself suddenly sprawled in the mud, with someone on top of him. He jerked himself round and threw his assailant to one side. Turning quickly as he jumped up, he saw David scrambling in the mud and preparing to hurl himself at him again, his face contorted with tearful rage. Then fists were lashing out at his face. He dodged and ducked and warded off the aimless blows. They came together again and fell to the ground and there grappled, rolling about and trying to get on top of each other. David's hands tore at his face and hair and shirt, and Philip had to work hard to avoid injury. He managed to push David off again and struggle to his feet. It was only a moment's respite. David was up again and rushing at him blindly.

"I'll get you!" he said, as he came at him, in a high, tearful, childish voice.

But Philip's fist got him instead, and David fell to the ground. With a bruised eye, seeing crooked, he got to his feet once more. More warily this time, he moved towards Philip. The fight had now started in earnest. Both boys raised their fists. Within a few seconds, they were both on the ground again, punching at each other's stomachs.

The other boys had encircled them, most of them shouting for Philip. But suddenly the circle was broken by Mr Lynch. He said nothing, but simply strode up to the fighting boys and, grabbing hold of them, dragged them to their feet. They struggled at first, until they realised who it was, and even then David still tried to break free and get at Philip again.

Mr Lynch gripped him tighter by the arm and shook him. "Be still and shut up!" he shouted.

At last, David seemed to realise, and stood still.

"Can't I leave you for five minutes?" shouted Mr Lynch.

"It wasn't my fault, sir," said David.

"Shut up, boy! I don't care whose fault it was! I'm sick and tired of every one of you."

He shook them again and then pushed them away from him.

"Sick and tired! Well, I'm washing my hands of you. That's it now. I've finished. And you've finished. There'll be no more rugby. No more team. Finished! You've had it! Now get back up to school, get changed and go back to your classroom. And wait for me there. Go on! Quick!"

The boys turned and made their way despondently back to the school.

"I said quick!"

They broke into a trot. Mr Lynch stood on the field for a few moments, watching them go. He bent down and picked up the ball.

"Damn the bloody lot of them!" he said.

For both Mr Birkett and Mr Lynch, who had been at The Meadows for so many years, being told that the school was to close down at Christmas was rather like being told that they had only eight weeks to live. Consequently, their preparations for whatever was to come after were rather vague and half-hearted, arising more from a morbid introspectiveness than from any practical effort to sort out their future. For the future bore the cast not of reality, but of heaven or hell or, more particularly, purgatory.

Fred's evenings in the village pub began to be more than occasional, started sooner and ended later. His appearance during the day became more haggard. His manner during the school day, and his treatment not only of the boys but also of his colleagues, became rough and callous and overbearing. Suddenly, he loathed the school and everything to do with it. But once he was away from The Meadows, and especially when he was sitting at a table in the pub, he became cheerful and talkative. Always a familiar face, he now became well-known and popular with the regulars, and friendly greetings met him as soon as he went in through the door. But occasionally, if he had been talking too much and not drinking enough, the gloom he had left behind would catch him up again and he would feel suddenly depressed. But another drink would soon send him racing on ahead, leaving his misery standing. The way he drove also suggested that he was trying to leave something behind, and it was fortunate that the road between the village and The Meadows was a quiet one.

It soon became common knowledge in the village that The Meadows was closing down at Christmas, Fred being one of the main sources of the villagers' knowledge. He didn't mind talking about the school, so long as he was away from it, and he supplied them with all the information they could wish for. The villagers' curiosity about the school had never been greater nor so well satisfied. In particular, they were curious about Mr Jones. Naturally, there were rumours. So Fred was often asked what kind of man the Headmaster was, and whether there was any truth in the rumours.

"He's getting old, that's all," and that was all that he would say. In answer to more direct questions, he would simply shrug his shoulders and say that he didn't know. Because for all his detestation of the school, he bore no grudge against its Headmaster. He didn't look for causes or a scapegoat. He just loathed it and wanted to be rid of it, because it had gone bad and made him miserable, and he let Fate bear the burden of the blame. For the rest, he took it out on the boys or drank to make himself feel better. He had no idea what he would do after Christmas. They were to be paid their salaries until Easter, in lieu of notice, during which time, he presumed, he would be able to find another post, presumably at another prep school, but he didn't relish the idea.

For Mr Birkett, the long awaited and oft predicted cataclysm had finally arrived, or was at least in sight, but he, the prophet, seemed now to be unaware of it. He continued to fuss and fidget through the daily routine of the school with undiminished briskness and an attention to detail which seemed to the others, and to Fred in particular, quite out of place under the circumstances. But Ron was taking very seriously the injunction of the Chairman of the Governors to act as Headmaster for the time being.

"Old Ron obviously can't face up to it," said Mr Hopper one day in the staffroom. "He won't admit that it's all over."

Certainly, Ron spoke less than the others about the school's imminent closure, and would brush off questions about the future with remarks such as, "Time enough to think about that when the time comes," or "I can't waste time speculating about the future, I've a school to run."

"Perhaps he knows more than we do," suggested Malcolm.

"He seems to think we might still be here next term. Perhaps the Governors are trying to save the school. Perhaps we won't have to go after all."

"I doubt it," said Geoffrey. "If Ron had been told anything like that, it will just be them trying to soften the blow. After all, they've got to make it seem as though they're trying to do something."

"Let it bloody die and be finished," muttered Fred.

"We might as well face facts," Geoffrey went on. "The day of the small private school will soon be over. I can tell you one thing. I won't be looking for another job in a prep school and have the same thing happen again. It will be a State school for me next year."

But Malcolm was troubled by unhappy memories, and hoped for the best.

A few days later, when he came across Mr Birkett sitting alone in the staffroom, he took the opportunity of asking him whether he thought there was any chance of the school's staying open after Christmas.

Mr Birkett looked up with raised eyebrows. "After Christmas?" he said. "You never know, you never know. We must keep our fingers crossed, mustn't we? Mmm?"

"You mean, there is a chance then?"

"Mmm? Who knows? Who knows?"

With that, Mr Birkett stood up and walked out of the room, leaving Malcolm to cling fearfully onto the hope his words had given him.

It was a curious time of inactivity, like the moments of still water between tides. Everyone waited for the turn. The school seemed more remote than ever from the real world outside its gates, as if it had been taken out of time. Harbourmaster Ron bustled about in his office and seemed not to notice that the clock on the wall had stopped. Activity of a kind continued on the quayside. They found things to do, ways of filling their time. But the water never moved. The strange atmosphere held sway especially over Malcolm, who, with a lover's intentness, was always in tune with the moods of the school, his beloved. He became very observant and seemed to see with great clarity. Watched the sky, saw the shapes and colours of the clouds; noticed the detail of frost on his window; saw the way the leaves curled and the way the bare branches trailed out into the sky. The keenness of his perceptions gave him great delight, and it was hard to believe that it was all over. Impossible. He did not believe it. During these days, he felt the presence of the school more strongly than ever before, almost as an actual physical presence. Sometimes, watching the mist on the meadows, he could imagine that it embodied the presence of the school. Sometimes, sitting alone in his room at night, he could imagine himself wrapped in the mist, or held inside a hand. The idea became so real to him that it was like a physical sensation, making his skin tingle.

And Alice, once again, fell away to the periphery of his life. He did not often think of her, and when he did it was without feeling, absent-mindedly. He had to struggle to remind himself that it was more or less settled now that they would get married. He knew that sometime soon he would have to do something about that, but at the moment it seemed too far off. Unreal, like everything else outside The Meadows.

Then, one evening, he had a strange and unnerving experience. He was sitting in the staffroom alone, working his way slowly and sleepily through a pile of exercise books. It was very quiet, very still. His mind wandered frequently from the marking and he would read several sentences sometimes before realising that he hadn't taken any of it in and would have to go back and start again. Eventually, after finishing one book, he put it down and did not at once pick up another, but leaned back in his chair instead and gave himself up for a while to his undisciplined thoughts. He fell into a waking doze and his mind wandered, as it were, leaving him behind.

After a little while, the door opened. Malcolm looked up and saw Mr Jones come in. He looked very thin and rather weary. He smiled faintly in Malcolm's direction, closed the door and walked slowly across the room to the window. Malcolm pulled himself up a little in his chair and tried to think of something to say. Mr Jones pulled one curtain back slightly so that he could see out of the window.

"Misty," he said.

"Is it?" said Malcolm.

Mr Jones nodded. "Misty and pale," he said.

Malcolm could not help feeling a sense of strain and embarrassment. He glanced down at the pile of exercise books. What could he say? He looked up again, and the room was empty. A shiver ran down his spine. Surely there hadn't been time for Mr Jones to have gone out again. He would have heard him. He would have heard the door.

He lit a cigarette. He must have imagined the whole thing, he thought. But they had spoken. It was all rather disturbing, and he was glad when, a few minutes later, someone came into the staffroom. But he didn't tell anyone what had happened.

David sat at his desk by the window with his arm stretched out along the radiator and his head resting on his arm. A few inches away, on the other side of the window pane, snow was falling. His pen lay on the desk beside a sheet of note-paper.

"Dear Mum and Dad,

It is miserable here."

The room was quiet. No teacher was present, but none of the boys seemed to want to take advantage of the fact to talk or fool around, and whenever the silence was broken—by a whispered word, or a chair scraping—the sound was swallowed up at once and the silence flowed in again to fill the space.

Letter-writing had been in progress for twenty minutes. Mr Birkett had been in at the start to see them settled, and had then gone out again, as was his wont. There had been a burst of chatter, as soon as he was well out of the way, but it subsided more quickly than usual. The boys all seemed to have plenty to write about. All except David that is, who, having written his one sentence, felt he had said all there was to say.

There soon grew an atmosphere in the formroom, an air of quietness which no one wanted to dispel. It settled on them as the snow was settling in the quadrangle outside. When Mr Birkett came in again at half-past-seven, the boys all looked up and stared at him as if he were an intruder. But when he too was settled at his desk at the front and had lowered his head to the work he had brought in with him, the silence descended again.

David did not move. His eyes stared at nothing. His face was blank. But inside all was anguish. This evening, his misery was absolute. He had never in his life known such a feeling of desolation. All day, he had scarcely uttered a word; scarcely a soul had spoken to him. Since his outburst on the rugby pitch, one minute of uncontrolled emotion which had cost the form their games lessons for the rest of the term and brought about the premature end of the rugby team, he had been more or less discarded by his friends. He felt like a thing of the past. Carter had defeated him. Philip had taken over from him. Philip was the one they all followed now. During the days following the games lesson, he had been simply ignored. Nobody took any notice of him. He did not know whether it was deliberate or not, whether the form had agreed not to speak to him, or whether it just happened. But, in case it was a deliberate plan, he tried not to betray any signs of being hurt by it. He set great store by 'manliness' and was determined to be brave. But today the struggle had been harder than before. Perhaps because it was Sunday and there were no lessons to distract his mind. His loneliness drove into him. He fought hard all day to maintain an appearance of sang-froid. But as the day wore on, he felt his isolation more and more and his resistance slowly diminished.

Now, as he leaned miserably against the radiator, his head on his arm, he felt like giving up. Why bother being manly? He was too tired. Perhaps he would go on with his letter and pour out his heart to his mother and father. But he could not quite bring himself to do it. It was such a let-down. He sensed the tears coming from deep down.

Philip, sitting at the back of the formroom, was watching him, as he had been watching him, carefully, unobtrusively, since the ostracising of his former friend had begun. It had not been Philip's idea to send David to Coventry, but he had agreed when the suggestion was made by one of the others, and in the days that followed he had awaited with interest the results of their action. He wondered whether David might run away, and would have liked, somehow, to suggest it to him. But so far nothing had happened.

"You, boy! Wake up! Get on with your letter!"

Mr Birkett spoke quietly but sharply. David sat up and picked up his pen. Everyone was looking at him. His face burned. He tried to think of something to write.

"Everything seems to have gone wrong. I don't know why. I want to come home."

He stopped writing and tried hard to stop himself from crying. He mustn't show them they had won. He mustn't. But the tears came.

Mr Birkett heard the snuffling sound and looked up. He couldn't make out at first what it was or where it was coming from. He frowned. Then he saw, and the boys too noticed one by one what was happening. David struggled to control himself, but could not. He was crying, and everyone had seen.

Mr Birkett was puzzled. He had only told the boy to get on with his letter. There must be more to it. But he had been a teacher too long to be greatly concerned by a boy's crying. He looked at his watch. Five-to-seven.

"All right, get back to your letters. Finish them off and get your envelopes done. It's five-to-seven." He stood up as he spoke and walked across to David's desk. He picked up the letter and read it. "Stay in at lunchtime tomorrow and write another letter," he said, then crumpled the letter in his hand and dropped it back on the desk.

It stopped David's crying. He put the letter in his pocket and pulled out his handkerchief. Mr Birkett walked back to the front of the formroom.

"Collect the letters," he said, pointing to a boy at the front.

When Mr Birkett had all the letters in his hand, he turned and walked out of the formroom. Everyone stood up and began talking, but David remained in his place. He wanted to go out and wash his face, but he felt that he couldn't move with everyone there to look at him. Gradually, the formroom began to empty. He decided he would go up to the dorm, which should be empty, because no one was allowed there except at bed-time. When there were only a few boys left in the room, he stood up and quickly walked out, without looking up.

The dorm was empty. He did not turn the light on, in case it was seen by any of the teachers. The light from the corridor shone through the door and he could see by that. He bent down over one of the washbasins and splashed cold water over his face and onto his eyes. He went on doing so for two or three minutes. The water was icy cold and made him feel better. He was anxious to get rid of any signs of crying. When at last he turned the tap off and turned round to look for a towel, Philip was standing in front of him. It gave him a fright.

"Sorry," said Philip. "I came to see if you were all right."

David didn't know what to think. "I'm all right," he said. He walked over to his bed and took out a towel from the locker beside it.

Philip followed him and sat down on the bed. "It must have been rotten these last few days," he said. "Most people would have cried much sooner than you did."

It made David feel better to think that.

"Let's be friends again," said Philip.

"What?"

David felt bewildered. This was the last thing he had expected.

"We might as well be friends again now," said Philip. "We've only got another few weeks. We might as well let bygones be bygones now. Don't you think? Come on. Let's shake hands."

He stood up, facing David, and held out his hand. David hesitated a moment longer, still bewildered by this unexpected change, and then took the offered hand, and shook.

"Thanks," he said.

"Good," said Philip. "Let's go back down to the formroom."

"O. K.," said David. The after-effects of his crying, the shock of the cold water and of the sudden renewal of his friendship with Philip, left him feeling dazed but refreshed, and he followed Philip happily back down to the formroom.

The room was empty.

"Wonder where they all are?" said Philip.

They heard shouting from outside. David looked out of the window.

"There's a snowball fight going on in the quad," he said.

"Shall we go?" asked Philip.

"If you like."

They went out into the cold blur of the snowy quadrangle, where the air was filled with big snowflakes and the snow lay already three or four inches deep and twenty or thirty boys were throwing snowballs at each other. They ran across to one side, clinging on to each other and dodging snowballs.

"He's on our side," said Philip.

David waited for their approval, but it came straight away, without question.

"O. K.—come on!"

David's face broke into smiles. A snowball hit Philip on the shoulder, and both boys joined in the battle, which raged on for several minutes, until Mr Birkett came out in a temper and shouted at them all to get inside.

The snow lay smooth and white across the meadows. The sky too was white, but since the early hours of the morning no more snow had fallen. The air was cold and clear, and a bright but shadowless light filled the wide spaces of the black and white landscape.

Mr Jones, walking down to the village, stopped on the bridge and looked over the parapet across the meadows to the school. Lacking colour, the landscape seemed more pure, reduced to its essential form, pure and simple. Groups of trees in foreground and distance, a few straight lines denoting the school, the white plain of the meadows. And what next, he wondered. Next year—what then? He shook his head, and walked on.

The landscape remained still and empty, unchanging. The white sky reflected the white earth. Nothing moved. Then, very faintly, a bell began to ring. It ceased. Still nothing moved.

Then a speck appeared on the whiteness in front of the school buildings. More specks joined it. They moved like tiny insects that had crept onto the corner of a white sheet spread out for a picnic. Slowly, by their movement, a small area of the pure whiteness of the snow became smudged, and the stillness of the air was disturbed for a while by the faint sounds of shouting from across the meadows.

Twenty minutes later, the faint sound of a bell ringing could be heard again, and the specks disappeared, leaving only a smudge behind them to show where they had been.

At half-past-eleven, there was a quiet knock on Mr Birkett's study door.

"Come in!" he said. But nothing happened.

"Come in!" he shouted, irritably.

The door opened, and a second form boy came in.

"Well?"

"Please sir, Mr Hopper sent me, sir."

"What about?" snapped Mr Birkett. "Come in properly, boy, and close the door behind you. You're letting all the cold air in."

The boy did as he was told.

"Please, sir," he said, "Mr Hopper said I was to tell you what I'd done."

"Well?"

"Please, sir, I was throwing snowballs."

Surely Mr Hopper could have dealt with this himself, thought Mr Birkett. "Throwing snowballs?" he said.

"Yes, sir. In the classroom, sir."

"You were *what*?" Mr Birkett exploded.

"Throwing snowballs in the classroom, sir," repeated the boy, scared by the explosion.

Mr Birkett stood up, glowering. The boy took a step backwards.

"And would you," stormed Mr Birkett, advancing round his desk, "take snowballs into your own home and throw them round the sitting room? Would you?"

"No, sir."

Mr Birkett reached out and took hold of the boy by his

shoulder. "Then why do you do it here? Eh? Why do you do it here?"

He shook him.

"I don't know, sir."

Mr Birkett pulled the boy closer to him and bent forward. He shouted into his face. "Why do you do it here?"

"I'm sorry, sir."

"Sorry? *Sorry*? That's easy to say. How many times do you think I've heard that since I've been teaching? Eh?"

"I don't know, sir," said the boy, nearly in tears.

"And do you think I ever believe it? Eh?"

He shook him violently.

"Eh? Do you think I ever believe it?"

"No, sir."

"No." Mr Birkett lowered his voice and released his hold on the boy. The boy's shoulder was hurting and he wanted to rub it, but he didn't dare. "No, I don't believe it, because it isn't true. You're not sorry. But you will be. I'll make you sorry."

The boy swallowed. Mr Birkett returned to his desk, and while his back was turned the boy quickly rubbed his aching shoulder. Mr Birkett bent down and pulled open a drawer in his desk. He took out a short cane.

This, he was saying to himself, is what this school has been lacking. Discipline. For the lack of that, we have come to this state. His weakness has brought us almost to collapse. If the school is to be saved, discipline must be instilled now. It is the only chance.

"Before I cane you, you will say, 'I am sorry for throwing snowballs inside the school,' and you will continue to say it after each stroke of the cane until I am satisfied that you mean it."

Mr Birkett walked round to the front of his desk again and went up to the boy.

"Hold out your hand. Now."

"I'm sorry for throwing snowballs inside the school," said the boy, and almost before he had finished Mr Birkett brought the cane down hard across his hand. The boy winced.

"Again."

"I'm sorry for throwing snowballs inside the school."

The cane came down again, hard.

"Again."

"I'm sorry for throwing snowballs . . ."

Before he could finish, the cane was brought down again hard across his hand. The boy yelped with pain and surprise, and withdrew his hand.

"Keep your hand out," said Mr Birkett. "You do not convince me. Say it again."

"I'm sorry for throwing snowballs inside the school."

The boy suffered ten strokes of the cane before Mr Birkett allowed himself convinced of his remorse, by which time the words, accompanied by choking sobs, sounded tolerably genuine.

"Now go back to your lessons," said Mr Birkett.

"Thank you, sir," said the boy, as he had been taught.

Mr Birkett sat down behind his desk and put the cane back in its drawer. For the good of the school, he said to himself. There is much to be done, if the school is to be saved, and nothing is achieved without suffering. But there is hope, he thought. If we are determined enough, there is hope.

By then it had begun to snow again. Mr Jones walked slowly up the lane from the village, and the snowflakes fell gently onto his head and shoulders, melted and glistened. He stopped again when he came to the bridge. He looked across the meadows as he had done earlier, but now, as the air filled with snow, the landscape seemed less precisely drawn, as if it were being rubbed out.

The ledge of snow on the parapet of the bridge thickened, and the snow began to settle and build up on Mr Jones's shouders. Soon the air was so thick that the school was all but invisible to him and he himself was wrapped in a cocoon of snow, all alone.

Philip had won. He was the hero, the leader. David, having suffered the miseries of rejection, scorn and exclusion, was simply glad to be accepted again under Philip's wing. He no longer craved the limelight. Carter had won his battle against David, he had asserted his rights. He had no grudge against Minchip. Indeed, in a way, he admired him for ousting Lundy. Tomlinson, who had always found Philip interesting, found him even more interesting now. Then there were Finch and Wilson and other lesser satellites. All followed Philip Minchip. The greatest were most under his spell, the least naturally followed, or were of no account. He held sway over them all, and there was no one to challenge him. But his reign had only a little more than two weeks to run before the kingdom would dissolve and his subjects, like Prospero's spirits, vanish into thin air. So he made the most of what was left to him.

"Not much longer to go," said Tomlinson to Philip one day.

Philip almost took it for granted now that Tomlinson could see further than most people into his mind and could even, on occasions, read his thoughts. He nodded.

"Are you sorry?" Tomlinson asked.

Philip nodded again. "In a way."

"It's not over yet though," he added.

"Oh?" said Tomlinson, interested. "What's to come?"

"I'm not sure yet. We can't just let things end, though."

"What do you suggest? Another rugby match?"

Philip scowled, then laughed and shook his head. "No thanks," he said. "Something else. I've a sort of idea."

"I can't wait," said Tomlinson.

A great community spirit existed in the school at this time, which contributed more than a little to Philip's ease of leadership. Several things had brought this about, not least of which was Mr Birkett's increasing despotism. He had suddenly begun lashing out with punishments for breaches of rules which most people had forgotten long ago. Under the circumstances the boys thought it very unfair of him, and it created a sort of war-time spirit among them, sticking together against the common foe. The fourth form suffered especially at the hands of Hitler, as he was now known, since he was their form-master. He seemed to be forever inspecting their desks and their clothing and keeping them in for every little thing he found wrong or out of place.

They were full of resentment.

Not even Wilkins escaped Hitler's wrath.

"What's this?" snapped Hitler, stopping behind Wilkins' desk.

The rest of the class looked up expectantly from their letters.

"Please, sir, it's a notice about the Stamp Club," said Wilkins, confidently.

"And what business have you writing notices about the Stamp Club during Letter Writing?" asked Hitler, testily.

"Please, sir, I've finished my letter," said Arnold, confidence still unshaken, and held out four pages of closely written note-paper for Hitler to see.

"You do not finish your letter, boy, until Letter Writing is finished. When you have said all you have to say to your parents or guardians, you check over your letter for mistakes, and when you have done that you sit with your arms folded until the period ends," said Hitler, as if he were quoting from the statute book, "which you will now do, and then you will copy out your letter again and bring both copies to me in supper."

"But, sir..."

"Don't you dare to answer me back, boy! Fold your arms! The rest of you, get on with your letters, or you'll all be doing the same!"

Hitler marched back to the front and sat down, while the whole class, except poor Arnold, bent their heads hurriedly to their letters and went on writing.

They all gathered round to offer Arnold their condolences after Hitler had gone. Arnold was indignant. It was the first time in living memory that he had been in trouble. He was appalled by Hitler's injustice. The others sympathised, although they were amused too, in a way.

"It's time we did something about it," said Philip.

"What can we do?" said Arnold, with a gesture of despair. "Mere pupils!"

"There must be something."

"I'd better start copying out my letter again," Arnold sighed. "That's the last long letter I'll write!"

"Blimey!" said one of the others. "That's more than I've written all term."

And so even Arnold was drawn into the group.

Philip and his friends wandered outside into the cold and huddled against a wall for shelter. They would have gone up to the room above the old stables, but Hitler had recently put it out of bounds. So they stood outside and froze, to put an edge on their resentment.

"I bet it snows again tonight," one of them said.

"I hope so," said another.

"Why?" said David. "We're not supposed to throw snowballs any more."

"You'd think they'd let us enjoy our last days here, wouldn't you? Not make them miserable."

"Just think! The Headmaster's loony and the Deputy Head's a sadist. It's not safe. We might all be murdered in our beds."

"Yeah, and if they don't get us, the ghost will."

They all laughed.

"Hey, what about the ghost, Phil? Have you seen it lately?"

"I wouldn't joke about it, if I were you," said Philip. "It's probably here, listening."

"Ah, belt up. You're making me nervous."

"It's a dark enough night," Philip added.

"Do you really believe in it, Phil?" asked David, in a serious voice.

"Of course I do," said Philip, just as seriously.

A few minutes later the cold, or the ghost, became too much for them and they went back inside.

"Have you got a diary, John?" asked Philip, just before supper, as he came across his first friend sitting alone as usual in the formroom.

John handed over a small pocket diary. Philip searched through the pages and then seemed to find what he was looking for. His face lit up.

"Great!" he said. "Thanks, John." He returned the diary to his old friend.

"What were you looking for?" asked John.

"Tell you later."

But Philip kept his own counsel for a day or two, waiting for the right moment. On Friday morning, just two weeks before the end of term, he called a meeting of the inner circle for after lunch, outside the old stables.

When the time of the meeting arrived, they were all expectant.

"Well?"

"What is it?"

"What's it all about?"

"I've decided to do something tomorrow night," said Philip, mysteriously, "and I want to know if any of you are willing to come with me. I'll do it on my own in any case. But if some of you want to come, you can."

"Where?"

"What are you going to do, Phil?"

"I'm going to go down to the river at midnight and wait for the ghost. It's a full moon tomorrow. If the ghost comes out at all, it will come out then."

None of them spoke at first, each waiting for somebody else to say something.

"I'll come," said David, at last.

"Me too," said Wilson.

"And me,"

"And me."

"Good," said Philip. "I knew you would."

"Hitler'll massacre us if he catches us."

"Ah, who cares?"

So it was settled, and the excitement mounted from that moment on, as they waited for the appointed hour.

"Was that it?" asked Tomlinson later.

Philip nodded. "That was it," he said.

The Rev. Morris Field, Chairman of the Governors, arrived at length within sight of the school and breathed a sigh of relief. The worst thing about The Meadows was getting there. Although, even when you were there, there was little likelihood of being afforded much comfort or even decent conversation under present circumstances. He pulled off his scarf, now that he was nearly there, and felt the cold air wrap itself round his neck in its place. His bulky overcoat was uncomfortable, too heavy for walking, but it was too cold to do without it. Four hours it had taken him to get here: a taxi, two trains, a bus ride, and now this walk from the village. Anyway, it was almost over now, and in all probability this would be his last visit. Thank the Lord!

What a distressing and disruptive business it had all been. But, from what he had seen so far of the people at The Meadows, he was inclined to think that the school's bankruptcy was a blessing in disguise. Jones was obviously not right in the head, and Birkett was getting past it—a fussy, obsessive little man he seemed. These little prep schools had had their day. He was on the Board of Governors of a little primary school in his parish that was doing wonders, trying out new methods. No comparison. The day of the little private school was definitely over, or ought to be. No, The Meadows would not be missed.

Nice-looking place, though, he thought, as he came round the bend in the drive and saw the old house looking peacefully down across the pale green, snow-patched meadows to the river. Pity, in a way. Who would buy it? He wondered. The agents seemed to think a small hotel was a possibility. Very nice it would be, too. Perhaps he would come and stay sometime, if that was the way it turned out.

The thing now was to round things off smoothly and neatly, with as little fuss and as few hurt feelings as possible. Not easy. Things had gone surprisingly well so far with the parents. No one had made any difficulties. But then what could they do? Anyway, they were all at a safe distance. The problem now lay in dealing with the staff, and in particular with Jones and Birkett.

There was no doubt that Jones should have informed the Governors much sooner than he did of the state the school's finances were getting into. Two, even three, years ago, he should have realised how things were going. If action had been taken then, the school might well have been saved. There was something a little odd, in fact, about the whole business. It was hard to believe that Jones had not realised the way things were going. During the first days of their inquiries, after Jones had written to the Governors, there had even been suspicions of embezzlement. Fortunately those suspicions had proved to be unfounded, but there was still a doubt in his mind, and in the minds of the other Governors, about Jones's behaviour. It seemed to him sometimes almost as though Jones had seen where he was heading but had gone driving on regardless, without telling anyone, until they crashed. Not that he engineered the disaster, just that he did nothing to try to avoid it.

He seemed quite unperturbed by all that had happened, almost as if it did not concern him. It was easy to see why Birkett should be so irritated by him. But the question was, what was to become of him? The Board had more or less decided on the course of action they felt should be taken, but the final decision was left to him after consultation with the men concerned. Hence his visit today.

The Board had been unanimous in their determination to avoid any kind of recrimination. Whatever part Jones might have played in the events leading to the closing down of the school, they wished him to be treated as an innocent victim.

The other staff were much more easily dealt with. He had told them unofficially, after his first visit, that they would each receive one term's full salary in lieu of notice. That was all fair and proper, and no more was required. Today, he brought with him the official letters from the Board of Governors, one for each of them, stating the exact terms on which their appointments would be terminated.

Then there was Birkett. His was perhaps the most difficult case, as he was yet several years away from retirement age. It was a question for discussion and negotiation, and it would not be easy.

He raised his hand and knocked on the Headmaster's study door. There was no reply. He opened the door and looked inside. No one was there. So he went out again and made his way to the staffroom. That too was empty, but he took the opportunity of ridding himself of his heavy overcoat and hung it, along with his hat and scarf, on the coat rack behind the door. Feeling better for that, he then noticed the kettle and tea-things over in the corner and realised that he could not do another thing until he had sat down and drunk a cup of tea. So, since no one seemed to be about, he made himself one.

A few minutes later, holding a cup of tea carefully in his hand, he lowered himself into an old chair, the seat of which had collapsed to such an extent that it was almost like sitting on the floor. Not the kind of chair one gets out of in a hurry. So he leaned back and sipped his tea. Delicious!

Why do they come here, I wonder, he thought. I wonder what brought Jones here in the first place. Or any of them. Living in an old, out-of-the 3/4-way place like this for most of the year, with sixty boys and four other men for company. Odd kind of life. Pleasant though, perhaps, in a way. If you like it quiet. Nice surroundings anyway. I daresay it could grow on you.

It was very quiet. Very still. The long hours of travelling began to tell on him. Now that he was sitting down, sipping his tea, waves of sleep began to roll over him and he began to doze. Catching himself nodding off, he decided wisely to put his cup down on the floor. He closed his eyes and thought he would just take forty winks, to recover from his journey.

Malcolm was the first to enter the staffroom at the end of afternoon school. The ringing of the bell had not penetrated Mr Field's sleep. He had sunk a little lower in the armchair and was looking rather crumpled, with his jacket collar riding up the back of his head and his mouth hanging open. He began to snore.

Malcolm was puzzled at first, until he realised who it was. He wasn't sure what to do, and was still standing staring at him when the Rev. Field woke himself up with a particularly loud snore and opened his eyes.

Malcolm was even less sure what to do now. "Good afternoon," he said. "Enjoy your sleep?"

"What? Oh! Have I been asleep? Must have nodded off."

The Minister was struggling to raise himself in his chair, but seemed unable to do so. Malcolm watched and wondered if he should help, but at last he managed to get himself up onto his feet. He came forward and held out his hand.

"How do you do?" he said. "There was no one about, so I made myself a cup of tea while I was waiting." He glanced down at the cup of tea, which had hardly been touched. "Then I must have dozed off. Journeys are always tiring, don't you think? Probably cold by now."

"I'll make some more," said Malcolm.

"Don't put yourself out for me."

"No trouble," said Malcolm. "I'd have been making some anyway."

Geoffrey Hopper and Fred Lynch came in, and they all had a cup of tea. Mr Field gave them their official letters.

"Of course, it's very sad," said Geoffrey Hopper, "that the school has to close. But it was bound to happen one day. I could see it coming. I only wish I'd got out and into a state school a bit sooner. That's where the future lies. These places are finished. We've got ourselves into a rut. Bound to happen."

"And this is only your first term here, Mr Drew," said Mr Field. "It's very unfortunate in your case. I hope you're not too resentful."

"No," said Malcolm, realising now that there was no hope. "It couldn't be helped. Just bad luck, I suppose."

"I'm glad you see it like that," said Mr Field, taking the opportunity to settle one point. "The important thing is to realise that it was no one's fault. No one is to blame. It couldn't be helped."

"Oh, absolutely," said Geoffrey Hopper. "We realise that. Not an accusing word has escaped our lips. It was to be expected. We all have the greatest respect for the Headmaster. He's been a fine man, though past his prime now, of course."

"The Governors are only anxious to treat everyone as fairly as possible and avoid any sort of unpleasantness."

"Of course," said Mr Hopper. "Of course. I speak for us all, I'm sure, when I say how generously we feel we have been treated by you and the other Governors."

The others murmured their agreement.

"I'm glad to hear it," said Mr. Field, who was beginning to wonder whether Hopper was leading up to something, so ingratiating was his manner. He decided to escape. "I think I must try to find either Mr Birkett or the Headmaster," he said. "I haven't seen either of them yet. If you'll excuse me."

"Certainly," said Mr Hopper.

Mr Field left the staffroom to begin the second part of his commission. Once more, he tried the Headmaster's study and once more he found it empty. So he went upstairs to Mr Birkett's room and found him in.

"Ah, Mr Field," said Mr Birkett, briskly. "Come in. Take a seat. Good to see you. Now, how are things progressing?"

"Progressing?"

"How are things developing? What have you and the Governors been able to arrange?"

"Ah, well, that is why I am here. We've given the matter a lot of thought, but before we come to any final decision on the matter we would like to hear your own views."

"My views," said Mr Birkett, standing and moving into an open space, "are that we must not give in. Where there's a will, there's a way. As far as I and the other staff are concerned, we would like to see any measures tried that could enable the school to continue to operate. I am assuming, of course, that Mr Jones will cease to be Headmaster as from the end of this term. Officially, I mean. He has been Headmaster in name only for some considerable time. I might even say for some years. The effective running of the school has been in my hands for a long time. Mr Jones is weak. He always has been. Now he has given up altogether. I am beginning—just beginning—to pull things together. But it will not be easy. It cannot be done all at once. Discipline has grown very lax. Stern measures will have to be taken. But I feel sure that if you were to come back at this time next term, certainly at this time next year, so long as I have the authority to apply my remedies effectively, you would see a big difference in the standards of work and behaviour here at The Meadows. It is a challenge, but I feel sure that we can succeed."

Mr Field was at a loss to know what to do. How could this man have got the idea that the school would still be open after Christmas? It had been made quite clear that it would be closing. All the parents had been informed. Clearly, there had been a misunderstanding, but he did not see how it could have come about.

"My dear chap," he began, "there seems to be some sort of misunderstanding."

"I know what you're going to say," said Mr Birkett. "I realise I've jumped the gun somewhat. Of course, the post of Headmaster will have to be advertised. But there is so much to be done, and I have started already on the task, that I can't help but think what I could achieve if I were appointed to the post. No one knows better than I what the school needs to get it going again. I hope you and the other Governors will recognise what a unique position I am in to be able to see what the problems are and how to set about putting them right. But I am speaking out of turn, I know. I apologise. But it is difficult for me to remain silent on a subject about which I feel so strongly, and which is, after all, so very urgent."

Mr Field was thoroughly confused. He did not understand how anyone could have managed to get hold so firmly of completely the wrong end of the stick and to be waving it about so dangerously. He felt that it would be advisable to exercise caution.

"Your loyalty to the school," he began, "your devotion to—to its cause, are both—very praiseworthy. Very praiseworthy indeed. I have no doubt that the Board of Governors will be influenced by what I have to report about you in their future treatment of you."

"That's very kind," said Mr Birkett, whose face however wore a frown. "I am interested only in the good of the school. I'm not looking for personal advantage."

"Good heavens, no! I wouldn't dream of imputing such motives to you. By no means."

"I shall continue to serve in whatever capacity the Governors see fit to use me."

"Highly commendable. Just what we would expect of you,

Mr Birkett. We have always been most pleased..."

He tailed off, not sure what to say next. Mr Birkett's manner was intense. His eyes had a visionary gleam.

"The Governors," he began again, choosing his words carefully, "have of course explored every avenue, considered every means, every possible means, of saving the school."

"Never say die, never say die. Where there's a will. We put our faith in you entirely to give us the means to continue. I myself have never doubted that a way would be found."

Mr Birkett sat down again, smiling, radiating confidence. He was unshakeable.

"Well," said the Minister, "your faith is an example to us all, I will say that. However, I must point out that all the parents have been told that the school will be closing at Christmas and advised to make alternative arrangements for their children's education after that date. Most of them, I am sure, will already have done so."

For a moment, a troubled look passed across Mr Birkett's face. "If you will allow me to express myself frankly," he said, "I must say that I consider that to have been hasty and premature. I would not have done that until everything had been tried. However, I recognise that it would have taken courage to do otherwise, and the Governing Body as a whole, perhaps, could not be expected to display such courage. That is always the trouble with committees. In any case, the parents will be as pleased as anyone else when they are told that the school will be staying open after all. They will gladly cancel whatever other arrangements they may have made."

"Perhaps," said Mr Field.

"Definitely," said Mr Birkett.

"Let me put one question to you," said Mr Field, trying once more to break through his opponent's apparently impregnable defences.

"Certainly," said Mr Birkett, smiling.

"Put the case like this. If—and I stress *if*—The Meadows has to close down..."

Mr Birkett shook his head, and still smiled.

"...have you thought what your position will be? Have you made any plans?"

Mr Birkett stood up and faced the Minister over his desk. "I have made plans," he said, slowly and firmly. "I have made plans for the improvement of this school. I have made plans for a revised timetable. I have made plans for a new set of school rules. I have made plans for a greater sense of discipline in the school."

His voice was rising with each sentence, his eyes burning with the strength of his emotion. Rev. Field stared up at him, surprised and not a little disconcerted.

"I have made plans which, when they are put into action, will put The Meadows right at the top of the league of prep schools. I have made plans which will give us a waiting list a mile long. I have made plans all right. I have done little else these last few weeks. And they are the only plans I have made. I refuse to consider any other matter but this. I will make no more plans but these. And I will go on making these plans, and I shall start putting them into action, and I will not be stopped, and I suggest that you go back to the Board of Governors and that you spend as much time finding ways of keeping this school open as I have spent in finding ways of making it great. Go back and tell them that. Tell them what I've said. Tell them. The Meadows must stay open. It must stay open."

He sat down again, worn out by his outburst, red in the face, perspiring. He was breathing heavily. He took off his glasses, fumbled in his pocket for a handkerchief and began to wipe the lenses.

Acutely embarrassed and shocked, Mr Field remained for a few moments seated in his chair in silence. He didn't know what to say. But obviously there was no point in going on.

"I will tell the Governors what you have said."

He stood up.

"The Governors will be writing to you," he said.

Mr Birkett made no reply but went on wiping his glasses.

Mr Field went out and headed straight for the staffroom to collect his coat. He was leaving at once. He could not face the prospect of another such interview with Mr Jones. He was going, and the sooner this place went too the better. But that was the last visit he intended to make.

"I wonder what we would do if we did see a ghost," said David.

"We'll find out tonight," said Philip.

David looked at him, with a look that mingled doubt and admiration. "Do you really think so? I mean, do you really think there might be a ghost?"

"I know there's a ghost," said Philip, with absolute conviction in his voice.

David wanted to believe, but couldn't quite bring himself to do so. "How do you know?" he said. "I mean, how can you be sure?"

Philip shrugged his shoulders. "I just know," he said. "That's all. I know."

"Is that what they call being psychic?" asked David.

Philip again shrugged his shoulders.

"Well, we'll find out tonight, perhaps," said David.

Soon everyone know about the ghost-hunting expedition and other boys began to ask if they could come too. They were referred to Philip.

Philip considered each request carefully and asked a lot of questions and laid down a lot of conditions, but turned no one down. By the end of Saturday morning, the size of the expedition had grown to about a dozen. By the middle of the afternoon, nearly twenty were going.

Some of the original group were sceptical and thought it would spoil it if too many people went. "They'll scare it away," they said.

Then it began to snow. Some of them thought the snow would ruin it, since no one would want to go out in the cold. But Philip was equal to the situation and adapted his plans accordingly.

"I know," he said. "Instead of just going out to watch for the ghost, let's sneak out a bit earlier and build a snowman on the meadows. Let's get everyone out building a snowman."

The others looked at each other, and their eyes lit up.

"Great!"

"But I mean everyone," said Philip. "The whole school!"

"Hey, yeah! That would be great!"

"Do you think we could?"

"Of course we could. Split up now and spread the word. We'll sneak out at half-past-ten. Right? That'll give us time to build the snowman, and then those who dare can stay on to watch for the ghost. O.K.?"

"O.K."

The group dispersed, and by the end of the afternoon each of the sixty boys in the school knew of the plan. It would be a gesture of defiance against Hitler, and it met with universal approval.

Excitement ran at a high level that evening in the school. The formrooms murmured with conspiratorial whispers, and no one spoke without first looking over his shoulder. They didn't think of it as a mere practical joke, but rather as a military manoeuvre. Everyone took it very seriously.

Philip's generals were rather worried about the first formers.

"They might get too excited and make too much noise."

"They might get scared."

"Someone will have to be in charge of them," said Philip. "We ought to have someone in charge of each form really."

"I'll be in charge of the first form, if you like," said David.

"O.K. Tomlinson, you can be in charge of the third form. Wilson, you can have the seconds. I'll be in charge of our form."

They all agreed to this division of command.

"So this is what we'll do. At half-past-ten, or just before, you three can go to your forms and lead them out. You'd better send them out in twos and threes, and you come last. Right?"

"Right."

During the evening, each of the generals saw his troops and briefed them. Everyone knew the plan. Everything was ready.

When Hitler did the rounds of the dormitories after lights out, all was quiet. He had no reason to suspect anything. The dorms remained quiet for ten or fifteen minutes afterwards, but then they began to whisper.

"What time is it?"

"I don't know. Just a minute."

"Sssh!"

"Half-past-nine."

"Is that all?"

"Ssssssh! Someone might hear. Hitler might come round again."

"'Course he won't."

"He sometimes does."

"Belt up, will you!"

And so on. Sporadic bursts of whispering in all four dorms.

"What time is it now?"

"Not again!"

"Not so loud!"

"Quarter to."

A groan.

"Surely it's after that. Your watch must be wrong."

"No it's not."

"I bet it is. What time does your watch say?"

"Quarter to."

Another groan.

"See!"

The quietest was the fourth-form dormitory. Like old soldiers, they waited in silence.

At twenty-past-ten, Philip slipped out of his bed and began to get dressed. Not a word was said. The others began to do the same. As soon as they were ready, Tomlinson, Wilson and Lundy picked up their wellingtons and tip-toed out of the dorm and down the corridor to marshal their troops.

Philip, standing by the door, nodded to two boys who were standing ready, waiting, with their wellingtons in their hands. They looked at each other, then at him, and then quickly and silently slipped out of the dorm. The others, as they were ready, came down in ones and twos to the door and waited for Philip to signal them to go.

The plan, so far, was going like clockwork.

It had come to Malcolm on the bus that he must break off his engagement to Alice. He had known all along, he realised now, that it was a mistake, but until now had lacked the courage to admit it. But it was one thing to admit it to himself, and another to tell Alice. He wondered how on earth he could do it without causing her too much pain.

Still, it was a relief to have made the decision at last, to have been honest with himself. Now that he had been forced finally to abandon all hope of being able to stay on at The Meadows, he had been wondering what to do next term. Nothing he could think of seemed to hold out any hope of satisfaction, anything like the happiness he had thought he could achieve at The Meadows. Except perhaps to make a complete break, to break off all ties and go somewhere new in a job that was entirely different. Perhaps not even a teaching job.

As the bus jogged along through the bare, depressing December countryside, he fastened his hopes on this one idea, which seemed to hold out some prospect of happiness, and tried not to think about the awkwardness of the coming afternoon with Alice.

Alice wanted to go Christmas shopping, so they went out into the town, and when they had finished shopping they went into the park. Malcolm knew that he would have to tell her now. Find a seat, he thought, and sit down and then... How to begin?

But Alice got in first.

"Malcolm," she said. "I've got something to tell you."

He should have guessed, but he didn't. He was too busy thinking about what he was going to say.

"What?" he said, only half-listening.

"I think I'm pregnant."

He stopped walking. It took a second or two for it to sink in. But when it did, his reaction surprised him. There was no panic or horror or anger or anything like that, just a sense of deflation.

He seemed to see everything suddenly float away from him and disappear into the distance, and he was left only with bare reality. He felt sad, as if he were saying goodbye to something, but that was all.

"Are you sure?" he said.

Alice nodded. "I'm sure."

"Well," he said. "It's all right. We'll get married after Christmas, shall we? New Year's Day perhaps. How about that?"

"That would be marvellous," said Alice, beginning to show signs of tears. "You still want to marry me then?"

"Of course I do."

"Only I'd been wondering lately if you might be changing your mind. You didn't seem... I don't know... I suppose it was just that you were preoccupied, with the school closing down and everything."

"Yes," said Malcolm. "I suppose so."

"I didn't know whether to tell you or not. I don't want to force you into marrying me. Only if you want to."

"Of course I do."

"Oh, I hope so."

Alice looked thoroughly miserable, standing there in the cold, grey park, surrounded by empty spaces, holding onto his sleeve. He felt sorry for her, and that helped him. He kissed her, and she rested her head on his shoulder.

"Have you known long?" He asked.

"Two or three weeks."

"You should have told me sooner."

"I wasn't sure whether to tell you at all. I didn't know what your plans were, whether you wanted to stay here or what. I didn't know whether you still loved me. So long as you still love me, it's all right. Don't marry me just because of the baby."

She had begun to cry, and he comforted her, assuring her that he would not marry her out of a sense of duty. that he really did love her. When she had stopped crying, they began to walk again.

"I'm sorry it had to happen like this," she said, after a little while.

"Never mind. Perhaps it's not such a bad thing. We're getting married sooner as a result. So it can't be bad."

"Oh, Malcolm!" she said, stopping again and kissing him. "Thank you. Thank you for being so kind."

Malcolm smiled, and they walked on again.

There was a small part of him that remained detached and merely looked on, while the rest of him talked with Alice. He watched himself not just pretending but actually feeling pleasure in anticipation of the baby, and saying so to Alice. He watched himself deriving satisfaction from seeing Alice grow more cheerful as he talked to her. He watched himself being proud that he was to be a father.

"I'm glad. I'm really glad," he said.

Alice too seemed almost elated now. He had convinced her, as he had convinced himself.

They came out of the park and into the busy pre-Christmas streets again. He took her into a cafe for tea and made her laugh by fussing over her as if the baby was due any day. For a little while, they were really very happy.

It started to snow, and they watched the flakes falling outside the window.

"You haven't told your mother and father," he said.

"No. That's what I'm dreading."

"How do you think they'll take it?"

"I don't know. I daren't think."

They went out into the street again and set off to walk back to Alice's house through the snow.

"Will you tell them we're going to get married," said Alice, "when we get home? You'll stay to tea, won't you?"

"Yes," said Malcolm. "Of course I'll tell them."

Throughout the evening, when he was with Alice and her parents, he continued to watch himself with that small part of his mind which remained detached. Only when he was alone again later did the two parts of his mind begin to come together again and form one self. Then he allowed himself to feel regret and admit to himself that things had not worked out well.

As he travelled back on the bus, he wondered what might

have happened if he had spoken first in the park and told Alice that he wanted to break of their engagement. But he didn't think about it much, realising that it was a futile speculation.

He had not realised what a good actor he was. He had announced his and Alice's intention to marry early in the New Year with great aplomb and had swept away any doubts her parents may have felt by the force of his enthusiasm and his exuberant manner. Quite a celebratory atmosphere was created. Her father went out to the off-licence to buy some drinks.

"What an exciting Christmas this is going to be!" exclaimed her mother.

He stared out at the snowflakes which mingled with his own reflection in the bus window, and thought how absurd it was that the course of the rest of his life should be decided so suddenly and so irrevocably, whether he liked it or not. But perhaps, he thought again, it is all just as arbitrary really. Only sometimes it's more noticeable.

The bus was going very slowly, because of the snow, which had been falling continuously and heavily since the middle of the afternoon. The country roads had not been cleared and conditions were hazardous.

It was a long, cold, difficult walk up from the village to the school through the snow, but in a way it suited him. His feet were soon wet through and frozen, but he didn't mind. With his head down and his hands thrust deep into his pockets, he plodded slowly on up the lane.

After about half-a-mile, he heard the sound of a car engine revving loudly, and as he walked round the next bend he saw a car stuck in the snow just ahead. The engine roared and the back wheels spun, but the car did not move, As he came closer, he saw that it was Fred Lynch's car

He tapped on the window.

"Am I glad to see you?" said Fred, winding the window down. His breath smelt of beer and his speech was rather slurred. "Bloody snow! See if you can give us a push."

Malcolm pushed, but to no avail.

"You need to get something under the wheels," he said.

Fred switched off the engine.

"Bloody snow!"

He opened the door and started to drag himself out of the car. "I'll see if I can get some branches," he said. As he walked away from the car he slipped and fell full length in the snow.

Malcolm almost laughed, and then went to help him, but Fred picked himself up, muttering, "Bloody snow!" and walked on again in search of branches. Malcolm followed him.

The plan worked and they drove off, but in another hundred yards they began skidding and sliding about on the road and soon they had ground to a halt again. Fred's handling of the car was none too skilful. His steering was rather erratic. He seemed to be constantly trying to fling the car from one side of the road to the other.

They went back to fetch the branches, but this time, when Fred tried to start the engine, it wouldn't.

"Damn the bloody thing!" he shouted.

"We're nearly there now anyway," said Malcolm. "Perhaps you'd better leave it and come back for it in the morning."

"I think I'll go to sleep here," said Fred.

"You can't do that," said Malcolm. "You'll freeze."

"I don't care." He struggled to pull something out of his pocket, which, when it emerged, turned out to be a small bottle of whisky. "This will keep me warm," he said, and took a swig. Then he passed it to Malcolm, who, after a moment's hesitation, took it and drank some. It made his throat burn, but it warmed him up.

"Come on, then," said Fred, taking the bottle back. "Let's go."

Once again, he climbed out of the car, slammed the door, and began to walk very unsteadily up the lane towards the school. After a while, he began to sing. But then, as they were crossing the bridge, Fred stopped and looked over the bridge towards the meadows.

"What the hell's going on?" he said.

Malcolm looked too and saw, hazily through the snow, a large crowd of boys on the meadows. It looked as though the whole school was out there. And in their midst stood a huge snowman.

After the last boy had left his dorm, Philip crept down the stairs to where David was putting on his wellingtons in the doorway.

"The dorms are empty," Philip whispered.

David nodded. "They didn't make a sound."

"You now," said Philip.

David nodded again, smiled, stepped out into the snow and ran quickly alongside the wall and round the corner under the archway. Philip waited a second or two, glanced round, and then darted after David.

Down on the meadows, work had already begun. As Philip and David walked down the slope away from the school, they could see through the falling snow the dark shapes of sixty boys moving about on the white surface of the meadows, all bent down rolling snowballs and carrying them over to the middle of the open space, where a mound of snow was beginning to grow. The two boys quickened their pace and were soon standing by the mound in the middle. Few words were spoken. Everyone was too busy. But when they saw Philip, they nodded and grinned. David ran off to find a patch of snow which he could use, but Philip stood by the central mound looking about, his eyes glistening. No doubt he was pleased with the way things were going. But there was also something a little unearthly about the scene which appealed to his imagination and stimulated it to further activity. He watched the mound growing by his side, as the boys, all with intent and eager expressions on their faces, went to and fro with their loads of snow, all in silence. The school could not be seen, the snow was falling so thickly. So they were more or less safe from detection. The air was full of snow, swirling, drifting, falling, ceaselessly falling. Philip looked up, and all he could see was snow. It seemed impossible that the sky could hold so much.

He became aware of Tomlinson standing beside him.

"Working like slaves, aren't they," said Tomlinson.

"Yes," said Philip.

"Isn't it quiet though?"

"Yes."

Philip looked up at the sky again. "Where does it all come from?" he said.

Meanwhile, the snowman was growing in stature. It was obviously going to be a magnificent creature. It was now so high that the boys were having to throw their loads of snow onto the top. Nobody was quite sure what its final height was going to be. They only knew it was going to be big.

Someone had the idea of making foot-holes in the side of the mound, so that it was possible to climb up to reach the top. So more and more snow was piled on and hammered down hard. Eventually, at about six feet, the shoulders began to be formed.

The intensity of the activity had begun to slacken a little now. Boys brought their load of snow and then stood around to watch, instead of rushing off at once for more, as they had been doing. The work of the final shaping of the snowman fell to just half-a-dozen of the senior boys, the craftsmen as it were. Now, if they wanted more snow, they would send someone for it. Another half-dozen or so of the younger boys did this labouring for them. So, gradually, the head was built up and a face made. At last it was done, and they all stood back to admire the finished work.

"Great!"

"Fantastic!"

It was about eight feet high, and it looked rather awesome, standing there in the middle of the meadows, with the snow falling round it. They stood and stared, and then someone noticed that Philip was not there.

"Where's Phil?"

They looked around, but he wasn't there.

"Looking for the ghost, maybe."

"There he is."

They all looked round, and saw Philip walking slowly up towards them from the direction of the river.

"Isn't it great, Phil?" they said, as he came up to them.

"What do you think of it?"

"What does it look like from the river?"

"Eerie," said Philip. "It looks like some monster, a weird creature. The god of the snow."

They all looked at it.

"You can only just see it from down there," he went on. "All you can see is this big white shape looming up through the snow."

They all stood round him, listening, wondering what they were going to do now and when the ghost hunting would begin.

"Once," said Philip, "about two years ago, I had dealings with devils. With real devils, I mean. Through witchcraft. Some people say there's no such thing. But I know there is. I saw the witches, conjuring up devils. Up in the hills in Wales, where I used to live, witchcraft still goes on. There's a certain spell they use to conjure up a certain devil, for which they have to have a child. They use the child as a sort of bait, to attract the devil. Then they trap it. Well, one night they took me and used me for their spells."

Not one of the boys—except perhaps Tomlinson—wasn't at least half-convinced. Philip spoke so confidently.

"Well, that's why I got you to build the snowman," he continued. "As bait. Bait for the ghost. For the spirit who walks here, the ghost of the meadows. You need something to draw a spirit. Spirits are curious. But now everyone has to stay. Either we all stay or we all go back in. One or the other. Are we staying? Do you want to see the ghost? Do you want me to show you how the witches conjure devils and raise spirits?"

There was a slight pause, while they all waited for someone to speak.

"Yes," said David. "I'm staying."

One by one, they all agreed. They would stay.

"Come a bit closer," said Philip.

The sixty boys moved in closer to him.

Philip looked at his watch. "It's half-past-eleven," he said. "In half-an-hour's time, at midnight, the ghost will begin to walk. We have to draw it towards us and make it show itself.

There's no need to be scared. It won't harm anyone. Sometimes devils can burn and bite. When I was devilbait, it got inside me and threw me on the ground. But this isn't a devil. Ghosts are sometimes sad and sometimes angry—always one or the other—but they never harm anyone. The ghost of the meadows is the ghost of a woman who drowned. It comes out of the water at night and walks on the meadows, and sometimes comes into the school, looking for someone perhaps. Some of us have seen signs that it has been in school."

"Yes," said David. "That's right."

"Seeing this," Philip went on, pointing to the snowman, "the ghost might come, thinking it's what it has been looking for. But there must be silence, or it won't come. We have to create the right atmosphere. An old man I knew in Wales taught me that. The atmosphere has to be right, or the ghost won't come. This old man taught me some words to say. I'll say them in a moment, but first of all, you'll have to do something. I must teach you first of all how to defend yourselves if anything goes wrong. There are lots of shapes in magic—stars and circles and things like that. A circle is a protection. You draw a circle to trap a devil in. If anything goes wrong, we must quickly join hands in a circle round the spirit-lure—the snowman. Then we'll be safe. But to draw the ghost in, we use the horse-shoe. That's good luck. A welcome. Opening the circle. So, we must be silent now. We've got to build up the atmosphere. Put them in a horse-shoe," he said to his three generals, "with the opening towards the river, everyone facing out. When the ghost enters, we can turn in, slowly. When the horse-shoe is made, I'll say the words."

Everyone was taking it very seriously. No one smiled. Scarcely one of them who was not beginning to feel nervous, and some of the younger ones were quite scared. As they were put in position, facing outwards, they stared out apprehensively into the snow and, mistaking the swirling of the snowflakes for apparitions, grew more and more tense and expectant.

Philip stood with his back to the snowman, facing the river through the open end of the horse-shoe. He let the silence deepen. His breathing became heavy. He seemed to be going into a kind of trance. The boys, hearing the strange sound of his breathing, wanted to look over their shoulders, but did not dare.

Suddenly, there was a crashing, rolling sound and a long, wailing cry from the river bank.

"A circle. Quick!" shouted David.

But they were already running, and David was running with them, even while he was shouting. Once it began, it was like a stampede. No one stopped to think. It was blind terror and panic driving them. They ran and stumbled and fell in the snow and trampled on each other, and went on running, regardless of the noise they made, until they were back inside the building. Panting, out of breath, trembling, relieved to be safe inside again, but still confused and scared, they all got back into their beds as quickly as they could.

"What was it?"

"What happened?"

"I don't know."

"I thought it was the ghost."

"Or a devil or something."

"Sssh!"

"Shut up everyone, or Hitler'll catch us!"

In the senior dorm, the scene was the same. There were puddles all over the floor from the melting snow. But within a few minutes everyone was in bed. All, that is, except Philip.

"Hadn't we better go and look for him?" said David.

"You can if you like. I'm not. We don't know what's out there."

"But he might be hurt or something."

"Serves him right for conjuring up devils."

"Did you believe all that?"

"I don't know. Sort of, I suppose. It was dead spooky out there."

"I wonder if it got him."

"Don't be stupid!"

"Well, there was something there, wasn't there?"

"Hey! We'd better be quiet. We don't want Hitler

coming up now."

Gradually, silence fell over the dormitories. But the silence was shattered ten minutes later, as the light came on in the corridor outside and the sound of heavy footsteps was heard. One by one, Mr Birkett burst open the doors of the four dormitories and switched on the lights.

"Up! Out!" he shouted.

The boys scrambled out of their beds.

Mr Birkett returned to the first dormitory, the senior one. He was in a rage the like of which none of the boys had seen before.

"You will be punished," he bellowed. "Every single one of you you will be punished. If you think you can get away with a prank like this, you've got another think coming. Every one of you will be punished."

Then he rushed out and down to the next dormitory, and he was heard by all the boys storming in similar terms in each of the remaining dorms.

"Now get back into your beds, all of you!" he shouted at last, at the top of his voice. "And remain silent. Absolute silence! Any boy who speaks will be caned now!"

One by one, he switched off the lights in the dormitories, but left the doors open. The boys climbed quickly back into bed. No one spoke. Mr Birkett lingered in the corridor for a while, and then his footsteps were heard retreating, but still no one spoke, and within quite a short time everyone was asleep.

Much later, after two o'clock, Philip entered the dormitory, passed quietly between the sleeping boys, undressed quickly and quietly, and got into his bed.

The boys had been standing in the hall now for well over an hour. It seemed like longer, but none of them dared to look at his watch in case Mr Birkett should see. The Deputy Headmaster sat on the big chair at the front, and stared at the sixty boys. He never seemed to take his eyes off them for more than a moment. On the floor beside him lay his cane. The threat of the cane hung over their heads, should anyone move or whisper or do anything but stand up straight and face the front.

How much longer? they wondered. How long did he intend to keep them like this? Surely it couldn't be for much longer. They had been there since returning from church. The sun began to shine outside, and beams of sunlight poured in through the tall windows. Their eyes flickered, but no one moved.

Outside, the snow glistened in the sun. On the meadows, the snowman stood alone surveying his pure white domain. Fresh snow had covered over the marks left by last night's visitors. Mr Jones stood at his study window, looking out at the clean sheet of snow and at the snow piled up in the branches of the trees. The bright sunlight reflecting off the snow was dazzling, and he had to shield his eyes with his hand.

The sunlight dazzled Malcolm, too, who was standing at the staffroom window, looking out at the same white landscape. At this moment, he was regretting more than anything else the fact that from the end of this week he would no longer be able to stand looking at the meadows. He remembered, often, the first time he had looked at them, early on his first morning here in September, draped with mist through which hazy sunshine gleamed and glistened. He had never seen anything like it. Nor like this—the meadows pure white, bathed in brilliant sunshine. Only it was spoilt rather by the snowman in the middle.

It was a far cry from how it had looked last night, with the snow falling and all the chaos and panic. But some things he could remember quite vividly. First of all, the strange sight of all those boys seen vaguely through the falling snow, gathered around the snowman. Then, when they began to move—that was when Fred began creeping over the bridge and trying to climb over the wall and down the bank to catch them—they seemed to move into a sort of horse-shoe shape around the snowman. He had crouched down behind the wall to watch them, wondering what they were doing, while Fred began to clamber down the side. Then he heard Fred fall and shout, and he jumped up and ran across to where Fred had climbed over the wall, thinking he might have fallen in the river. At first, he couldn't see him, and he feared the worst. Looking up again to the meadows, he saw that the boys had gone. He could only see the snowman and the snow swirling round it. Then he heard Fred's voice, groaning and swearing.

"Bloody snow! Oooh! Come and get me out! Ohhh!"

Malcolm saw him now, sprawled at the bottom of the bank, well away from the water's edge, behind a bush, half covered in snow. He was obviously unable to extricate himself.

"Are you all right?"

"No. I think I've broken my bloody leg."

It turned out he had sprained his ankle, but Fred was not in any mood to play down his injuries. Malcolm scrambled down the bank and tried to help him out, but Fred declared that he was unable to walk and told Malcolm to go and get help. After a moment's hesitation, while he wondered what to do and which way to go, he set off across the meadows.

"Ring for an ambulance," Fred shouted after him.

Malcolm remembered thinking he saw a boy still on the meadows as he ran and stumbled up to the school, but it was difficult to be sure in the snow, and he didn't stop. He remembered all the footprints which led up to the school and in under the archway. What had it all been about, he wondered. Just an end-of-term lark, presumably, going out to build a snowman on forbidden ground.

He was just coming across the quad, when he saw that someone was standing in the doorway. As he came closer, he saw that it was Mr Jones.

While Malcolm was thinking about these events in the staffroom, the first caning was taking place in the hall.

"You, boy!" shouted Mr Birkett, making everyone jump, hoping it wasn't them he meant. "Come out here," he said, pointing to the boy who had done wrong.

The boy came out to the front of the hall.

"Can't you stand still?" shouted Mr Birkett.

"Please sir, my legs are . . ."

"Silence!"

The boy looked aggrieved but said nothing. The rest of the boys tried to keep their eyes staring straight ahead, not looking at the unfortunate boy or at Mr Birkett.

"Your legs were strong enough to take you out of bounds last night. They should be strong enough to hold you up now without shuffling. Hold out your hand!"

Mr Birkett had already picked up his cane and now stepped forward. The boy held out his hand, and Mr Birkett quickly snapped down the cane four times.

"Back to your place!"

Malcolm could hear Mr Birkett's voice, but not the words. He wondered what was happening. Mr Birkett was taking it all very seriously, taking it indeed almost personally. When Malcolm had gone up to his room last night to tell him what had happened, he had at first appeared not to comprehend, perhaps because Malcolm's account was itself fairly confused, but once he did realise what it was all about he suddenly went into a rage. Malcolm remembered how embarrassed he had felt.

"Where are they now?" screamed Mr Birkett.

"I don't know. Back in the dorms, I think. The Headmaster is . . ."

"The Headmaster? He's the one to blame. This is the result. It's impossible. Well, I'll teach them. I don't care if the school is closing tomorrow, I'll teach them. They can't do this."

"What about Mr Lynch?"

"What's he got to do with it?"

"He's . . ."

But Mr Birkett had already gone and was marching away at top speed to vent his fury on the boys in the dormitories.

So Malcolm, not sure what to do next, went back downstairs to find Mr Jones, who was still standing in the doorway.

"Mr Birkett's gone to deal with the boys," said Malcolm.

"I know," said Mr Jones, smiling. "He's just passed through. He seemed very angry."

"He was rather," said Malcolm.

Malcolm began explaining to Mr Jones about Fred Lynch, asking what he thought they should do, when Fred himself came limping through the archway into the quad.

"I can manage," said Fred, as Malcolm came out to help him.

"We were just coming for you."

"Looks like it."

"It's not broken then?"

Fred did not reply.

"Are you all right, Mr Lynch?" asked the Headmaster, as they came up to the doorway.

"I'll do," said Fred. "Kids! I've had my fill of them. What was going on anyway?"

Mr Jones looked at Malcolm. Malcolm shrugged his shoulders. "We still don't know," he said. "Mr Birkett's gone up to deal with them."

"God help them!" said Fred.

"Just an end-of-term lark, I suppose," said Malcolm.

"End of term," said Fred. "I wish it was." He shivered and sneezed. "I'm going to bed."

He refused Malcolm's offer of help and limped away laboriously up the stairs. He had still not shown his face that morning, and Malcolm wondered now whether he should go up to his room and see how he was. Perhaps he should take him up a cup of tea. He looked at his watch. It was after eleven. He went across and put the kettle on. There was his car still waiting in the lane to be fetched too.

While he waited for the kettle to boil, he thought about the conversation he had had with Mr Jones after Fred had left them.

"And where are you going next term?" Mr Jones had asked, after they had stood a few moments in silence looking out at the falling snow.

Malcolm was on the point of saying that he didn't know, when he recalled what had happened earlier, which the recent excitement and rush of events had driven from his mind. His heart sank a little, but he tried to sound cheerful.

"I'll be getting married early in the new year," he said. "I expect I shall be looking round for another teaching post in the area."

"So your future is assured."

Malcolm nodded. The phrase, it seemed to him, had a rather deadening sound to it.

"And what about your past? Tell me a bit about yourself."

It seemed an odd thing to ask, at this time, in this place, but Malcolm was glad to be able to postpone the time when he would have to go up to his room and face his thoughts alone again. So they stood in the doorway, and Malcolm sketched in the main points of his life so far. He told Mr Jones about his college days, about being left alone when his mother died, about his friendship with Alice, the school in Liverpool and his loneliness there, and how happy he had been coming to The Meadows after that.

"I think life is a matter of coming to terms with loneliness," said Mr Jones, when Malcolm had finished. "To have had an early start with this struggle, as you have done, may seem unfair and unfortunate at the time, but in the end it will prove to have been an advantage."

It seemed to Malcolm a peculiarly comfortless philosophy.

The kettle boiled and Malcolm made the tea. He poured out a cup for Fred, and went out with it. On his way up to Fred's room he passed Mr Jones.

"Good morning, Malcolm," he said. "Are you looking after Mr Lynch?"

"Just taking him a cup of tea."

"Good. Good."

Mr Jones walked on, smiling as usual. He came to the door to the hall, opened it and went in. All eyes turned to the door. Mr Birkett stood up. Mr Jones looked round the room, smiling kindly.

"All right, Mr Birkett," he said. "Thank you. Very well, boys, you may go now."

He stood and watched the boys go out. Their voices rose in chatter and excited shouting as they left the building and went out into the clear bright morning. When the last one was out, Mr Jones turned and followed them, leaving Mr Birkett to control his anger as best he could alone.

Philip and John sat on the wall of the bridge, and watched the ambulance drive away from the front of the school and disappear down the drive. Two or three minutes later, it drove past them, over the bridge, down the lane towards the village. They watched it go.

Philip had spent most of his time with John during the last few days. The mood of the school, and Philip's own mood, had changed since the weekend of the snowman and the ghost hunting. The boys' thoughts turned more and more to home, and Christmas, and presents, and as they waited for the end of term their interest in school steadily faded. Every day its hold on them slackened a little more. Philip's position at the centre of the group became less significant as the group began to drift apart again. Also, the reign of terror seemed to be over. From the moment when Mr Jones released them from the hall last Sunday morning, no further mention had been made of the incident, no further punishments doled out, and Mr Birkett seemed to become as lax as anybody else in the enforcing of rules. So that now, Philip and John could sit here in full view of the school, out of bounds, on a Thursday afternoon, without much fear of getting into trouble, even if they were seen. Nobody seemed to care any more.

Philip, aware that his power was on the wane, sensing a certain amount of resentment in certain quarters for the punishment that had followed their adventures on the meadows, taking a warning from the hint of sarcasm that began to creep into his friends' voices when they were talking of his dealings with ghosts and devils, wisely decided to stay away from them. So he turned back to John. Old, reliable, dead-faced John. The others had plenty of other things to think about, with all the changes that were coming, and more or less forgot him. When he was with them he was quiet and withdrawn, unobtrusive, much as he had been in his first days at the school, but as often as he could he escaped from them to be on his own, or with John.

"I'm looking forward to living at home all the time," said John, whose parents had decided to send him to the local grammar school.

"It'll be nice for you," said Philip.

"We've got quite a big garden at home. They're buying me a proper nesting-box for Christmas."

"Won't they let you sleep in the house?" asked Philip.

"What? Oh, belt up!"

The two boys laughed.

"Have you saved up enough for your binoculars yet?"

"Not yet, but I think I might get some money towards them for Christmas. I'd quite like to take up bird photography next. I think I might ask for a camera for my birthday. You can get quite good ones fairly cheaply second-hand. If any birds nest in the box, I might be able to photograph them."

"Sounds good."

"Yes."

Philip slid forward off the wall and began walking slowly up the lane, back towards school. John followed.

"The good thing about you, John," said Philip, after they had walked a little way in silence, "is that you're always the same."

"I should have thought that was the worst thing about me."

"No, that's the best thing. I'm always changing. I get impatient. I can't keep still for long. I'd never make a bird-watcher."

"Like when you scared the birds away that time."

"Yes," said Philip, a little surprised. It was the first time it had ever been mentioned. "You got on my nerves, being so still. I'm sorry about that."

John shrugged his shoulders. "That's all right."

"But I was interested, really. I think ornithology's fascinating. I just haven't got the patience."

"The thing is," said John, "I don't mind being on my own, whereas you like being with people."

"I suppose that's it," agreed Philip, and they walked on talking of this and other things.

Once again, most of the snow had thawed, and there were only lumps and patches of snow left by the roadside and in the fields, looking rather grey now. The weather had been comparatively mild since the heavy snow, and this afternoon was typically cloudy, with a slight breeze and an occasional moment of weak, hazy sunshine. As Philip and John entered the quad, they saw Mr Drew standing near the horse-chestnut tree talking to David Lundy. David saw them and nodded to Philip. Philip nodded in reply and walked on with John.

It was Malcolm's last day on duty, and he was going through it with very mixed feelings. There was an atmosphere in the staffroom of total apathy. Ron Birkett had more or less abdicated and declared that whatever happened now was of no interest to him. Geoffrey Hopper was scarcely ever there: he arrived in time for the start of lessons in the morning and went home again as soon as they were over. Malcolm just wished the end of the week would come now, so that the whole thing could be finished.

But he still regretted that he would not be seeing any of the boys again after Saturday. He had often thought, during these last days, of his first day in the school, and the hopes he had had. He remembered Geoffrey Hopper introducing him to a group of boys outside the old stables. Lundy had been one of them. What a contrast he had felt to the boys at his previous school. He remembered too all his feelings about David Lundy. It all seemed unreal now, belonging to a past age, a golden age. But he had sought out Lundy now, for old times' sake as it were, just to glance for a moment longer over his shoulder at that other world before it faded altogether.

"Looking forward to Christmas, David?" he asked, using the boy's Christian name for the first time, as a special indulgence.

"Yes, sir," said David, but Malcolm thought it didn't sound as though he really meant it, and wondered why.

"How do you feel about leaving two terms early? Do you mind?"

"So-so."

"Mixed feelings, eh? Like me."

"Yes, sir. It's been a bit of a mixed-up term really."

"It certainly has."

They went on talking rather vaguely for a while, but gradually David began to be more open and honest and started telling Malcolm about some of the things that had happened, the things that had gone wrong. Malcolm was delighted to find David so ready to confide in him and listened sympathetically, encouraging him to unburden himself of all his worries. Some of it he knew already, without having realised its full significance. David told him all about the rugby team rivalry, and the Amateur Dramatic Society and Stamp Club business, and about his friendship with Philip. He told him everything in fact. He became rather emotional in the telling of it, and came close to tears at one point, but Malcolm coaxed him along and got him over it. In the end, it had obviously done the boy a lot of good, getting it all off his chest.

"But I feel all mixed up, sir. I don't really understand."

Malcolm couldn't really help much, other than to say that anyway it was all over, and that there were always these difficulties between people. You just had to get used to it and do what you thought was right.

"I suppose so," said David. "Anyway, I'd better go now. Thanks for talking, sir. Listening, I mean. I feel much better now."

"Good," said Malcolm. "I've enjoyed listening."

David's smile was sufficient recompense, although it made Malcolm wish more than ever that things had worked out differently.

It was almost dark now. Malcolm looked at his watch and saw that in ten minutes it would be time to ring the bell for tea. He turned to go inside, when a shape he recognised emerged from the doorway.

"Mr Drew," it said, coming towards him.

It was Mr Field.

"I came as soon as I heard he was not well. But I couldn't find anyone. The place seems deserted. How is he?"

"The doctor saw him this morning and decided he would have to go into hospital. The ambulance came for him about an hour ago. He'll be in hospital by now."

"Oh dear. It is pneumonia then?"

"They think so."

"Dear me. What a thing to happen, right at the end. Mr Jones has not had an easy term, has he? What a pity! Ah well!"

They went in, and the boys began to gather in the quad.

It was the last day. Saturday morning. It had come at last. The school was bursting with excitement. Everyone was rushing up and down stairs with trunks and suitcases, and there was constant chatter. The school was noisy at breakfast. But then they had to go into the hall for the last assembly, which was taken by Mr Field, who, in view of Mr Jones's illness, had stayed on at the school to see it through to its close.

They didn't want to listen, but they did, and once they were listening they even allowed themselves to be moved by what was said. It was, after all, a momentous occasion in their lives.

Mr Field expected them to take what they had learnt from The Meadows and use it wherever they went. To carry the torch which had been lit here, and to keep it burning. And so on. They sang the hymn with great gusto. It was a useful way to release their enthusiasm for leaving.

A few moments later, they were all rushing out into the quad again, with renewed vigour. Already the first parents were arriving in their cars to collect their sons, and last farewells were being said. Others were preparing to walk down to the village for the bus to the station.

Malcolm went up to his room to finish packing. He could hear the boys talking in the quad below. He wanted to be away as quickly as possible now. It suddenly became a most urgent need, and if it were possible he wanted to slip away unnoticed, without any sort of formal leave-taking. But when he was nearly ready, there was a knock on his door and Fred Lynch came in.

"Well, that's it then," said Fred, briskly. "I'm off. No point in hanging around."

"None," said Malcolm.

"You in a hurry too?"

"I'm going as soon as I've finished packing."

"If you're dead quick you can have a lift."

"No, it's all right. You get away. I'll be a little while yet."

"Right. All the best then!"

He held out his hand.

"All the best, Fred!"

"Let her know who's boss."

"I will. Don't worry."

And Fred closed the door and departed.

The numbers in the quad were dwindling rapidly. One by one, the boys were going and the old building was growing quieter. It was a very still, white day, with no sun, light but without shadows. A peace was descending, but a rather desolate peace, as the quadrangle emptied.

Philip sat under the tree with John, still keeping in the background, watching people go, saying goodbye to those who noticed him. It was surprising who did and who did not say goodbye. Carter did, for example. But Tomlinson went without a word. David was anxious to say goodbye to everyone, but was rather embarrassed when he came to Philip.

"'Bye, David. Have a good Christmas."

"Thanks," said David. "Same to you."

There was an awkward pause.

"Come on, David!" shouted his father.

"'Bye, then," he said, and ran off to the car.

A taxi-driver walked through the archway into the quad. He looked at a piece of paper in his hand, and then at the boys and the few adults standing around.

"Philip Minchip?" he said, as though he might have got the name wrong.

Philip and John stood up.

"Goodbye, John," said Philip.

"Goodbye, Phil."

They shook hands, solemnly.

"I hope you get what you want for Christmas, the nesting-box and everything."

"Thanks. I expect I will."

"Good luck then!"

The taxi-driver was staring at the paper and scratching his head, convinced that he must have got it wrong.

"I'm Philip Minchip," said Philip, walking up to him.

"It was right then," said the man. "I thought maybe I'd got it written down wrong. I've never come across that one before. These your bags, are they? Here you are, I'll take them. What nationality's that then? That's never English."

"Japanese," said Philip.

"Get away! Is it?"

"Yes."

"Thought it couldn't be English. I felt sure I'd got it written down wrong. No offence meant. There you are then."

He slammed the passenger door shut, and swung into the driver's seat.

"Airport then, is it? That where you're going—Japan?"

"That's right."

"Lucky old you, eh? Japan! Well! Hey, but it won't be Christmas there, will it? Don't seem right, that. Folks live out there, do they?"

"That's right," said Philip.

And the taxi drove away.

Malcolm had soon finished his packing and, looking round his room for the last time, closed the door and walked away down the stairs. There was only a handful of boys left in the quad by this time. He said goodbye as he walked quickly through, and they all wished him a merry Christmas, but then he went through the archway and had soon left them, and the school, behind. What he felt most, as he walked away, was a sense of relief that it was finished. He thought about neither past nor future, just this present moment of relief.

Soon everyone had gone except Mr Birkett and Mrs Jones. Mr Birkett left late in the afternoon, having spent the day until then trying to convince himself that he was glad to be going, and fussing about irritably, getting his things together, taking longer over it than was necessary, until he could delay his departure no longer and was forced to go.

At about the same time, Mrs Jones was being told by a doctor at the hospital that her husband had died.

For years, no one had known what went on in Mrs Jones's mind, and that never changed. On Christmas Eve she attended her husband's funeral and then returned to The Meadows for the last time. She swept all the floors in her part of the old house, and dusted, and then put dust sheets over all the furniture, and when she had finished she packed her few clothes, put on her coat and hat and prepared to leave.

On the doormat an envelope lay. She picked it up and opened it. Inside was a Christmas card. "With best wishes for a merry Christmas, Arnold Wilkins," she read. But her face showed no reaction. She put the card down on a table, and opened the door.

And when she closed the door for the last time, she did so just as she had closed the covers of so many books over the years, sitting opposite her husband in the evening, silently, blankly and without feeling. She had no comment to make, and she turned impassively and walked away.